THE ACCIDENT

Julia Stone is a psychologist, trainer, coach and psychotherapist. She attended Faber Academy in 2017 and in 2018 won The *Blue Pencil First Novel* award. *The Accident* is her second novel.

Also by Julia Stone

Her Little Secret

The Accident

Julia Stone

First published in Great Britain in 2022 by Orion Dash,
an imprint of The Orion Publishing Group Ltd,
Carmelite House, 50 Victoria Embankment
London EC4Y 0DZ

An Hachette UK company

1 3 5 7 9 10 8 6 4 2

A CIP catalogue record for this book
is available from the British Library.

ISBN (eBook) 978 1 3987 0780 1
ISBN (Paperback) 978 1 3987 1065 8

www.orionbooks.co.uk

In loving memory of Graham Dean,
the original Billy Liar.
1958 – 2013

Chapter 1

The other witnesses had focused on the balloons in their description of the accident. Red, yellow, orange; bright lively colours. Hard to miss, you would think.

'Is there *anything* you remember?' The police officer was patient. This was the third time he'd asked me. He kept referring to it as 'the incident'. What did I remember about the incident?

He'd described the balloons to prompt me. Did I recall seeing them?

I raised my gaze to the ceiling of the hospital ward, trying to recollect. The strip lighting and hoist-rails were distracting, so I closed my eyes. I pictured the harsh playground colours of the helium balloons. In my mind's eye, I saw them rising above the bridge, bobbing against each other in their mission for freedom. The image was jarring to my frayed nerves, so I made it more calming. They became a drifting autumnal cloud of russet, rust and amber, hard to make out against the backdrop of the trees, their colours merging with the dying leaves.

I hadn't seen the balloons.

I wish I had and then I might have seen her – alive – if only for a fleeting moment.

'Shin splints,' I said, opening my eyes. 'I remember that.'

He looked up from his notes. I was aware there is a terrible irony in an overweight middle-aged woman suffering from shin splints, a condition that Dr Google says 'typically occurs in runners'. Lack of magnesium, not enough water, a sign of the approaching menopause – whatever its cause, when it struck it demanded my immediate attention.

'I could feel the cramp coming on in my shin.'

I patted my right leg, the one that did all the work when driving an automatic, as if this confirmed the veracity of my one pathetic contribution to the jigsaw he was piecing together.

'I was trying to find somewhere I could pull over.' A shiver ran through me and I tugged the thin hospital blanket up around my shoulders. I was unsure if it was the sudden memory, or the temperature of the ward, which – while not so cold that anyone would complain – was kept a tad too chilly for comfort. 'I'd spotted a sign for a lay-by. Up ahead, just past the bridge.'

He seemed to be struggling, his notes taking more time than my few words warranted. He was young enough to have been my son.

'That must have been when it happened.'

It was a feeling, a sense of something rather than a proper memory. Like a fleeting movement in your peripheral vision.

I didn't *recall* any noise. No scream as she fell, no bang on impact as she landed on the bonnet of my car.

There was just a deafening silence, a black field where the memory should be.

She fell backwards he'd said, in the fashion that people launch themselves from boats when scuba diving. I used this information to try to fill in the gaps in my memory – imagining her descent towards me like a slow-motion film, the sound on mute. I pictured her shoulders through the broken windscreen, her head lolling back over the steering wheel, her auburn curls cascading into my lap. Thrown forward by the force of the crash, my face next to hers; so close I would've seen her freckles, our cheeks almost touching.

I found myself crying. 'I'm sorry,' I said, wiping my cheeks carefully, dabbing around the cuts and grazes. 'I don't mean to cause a scene. It's just . . .' My shoulders heaved as I succumbed to my tears. 'I'm sorry . . .'

The police had informed me that the car was a write-off, having hit the concrete embankment, then the side of the bridge when I was knocked unconscious. They were amazed that I had no significant injuries: some bruising on my ribs and chest, a lump on my head, cuts from flying glass; nothing that couldn't be resolved with surgical tape and hospital glue apparently.

The doctor tested my reflexes with a tap to my knees, shone lights in my eyes and got me to follow her long thin finger as she moved it from side to side. She could have been a musician with hands like that – they'd easily span an octave on the piano. I was curious as to how she chose her career. Did she play hospitals with her dolls, bandage her teddies? Or was it something she discovered later when she realised she was good at biology?

I didn't ask.

They ended up keeping me in overnight, watching out for signs of concussion and waiting for my blood pressure to come down. The next morning a young nurse brought me a pair of paper scrubs to go home in, my own clothes having been destroyed following the crash. She helped me sit up and edge to the side of the bed before passing me the trousers.

'You can leave as soon as the doctor has seen you.' She untied the cord holding the hospital gown together at the back.

Wincing, I let her help me, thanking her profusely. I gingerly lifted my arms and disappeared into the green-grey top, thinking back to the day I'd got dressed to set off on my journey to Norfolk. So much had happened since. Pushing my head through the V neck I asked, 'What day is it?'

The nurse flashed a frown of concentration, possibly trying to assess whether I was amnesiac or struggling to remember the date herself.

'Monday,' she said. 'The eighteenth, I think.'

Oh no. Where had Sunday gone? I'd missed my weekly duty call with Mother. She would not be pleased.

They let me leave hospital that afternoon. I still felt a bit shaken but wasn't in serious pain. I touched the graze on my forehead gingerly. While sizeable, it was

4

shallow and already scabbing. I must've looked like an anonymous extra, turned into one of the walking wounded by the overzealous efforts of a TV make-up artist. Luckily there was no one I needed to impress.

As I left, they gave me Tramadol and the phone number of Victim Support, should I feel the need to unburden myself. I wasn't sure what, or who, I was 'the victim' of – hardly that poor, poor girl. It seemed that we were both the victim of fate.

I kept thinking of her.

It was a relief to be in the taxi on my way back to my own home. I was a bit peopled-out; not used to so much attention, so many questions, so much talking. With all the constant distraction it had been hard to focus my thoughts, my brain skittering in different directions, not allowing me to process the horror of the past days. Now in the dark warmth of the back seat of the cab, I was exhausted but unable to rest as my mind flashed up an assortment of sounds and images; a mix of memories and imaginings, which would no doubt haunt my dreams for days or weeks to come.

The moment the cab pulled up on the pebbled drive of my home I was brought back to the present by the sound of the ducks squawking from the pond, their cries like those of children demanding to know where I'd been. They'd become tame over the years, since I'd started feeding them; each generation bringing me their chicks to feed as soon as they hatched, abdicating responsibility for their brood to me, their surrogate mother.

It seems they'd missed me.

'Nice place,' the cab driver said. I forgot how imposing the old house looks when you first see it as you round the bend in the drive. Still named The Old Vicarage, there'd been no men of the cloth living here for over two centuries, but memories are long in villages. 'You've lived here a while?'

'My grandfather bought it between the wars. It's been in our family ever since.'

'I bet your kids loved growing up here, having all this space to play in.' I looked away, fumbled with my purse so he couldn't see my face. 'A kids' paradise!'

He meant well; he wasn't to know. Suddenly tired, I rested my head on the side window, watching as my breath steamed up the glass. 'If you take a left by the war memorial, you can avoid the back lane. The pot holes are worse than ever since all that rain.'

'Tell me about it!'

I gave him twenty pounds for the sixteen-pound fare, told him to keep the change. He gave me a hoot of his horn and a thumbs-up through the window as he drove away. I stood there until I could no longer hear the rumble of his tyres, the purring of the engine, and was left with only the country stillness, the call and response of distant owls.

'I nearly didn't pick up.' Mother's voice was curt, conveying the disdain on her face across the thousand miles between us. She lived in Spain with Georgio, her current gentleman friend.

6

'Sorry, Mother.'

A deep sigh. 'Hmm.' Was that faint tapping her nails drumming on the wooden arm of her chair?

My allocated slot was on Sundays: 5 p.m. GMT, before her first G&T. It was now Monday evening.

'I couldn't call. I'm sorry. I had an accident and had to go to the hospital.'

'What have you done this time? Always tripping over things and galumphing about the place. You should wear your glasses more often, then you might see where you're going. You get this clumsiness from your father's side of the family. I tried my best, but you've always been ungainly.'

The flash of an image: me at ten years old shuffling up and down the long corridors of the house, books balanced on my head to help my 'deportment', Mother listening out for the clatter of any dropping to the floor.

Mother was still talking. 'A graze here, a bruise there. Lord knows what people thought. These days you'd be whisked into social care. Did they have to give you stitches?' She didn't wait for me to answer. 'Do you remember that time you fell in the pond? You and your father had to wait hours at the hospital, just for two stitches. To be fair, he said you were quite good about it. Didn't make a fuss. Do you remember?'

'Yes.' My fingers find the small pale scar on my knee. 'But this wasn't my fault. It was an accident . . .' I sounded timid to my own ears, almost pleading. I shouldn't have mentioned it. 'It really wasn't . . .' But I'd lost her attention already.

She was talking to someone else, not bothering to cover the mouthpiece of the phone, her voice light and bright. A man's voice, something about dinner on the patio. With enthusiasm she expressed her preference for the new bottle of Pinot over the remains of yesterday's Sauvignon.

'Georgio says dinner will be in ten minutes and I have to freshen up. You really must be more careful, darling. I hope you're on the mend soon. I'll speak to you next Sunday.'

Chapter 2

A couple of days later the police came round to see me again. They wanted to check my statement, to find out if I'd remembered anything else. I'd been checking the newspapers to see if there was any mention of the accident, anything that might jog my memory. But it was only a side bar in the nationals, warranting just a few lines: '*A young woman fell from a pedestrian bridge over the A12 yesterday morning, landing on a vehicle passing below. She died at the scene. The car driver was freed from the car and taken to hospital. While the death is being treated as non-suspicious, enquiries are on-going and the police are appealing for witnesses.*' The following day it wasn't mentioned at all, the incident old news now. The world had moved on to the latest rise in crime/obesity/global temperatures/petrol prices.

I ushered the police into the front room, shutting the door firmly while I went to fetch tea and digestives. I only put the heating on in the rooms I used: the old house was big and damp, the sash windows ill-fitting, allowing in drafts and random insects that had to be ushered back outside. Other than these wild creatures, visitors were rare, so I figured the police deserved

Mother's best plates – the Royal Albert with the pink roses – although I had to give them a quick rinse first. It had been years since their use had been warranted.

Fred, the cat from Woodley's Farm, wound in and out of my legs as I walked back with the laden tray. He'd lost most of his tail in an accident with some farm equipment, but the stump waved vigorously, signalling temper or curiosity. The second I turned the door handle, Ginger shot from halfway up the stairs and they both zoomed into the front room, clamouring for attention. The male officer seemed happy as Ginger made herself comfortable on his lap, but the woman kept Fred at bay by rifling through her paperwork. I suppose he isn't very appealing with his missing eye and shredded ears. But I'm fond of them both and, even though they are meant to be feral and live in Woodley's barn catching rats, they prefer to spend most of their time with me.

The woman started talking before I'd even poured the tea.

'You say you saw nothing.'

I nod, waiting for her to say more, the pedant in me pondering whether it is possible *to see nothing*.

'The driver of the car behind yours gave a statement. He said he thinks he saw someone else on the bridge.' She checked the file although I'm sure it wasn't necessary. She was giving me time to think about what she'd said. 'He may have seen a man in a red hat, near the barrier, after the woman fell.'

The young policeman scratched Ginger under the chin. 'Of course, it could just have been another balloon.' He looked pleased with himself, proud of his deduction. 'A red balloon, you know, not a hat at all. In the chaos people think they see things they haven't. Happens all the time.'

The policewoman frowned at him, but he was too busy helping himself to a biscuit to notice.

'Has anything else come back to you about the events?' she said.

I shook my head. 'No, it all happened so fast.'

I proffered the sugar bowl and the policeman shovelled three spoonfuls into his teacup. He was young, probably still growing and needed the energy. The woman read back my statement, her voice conveying an edge of boredom.

'Do you have any questions for us?' she asked, once I'd reaffirmed what I'd told them before.

'Do you know the name of the young woman?' I asked. 'Do you know who she is?'

It seemed important for me to know.

'We don't know her name, no,' she said. She paused for a moment, as if considering whether she should share more. 'There was no handbag or mobile, which is unusual.'

'A real "Jane Doe", I'm afraid,' the policeman interjected, like an investigator in *CSI*. 'Even these days, these cases don't always get solved. We might never know who she is or how it happened.' He reached for another biscuit. 'Could be suicide. But who commits suicide with a load of balloons? Misadventure probably.'

'That's for the coroner to determine at the inquest.' The woman's tone was clipped. She was that bit older than him and probably fed up with having to tow around someone she saw as a lightweight partner. But I liked him. Even if he was a bit unpolished, he still had his raw enthusiasm.

The policewoman was already placing her paperwork in a large shoulder bag. I wondered whether this interview was just a box-ticking enquiry to her. The poor dead girl just another open case, another missed target if it couldn't be resolved. They probably have to build a tough veneer to cope. 'We've taken up too much of your time, Mrs Thomason.'

'Miss. Miss Thomason. Or Janice.'

She didn't apologise, unaware that she could have caused upset with her assumptions. Her eyes flashed something to her colleague, who bounced into life.

'Your belongings, Miss Thomason.' He held out a bulging plastic bag that had been resting at his side against the chair throughout the 'interview'. I'd been handed something similar years ago at the hospital when Father died. That one had had the hospital name printed on the side in grey, his clothes and few possessions jumbled inside. This was a gaudy orange, that particular shade favoured by Sainsbury's.

'The things from your car,' he said.

I took the bag. 'Yes, of course. Thank you.'

He handed me a card with a contact number, although I'd already been given one in the hospital. 'Call us. If anything comes to mind.' I noticed he'd scrawled his name and the incident number on the back. For someone less experienced in deciphering handwriting it would have been hard to tell the 1 from the 7.

Ginger seemed sad when they left, meowing at the closed front door while Fred stomped about, cross at changes to his routine. But sometimes it's nice to have a bit of company.

Nothing that two bowls of kitekat and a KitKat couldn't resolve.

I cleared away the tea things before I opened the orange plastic bag. I was relieved to find my manila client folder seemingly intact and, flipping through the paperwork, everything appeared to be there. On top, the hard copy of the original email request. It was from Mr Abbyss, my client, asking if I could research his family tree in time for his great-aunt's ninetieth. Beneath that a photocopy of my handwritten letter setting out the information I would need and my research plans. His reply, birth and death certificates appended; some photos and a sketchy family tree, hand-drawn by Aunty Marjory with lots of arrows and question marks.

On the day of the accident, I'd been travelling to a cemetery in the outer reaches of Norfolk. I was in pursuit of the records of an eighteenth-century farmer, the next generation in the genealogy of the Abbyss family. There was only so much research one could do at the computer before having to leave home to metaphorically dig around in graveyards and old records. I charge more for these trips, of course, my fee quote always stating 'plus incidental expenses'. Honest to the last penny about money, I always submit the receipts with my invoice.

I take great pride in my work tracking down people's forgotten histories, finding the poor souls lost in time and giving them back to the world. Reverence for the dead is at the heart of my business. I'd built a reputation for being caring, thorough and proficient – enough for me to have been asked to help out with background research for that TV show, *Who Do You Think You Are?* It was just the once, and of course I never appeared on the programme, but it was my one claim to fame, should there ever be anyone I needed to impress.

In my experience, Joe Public gets just as excited about knowing their roots as any star on the TV, even if most of their antecedents were coal miners or agricultural labourers. The stack of thank-you letters and invitations to join family reunions were evidence of that. Of course, I never went – it was important to keep professional boundaries. And a quiet night in with a cup of cocoa always seemed infinitely more attractive than a room full of strangers where I wouldn't really belong.

I put the Abbyss file on one side to take upstairs to my office later. Sitting at the kitchen table to retrieve the rest of my belongings from the plastic bag, I was pleased to see my trusty old Pentax had survived; a much better tool than my mobile for shots of tombstone inscriptions and registry entries. There was the book I'd planned to read at the hotel, a romance novel which had been well reviewed in the press, its cover scuffed and torn. My packed lunch lay sweating in my favourite Tupperware, the one that was just the right size for a couple of rounds of sandwiches and a chocolate bar. I peered through the lid, wondering momentarily whether any of the contents would still be edible – Gran had hated waste – but sanity stepped in and I put it to one side to go in the kitchen food-bin.

Having removed the larger items, I tipped the bag upside down on the table to empty out the last few things. Some loose coins fell out, small change for parking and supermarket trollies that I kept in the car ashtray. It was then that I saw it, among the minutiae of my life, entwined with my spare keys – a silver bracelet laden with charms.

I carefully untangled it, holding my breath to steady my hands. The chain was not the modern costume jewellery you buy in high street stores, but more solid and traditional. The clasp was broken.

It must've been hers.

It must have fallen from her wrist and been lying in the footwell of my car, waiting to be scooped up from the wreckage with the jumble of my belongings after the crash.

Gently, I laid it out flat on the table. Probably not valuable, but of sentimental worth. A hand-me-down? I should give it back, ring the police tomorrow. It was probably listed on an inventory somewhere; I wouldn't want to get in trouble.

My fingertips touched each of the charms in turn – the broken padlock, a teddy bear with a small sapphire

on his chest, an acorn, a heart with the initial S . . .
The bracelet was thick with them. Each a symbol of a
time, a person, a place. She'd lived her life to the full,
this young woman.

The more I considered these personal events in her
life, the closer I felt to her. Like she was sharing her
story with me. I can't explain it rationally, but I had
a strong sense that she meant me to have this bracelet,
to look after it for her.

A shiver ran through me as I realised — it was a
sign. Fate had brought us together in a cruel way, but
I was meant to be in her life and she in mine. We
were connected after all; I was the one who was with
her at the end, her face next to mine when she passed.

I had to find her.

This was not just another fascinating research project —
my quickening pulse signalled that. I wanted to breathe
life back into her; to give her back an identity so she
wasn't just another 'Jane Doe', lost and alone. No doubt
the police were doing their best, but they had other
priorities and targets to chase. It's their business to close
cases and move on; it's not in their interests to *care*.

I couldn't bear to think of her laying there in the
mortuary when I could help.

I looped the bracelet around my fingers and made
my promise to her. I *will* find you. I *will* bring you
back to your family.

Chapter 3

'Yes, Mr Abbyss . . . Of course, Glyn, sorry.' I tucked
the receiver under my chin to flick through the pages
of my diary. 'Hmm . . . 28th November. Yes, definitely.
All the work can be completed by then.' My schedule
looked delightfully clear; having high standards for my
work I don't cope well with pressure, don't like to feel
rushed. There was only one blot on the blank pages for
the coming months, a talk on family history to the local
Women's Institute. 'In fact, I plan to have everything
with you the week before.'

Reassured, he started to make signing-off noises.
Among the ritual goodbyes, I interjected, 'Oh, and
Glyn, please do thank Aunty Marjory for her diagram
of the family tree . . . immensely helpful.' It's important to recognise people's efforts to help and I liked to
leave client conversations on a warm note; a balance
of professionalism with the personal touch.

I set to work as soon as he hung up the phone. With
plenty of time before the deadline for my client work,
I could focus on my priority: collating the information
I had gathered so far.

I selected a beautiful turquoise box file from my

stock of stationery; brand new, not repurposed. I've always loved creating order out of chaos – folders, index cards and paperclips the tools of my trade. Of course, I could see the value of technology – I was no Luddite. A well-crafted spreadsheet was a joy to work with. But for some things paper couldn't be beaten.

When I was a teenager, Father used to give me his expense accounts to do. Not the maths part, but the sifting and sorting. Creating the system was half the fun; bullying all that paperwork into submission so it told a logical story – January to December, A to Z, low to high.

'She's off on another of her projects,' Mother would say, watching me scurry to my room with her recipes, no longer able to bear seeing them all jumbled together in the shoebox where she seemed content to keep them. Her cosmetics were the same, despite the fact I'd saved up my pocket money and bought her a make-up bag with separate compartments. Sometimes I wondered if she did it deliberately, to give me something to do.

I reached for the black permanent marker pen to label the new file. It was my favourite, the nicely chis-elled edge almost an italic nib. I prided myself on my penmanship; hours of practice when I went through my 'calligraphy phase', as Mother termed it. With the pen poised, I dithered – what to call the file? Since nothing *felt* right, I decided to use a Post-it Note as a temporary solution. In my best handwriting I wrote *'The lost girl'*, for that is what she was.

I'd cut out the original articles in the nationals – *The Times* and *Daily Mail* had both deemed the accident worth a mention. I'd also searched the news websites local to the accident to see if they'd given the incident more virtual column inches. In one there was a photo of the bridge festooned with yellow and black police tape, my car thankfully already towed from the scene. I'd printed the article to add to the file. It may seem of little importance now, but my genealogy work over the years had taught me that something small may yet turn out to be the hook on which everything hangs.

The McDougal family was a case in point. Born to an unknown father, Roger Bradwell McDougal was suddenly struck by a need to know more about his heritage when he turned sixty. He contacted me to ask whether I might be able to identify his father. Needles, haystacks . . . How could I track down an anonymous parent after all these years? Researching his mother's family, I noticed a theme of biblical names – boys were Mark, Matthew, Paul. There was a pattern of naming first-born sons after the father, with Bradwell as a middle name. Roger was not, to my knowledge, a common biblical character, so I deduced the father was possibly another Roger.

With the information he'd given me from the Barnardo's files and some logical deductions, I narrowed it down to two Roger 'suspects', right age, right place. I researched the family trees of these putative fathers, highlighting patterns in 'cause of death'. One family showed a propensity for alcohol, it would seem, given the number of liver failures; the other weak hearts. I handed over the files and left Roger McDougal to draw his own conclusions. He wrote to me that Christmas to say that he'd found two half-sisters, a pleasing result for both of us. The devil, it seemed, was in the detail.

★

I made myself wait until Friday before I called the young police officer. Once he'd looked up the case number and placed my voice, he was bright and friendly.

'Thank you for calling, Janice. Can I take it you've had some further recollections about the incident?'

'No,' I said, sorry to disappoint him. His mother was no doubt justifiably proud of him, having such a good career in the police service. 'I was wondering if you've identified the young woman.'

'I'm sorry to say we've not made any progress there yet. The inquest has been opened and adjourned until we know who she is. Now, if we'd had her mobile that would've made it easier but there was nothing of that nature on her person.'

On her person. Bless him. They must teach them to speak like that at Hendon. Or maybe they inadvertently pick it up from the TV shows, stashing a bottle of whisky in their bottom drawers to really get into role.

'You found nothing at all?' I said.

'No jewellery, other than earrings.'

Her bracelet lay on the desk in front of me, glinting in a ray of sunlight, and I swallowed a flash of guilt. He continued, 'She had tattoos but that's not unusual.'

'Oh?' I hoped he'd say more, give me something to help me envisage her; a clue, however small.

'Could you hold on, please,' he said. He must've put his hand over the receiver as I could hear a muffled conversation. The brevity and tone suggested something formal rather than office chitchat about the morning coffee run. His manner had changed when he returned to our conversation, something along the lines of 'We are not in a position to divulge any further information at this time.'

'I do a lot of research myself, have you thought about—'

'We have a detective on the case, Miss Thomason. I am sure she will consider every angle.'

I thanked him for his time before I hung up. It's important to be civil and show appreciation; it can help open doors and make friends.

Picking up the bracelet from where it lay, I pondered whether it could really help them find her. Or would it just end up logged on an inventory, then stashed in some evidence bag to be stored in a box in the basement, forgotten.

The blue sapphire twinkled at me, caught by the sun. If the balloons had been for her birthday, it would be her birthstone. It seemed we shared a star sign, me and this young woman. I wondered if we were alike in any other way. Not that I'm the type to believe in horoscopes, mediums and mystics, but twining the bracelet around my fingers, I felt a strong sense of her. Somehow I knew that it was not just another piece of jewellery.

A family heirloom? Passed on by her mother for her eighteenth? Left to her by a loving grandma? Whoever bought her these charms clearly adored her, each milestone marked; tangible evidence of every happy memory.

What must it be like to have a family like that, to give or receive that much love? How desperate her family must be, wondering where she was and what had happened. What if she were my daughter? How awful to not know.

The police didn't seem to know where to look next, but I could use my research skills to help. I had a small following on my genealogy blog and wondered if there might be someone out there who could identify the provenance of the bracelet. People interested in ancestry were often history buffs or experts in esoteric fields. Excited by my idea, I laid the chain on a sheet of white paper, arranging the desk lamp to illuminate the broken clasp. It seemed it would be too personal to place images of all the charms online, too exposing – like sharing someone's photo album without their permission. The clasp was a good place to begin – small controlled steps; someone may know when it was made, or where, which would give me a starting point. I set the camera to macro and zoomed in on the tiny hallmark on the back of the broken padlock charm. I posted the shots with a short message to my 'fans': 'Can anyone help me identify this bracelet on behalf of a client?'

Time would tell.

It was chilly in my room so I went down to the lounge, taking my notepad with me. I lit a fire then left it to catch while I made myself a large hot chocolate with marshmallows on top – a treat to help steel myself for my weekly call to Mother. At ten to five I herded Fred and Ginger out of the house, apologising for shutting them out in the drizzle that had just started. Fred leapt onto the fence, flicked his stub of a tail and was gone; off to find a small animal he could taunt, no doubt. Ginger took refuge in their Wendy house – I'd bought it at a garage sale in the village so they could shelter there if I wasn't around to let them in. Lined with old blankets, it was cosier than that draughty barn at Woodley's.

Settled in my armchair, my notepad beside me, I watched the hands on the grandfather clock approach the hour. I started dialling just before five o'clock. oo 34 . . .

'Hallo, Mother.'

'Oh, it's you. I hadn't realised the time.'

'How are you? How's Georgio?'

She set off on a rant about the challenge of finding a reliable cleaner in Madrid, which segued into the problems she'd been having with her hips, then the trouble she has getting out of the low-slung seats in Georgio's BMW.

'Which reminds me,' she said. 'Peggy tells me you've got a new car. Of course, I had to pretend you'd told me already. She saw it on the drive when she cycled past. She said it's not a very practical colour. Far too light for country roads and all that mud.'

Peggy. A woman who invented Neighbourhood Watch before it was 'a thing'. And frustratingly, she: 1) had been a friend of Mother's, 2) they were still in touch, and 3) she lived in the next village. Mother may as well have had a drone circling the house constantly spying on me. Not that I ever did anything worth reporting back.

I smothered a sigh. 'It's not a new car. It's a courtesy car from the insurance company . . .' It had been a week since the accident and I really didn't want to go back over it and start explaining to Mother; it was still far too raw. A white lie would do the trick. 'My car got stolen but it's covered by the insurance.'

She immediately launched into a diatribe about crime in the UK, which kept us going for most of my allotted time. When she paused for breath, I threw in Item One of the conversation topics on my prepared list: the rather nasty divorce of the Guilfords, something I knew she would relish. She never liked them when she'd lived here and was pleased that I'd harvested quite a lot of information from the conversation I'd overheard on the bus.

We ended the call on a good note.

Chapter 4

When I next phoned the police later that week, I was put through to the female officer who'd come to the house. She had no need of an armoured vest; she was born Teflon-plated – there was no way past her defences. As soon as I started to ask questions, she cut me short, turning the questions back on me, asking if I had the number of Victim Support.

'Thank you, yes, I do.'

'I wonder if it would be good for you to give them a call,' she said. 'The shock of an incident like this can present in different ways. It's their job to listen and offer support to victims who are struggling to cope with events.'

Closing the call, she told me that any updates would be available on their website and they would be in touch should they need a further statement for the coroner's court; the message 'don't phone us again' was unstated, but coming through loud and clear.

She was treating me as a nuisance, when I was only trying to help that poor lost girl.

★

25

Since the police had no answers for me, I phoned the coroner. I'd first found out one could do this after Father died. I'd been trying to make arrangements for his funeral but, because he had died while on a respite stay in a care home, there needed to be an autopsy. Bereft of information, I'd called them. It was a bizarre conversation and didn't instil confidence.

Apparently February was a busy time for postmortems. When I asked how long I would have to wait for Father's death certificate, the man asked me what he had died of. Incredulous, I spoke without thinking and was uncharacteristically abrupt, sounding just like Mother. 'I rather thought that was your job.' He was a little sniffy with me after that.

This time I would need to be professional, polite and diplomatic if I was to get any answers. I dialled 141 before the number of the coroner's office just in case awkward questions were asked – I didn't want anything traced back to me.

The police I'd been dealing with were from Chatford, the nearest station to the accident site. I'd watched enough police shows to know some of the jargon. 'I'm calling from the RTA Department at Chatford Police Station. It's about a case you're handling for us. An unidentified young woman. Died falling from a bridge. Would've been brought in sixteenth September.' My genealogy research has taught me that it's best to assume confidence and a level of authority with clerical staff and civil servants; speak their language, as it were.

The dead are not covered by data protection, it would seem. I was informed that she died before she hit the car, neck broken during the fall. No defensive injuries. Probably misadventure but the coroner's court would decide in due course.

When I hung up, I cried tears of relief: I wasn't to blame for the poor girl's death. There was nothing I could have done to save her, even if I'd had time to try.

I couldn't help her then, but I was doing everything I could to help her now.

Later that evening when I'd finished my scheduled chores, I shooed Ginger out of the room, then turned on my pc to check for any updates that the Teflon woman had refused to divulge to me in person.

The machine laboured through its start-up routines, but I was duly rewarded when I logged into the police website. They had at last issued a full description of my poor girl. I read it avidly, eager for information. Long wavy auburn hair and hazel-green eyes . . . mid/late twenties . . . five foot ten. Like me, tall for a woman. Multiple piercings in both ears. Tattoos, although they still didn't say of what, or where they were sited.

There was an e-fit graphic alongside the text which, like the average passport photo, probably bore no resemblance to reality. The eyes were wide-spaced under a broad forehead; an equally wide mouth and nose — everything about the features was generous. It was an enthusiastic face, a notice-me face; the opposite of my own. I swear I could be trapped in a train carriage for hours with half a dozen other people and, afterwards, none of them would recognise me if I passed them at the station. I was just too beige to be of interest.

This woman in the e-fit looked *vivid*, her personality full of colour – like her balloons.

She looked like someone who enjoyed life.

Had enjoyed life.

I signed on to social media with a heavy heart. My standard password, TIm3_Wa5t3, summed up my feelings towards this ghastly modern phenomenon. Observing the vitriol of many of the posts and the saccharine falseness of others I felt like a passive smoker, the toxicity seeping into my body just by being there. Still, even I had to admit, it had its uses. And this was one of them.

Twenty or thirty years ago the police would always have been your first port of call for help. But judging by social media, village email updates and posters on lampposts – whether you'd lost a dog, had a bike stolen, seen someone suspicious, or someone had gone missing – it seemed people often reached out to others first.

I searched #MissingPerson and was inundated with posts. The old and demented, the young and drug-addled, the vulnerable women, family men; so many people lost to the world, so many questions left unanswered. I narrowed my search to #MissingGirl, then #MissingWoman, both resulting in pages of messages. I settled in for a long evening, my pen and notepad close to hand.

There were a surprising number of auburn-haired women. Maybe a fashion thing. Some trend started by a pop star or actress that I'd be hard-pressed to recognise let alone name. I hadn't realised there were so many shades of red hair. Maybe I should consider it myself? I may have been approaching fifty, but I wasn't too old to make a change.

An hour or so later I'd found several viable options for my missing girl.

I'd based my search on the date of the posts, giving myself a range of a week before and after the accident; although she had died recently, in reality the poor young woman could have been missing for years – a runaway, an elopement, a bitter family row. Or she may not even be missed yet – an itinerant worker, a holidaymaker, a loner. But all those memories stored on her charm bracelet suggested that she was loved, someone people cared about; she'd touched others, had an impact on their lives. Surely someone would have missed her by now.

First up: Jac Pritchard, reported missing on 17th September 2018, the day after the accident. Last seen at a festival talking to a DJ. It was the cascading auburn curls that caused me to single her out, along with her age and the multiple studs in her ears, one through the cartilage like those tags you see on cattle. The 'missing' photo had been lifted from her account profile. She had seventy-two followers, mainly young people discussing fashion and music. Reading through each of her posts in turn, I found that she'd planned a 'wild new look' for the festival, which could mean anything, a new outfit, more piercings, a rakish hat. I skim-read through until I found the conclusive message: it clearly wasn't her. Back in early September, there it was: 'I am so over him!' it read, above a photo of her with *cropped* bleached hair. To be honest, it suited her better. Easier to manage too, I'd have thought.

Possible number two: Ella. She had that softer shade of ginger hair sometimes called strawberry-blonde. She'd applied for a place at college as a mature student and moved to the area over the summer to prepare for the start of term. It seems she'd changed her mind at the last minute and now no one knew where she was. Apparently that in itself wasn't so out of character, but she'd paid her rent for three months in advance and not tried to reclaim it – that was the giveaway to her family. They'd posted a photo of her. She had a tattoo of ivy that snaked over her collar bone and up to her left ear. Surely the police would have mentioned that in their description? Aside from this, she was a match: height, age, hair, eye colour all fitted. And the place she had rented was on the outskirts of Colchester, quite close to the A12 where the accident had happened.

She was a possible.

I set up a folder on the computer and saved the information. Thrilled with my progress, I decided a celebratory glass of wine and a hunk of cheese were in order.

Back at my desk, nibbling on my crackers and Jarlsberg, I researched my third possibility. As I read more about

Sunny, a missing barmaid, I felt the familiar excitement of homing in on my target.

The 'missing' message was posted under the name of a pub: the Pheasant and Grape, about fifteen miles from the accident site. *Trying to find Sunny Ryan. Not been seen since 15th September. Travelling from Australia. May be in London?'*

Her friends had responded with a thread of jocular posts over the first few days – it seemed they weren't particularly worried. *'He was* that *good????!!'; 'There's Celebrating your Birthday and there's taking the piss! Call me when you sober up. Dying to hear the goss!'; 'Get your Aussie arse back to work! I'm having to do double shifts.'* A riff on Vegemite and the drinking habits of Australians followed.

Over the last couple of days, greater urgency edged into the messages: *'Sunny, answer your phone or call me. Just let me know you're okay. If anyone's seen her get in touch by DM.'* I imagined myself in their shoes and goosebumps rose on my forearms.

One of her colleagues, JayCee, had a personal Instagram account. Clicking through, an image of a group of youngsters filled the screen. I scanned the happy faces searching for the red hair, my eyes flicking from one image to another until I found her. Disappointingly, in this first shot she had her head thrown back in laughter, her features distorted, half hidden. I scrolled down to find other photos.

And there she was.

I held my breath as I studied her, as if breathing on the screen too hard would blow her away again.

Something in my gut told me she was the one. But facts are more important than instincts and I would need to complete my research before reaching a conclusion.

She was not as beautiful as I had imagined. If it was her, then the e-fit was a fairly good representation. Maybe not so surprising, since they weren't reliant on the fanciful descriptions of witnesses . . . I pushed the mortuary slab from my mind, not wanting to imagine her there. I preferred to think of her alive and vibrant, living life to the full.

I copied and pasted the images onto my pc, along with any text I could find that identified the other people in the photos.

It was late and I was more tired and emotionally drained than I'd realised. I'd analyse all the information on my two girls, Ella and Sunny, tomorrow.

Step One complete.

Chapter 5

The next morning I'd decided to take my winter coat for dry cleaning and get a few other things off my to-do list. Clear the decks so I could focus on the next step of eliminating either Ella or Sunny. While I was always enthusiastic at the start of a project, this research was different. Knowing I was doing something worthwhile gave me a sense of purpose. I felt strangely energised and set off for the bus stop at a jaunty pace.

On the bus on my way into town, I considered my two young women – my money was definitely on Sunny. I ran through questions as they popped into my head: Assuming Sunny is a nickname, what's her real name? Were the balloons for her birthday? Who was the man her friends referred to? Why hasn't he come forward? Where are her family?

I was so wrapped up in my thoughts, I carried on up the high street and through to the market square, not pinging the bell until the bus had passed Asda, which should have been my first port of call. Once off the bus, I looked around to get my bearings and found myself outside a hairdresser's. Hair dye was top of my shopping list, and Asda frequently did a two-for-one offer. It was important to look professional and well turned out, but I'd been so distracted the past week or so that my roots were starting to show.

In the window of the salon there was a huge promotional poster: three smiling women, their heads so close together that the blonde, brunette and copper of their curls appeared to merge. There was something about those happy faces that called to me and, before I knew it, I had opened the door to the salon. I was hit by a blast of warmth and the sweet muggy smell of hairspray. It was a small place, a radio tuned to a seventies music station playing quietly in the background. The woman at the counter promptly put down an iPad and looked up. She seemed to be the only one there. 'Hi, can I help you?' Her manner was keen and professional and I imagined it was her own business. She was about my age, her hair in a neat shoulder-length cut.

I pointed to the poster in the window. 'I was thinking about hair dye.'

'You'd like an appointment to get your hair dyed?'

That wasn't what I'd envisaged – I'd thought maybe I'd be adventurous, buy a new product – but now she'd said it, I thought, why not? I could afford to treat myself occasionally; get my hair professionally coloured and styled.

'Yes please. As soon as possible.' It suddenly seemed imperative that I get it done that day, before I changed my mind.

'Were you thinking of the same colour? Or maybe something warmer?' She got up from her stool and walked towards me. She was short and stocky but nicely turned out, wearing a roll-neck tunic-dress which came to her mid-calf. I wondered if Tesco might stock something similar in my size. 'If you'd like to take a seat for a moment, I can show you the colour charts,' she said.

She handed me a book of swatches, pointing out the section closest to my usual shade.

'Natural Ash', apparently. Mother used to call it Field Mouse Brown.

'We could take it up a notch or two.' Her fingers hovered over a reddish-brown named Cocoa.

Recalling all those women with their various shades of red hair I thought *why not?* 'I'd really like to be daring – do something completely different.' I stroked the copper colour to indicate my choice. It had an energy and vibrancy.

Her face flagged her doubt.

'I always used to have my hair this colour until a few years ago,' I lied.

The woman pursed her lips slightly, but I guessed she wanted to please – after all, the customer is always right. I pressed on with my story. 'I'm meeting up with some old friends later in the week and I'd love my hair to look how it used to. Even if my face has aged a bit!'

Our eyes met in the mirror and she smiled. Her eyebrows didn't move and her unlined forehead suggested she may have had Botox injections.

'And I need something to distract from this!' I pointed at the healing scab on my forehead and the greenish bruise that had formed since the accident. 'I fell up the backstep, rushing to answer the doorbell.'

35

'I did wonder what you'd done. Looks painful. How about a choppy fringe to cover it?' She lifted my hair to show me the effect. Her hands itched to get the scissors, I could tell. 'A long bob cut? Maybe some layers?'

'That sounds great.'

A couple of hours later we were like old friends, me and Cathy. True to her profession, she'd started with the weather and holidays. Not wanting to be rude by being monosyllabic, I kept my end of the conversation up with the (fake) news that I was 'holidaying in Greece with one of my girlfriends', which set her off on an anecdote about an ill-advised fling with a waiter called Christos . . .

From there it only took a few questions for her to spill her life story, and I reciprocated with enough details to ensure the chat flowed pleasantly. Our reflections danced in time in the mirror: I smiled, wrinkled my nose, frowned whenever she did; obliged with shock or outrage – 'no!?' – when expected. Naturally curious, I prefer to ask questions and I've found that people enjoy talking about themselves. A good listener can put people at ease. She didn't ask me much and my contribution to the conversation could be summed up as: a preference for Asda over the new Morrisons, a love of animals, an enjoyment of gardening, and that I'd not watched the new series on Netflix because I'd stopped my subscription. Some of which was true.

I liked her and we seemed to have got on well enough that I would be comfortable to come here again. And who knew, maybe in time we could get to know each other properly and become friends.

'There!' she said, as she smoothed the last stray hair into place.

I put on my bifocals to take stock of my reflection and hardly recognised the vibrant image before me.

'Do you like it?' Her eyes met mine in the mirror, eager for approval.

'I love it!' Which was true. I was a changed woman. At least, from the neck up.

It was after lunchtime before I got home, all my missions complete. I was surprised not to have noticed my growling stomach before, but I didn't want to stop to eat now. I had far too much to do. I grabbed a plate and a couple of chocolate digestives and headed to my computer.

Comparing Google maps with the information I'd found on the post about Ella, I narrowed down her rental to one of three streets on the south side of Colchester. 'Triangulation', I believe they call it on crime programmes. A tingle of satisfaction ran through me; this felt like progress. It would be good to pop into the cafes and pubs nearby; ask some questions, see if I could find out anything useful. Like did she ever wear a charm bracelet? Maybe I'd drive there, later in the week, once I'd steeled myself to the idea. I'd still not had the nerve to get behind the wheel of the hire car. Maybe this mission would give me the courage.

★

Moving onto Sunny, I sorted through the images I'd downloaded. Enlarging one of the photos of the youngsters together in the pub, I zoomed in on her. Her T-shirt hung loosely off one shoulder, revealing a black bra strap; her jeans were cropped above the ankle and fashionably ripped. I scanned down to her hands: long scarlet nails, each finger laden with rings, and there it was – the charm bracelet hanging loosely around her pale freckled arm.

My fingers searched out the bracelet in its new home, tight around my left wrist, checking that the padlock was still clicked safely shut. The jeweller in the high street had done a good job.

I'd found her. The poor girl was Sunny. Sorry, Ella, I'm not going to be your saviour – Sunny is the one I need to help.

Be patient, sweetheart. I'll find your family and bring you home.

My plan was to make things easy for the police. I would find her family, collate all the information and hand it over to them, then step back into the shadows.

Envisioning that moment, I felt a thrill of excitement, familiar from my successful genealogy research missions. My professional life has been dedicated to finding links between the dead and the living, reuniting people across the divide of time and space. But this was different, more urgent and important than finding the missing link in a family tree. Time was ticking and still she lay there, alone and unloved, without a name.

Sunny's colleagues at the Pheasant and Grape *must* know something about her, even if she had been backpacking around the UK and only working there temporarily. Someone would have information that would help me – her full name would be a start.

The next step must be to go there, to Sunny's pub. But it would have to be anonymous – I couldn't face admitting to having been involved in the accident, couldn't cope with their horrified reactions, the risk that they would blame me for everything.

The decision made, I felt anxious just contemplating the journey. But I had to do it, for her. I studied the road map for routes that avoided the A12 and the bridge where this all started – I would take her flowers when I felt ready. Maybe a month from the accident.

Much as my priority was to find Sunny's family, my client work still needed to be done. I was conscious that the research visit, to the graveyard in Norfolk, remained an outstanding task and time was marching on. I decided to combine the two trips: an overnight stay in Norfolk to visit the graveyard and research their records; then, on the way back, call in at the pub to ask some questions without drawing attention to myself.

I looked up the Pheasant's website. Their menu was standard pub fare and they served scampi and chips, one of my favourites. A middle-aged woman calling in for a pub lunch on her journey home; what could be a better excuse?

Chapter 6

Thankfully the drive up to the Norfolk churchyard went without incident, despite my jangling nerves. Every time I felt anxious, I looked at the bracelet and thought of Sunny and it was as if she was there with me, encouraging me on.

When I arrived, the church warden was very accommodating, helping me identify the right volumes in the registers, before setting me up at a desk in the vestry.

'The light's not so good,' he observed as he manoeuvred a heavy standard lamp nearer to my seat. 'That handwriting's hard enough to decipher even when you *can* see it.'

I smiled my appreciation.

Later he led me to the Abbyss gravestones in the far corner of the cemetery. Rain was falling in a slight drizzle so he held a golf umbrella above our heads. The ground was uneven, as it often is in graveyards, with muddy puddles in unexpected places. We descended a slight slope pitted with shallow troughs – badgers' snuffle holes, he informed me. He offered his arm for me to lean on and I accepted gratefully; if I'd slipped, it wouldn't have been easy for me to get up and he certainly wouldn't have been able to lift me. He wasn't very tall and didn't have much meat on him.

After I'd taken photos of the headstones, he showed me the badger sett in the copse, pointing out the entrance ways and the fresh spoil from their digging. We made our way back to the vestry chatting amiably. I was gathering my paperwork from the desk and planning my goodbyes when he rubbed his hands together like an amateur actor miming cold.

'Cup of tea to warm you up before you get on your way?'

It was only later, as I struggled with the damp knot on my lace-ups back at my hotel, that I realised he may have been flirting with me.

It was odd for me to be noticed, for someone to show an interest in me. Maybe it was my new hairstyle. Maybe I should pop back to the church the next day before I headed south. I could leave my business card 'in case someone ever needs guidance with some research' . . .

As I ran my bath, stirring the water with one hand to ensure the correct balance of hot and cold, I let my imagination loose. *It's not long before the church warden phones me. 'A local woman wants to find her ancestors from the 1700s,' he says. 'Can you help?' When I visit to start the research, he's there waiting at the church door. He's thoughtfully collated the relevant records. 'Teach me,' he says. 'I'd like to learn what you do. The tricks of your trade.' He is a kind and earnest man. Pouring over the ancient marriage register together, our hands touch . . .*

Reaching for the flannel I caught sight of myself in the steamed-up mirror and swore I could almost hear Mother laughing.

The next morning, after a full English breakfast, I set off in the direction of home, via Sunny's pub. For most of the journey, I was pleasantly wrapped up in my thoughts, contemplating how to present my research to the Abbyss family. I loved finding the best way to tell the story, weaving the threads together in a way that brought each individual to life, adding a little colour here and there. My client, Glyn Abbyss, had opted for local history to be interleaved with the branches of the family tree. I had yet to collate the photos and background information. Google images and Wikipedia were my fallback if I ran short of research time. Wiki and my imagination could go a long way in creating an engaging story.

I was contemplating Aunty Marjory's possible reaction to discovering she descended from 'the Bastard Child of Margt Abbisse', when the sat nav man announced that I was approaching my destination: the Pheasant and Grape. I'd been following the directions mindlessly for over an hour and it was unsettling to be pulled from my reverie into Sunny's world. Like the first time you step off a plane in a foreign country – I felt a mix of excitement and nerves. My heart pounded as I pulled onto the forecourt. This was the closest I'd been to Sunny, to her life. I turned off the engine and sat for a while to gather my thoughts.

Pushing open the door to the bar, I was met by the smell of stale beer with a top note of air freshener. This place was not what I'd expected. The romantic in me had imagined Sunny working in a chocolate-box country pub: boot scrapers, roaring log fire and requisite muddy Labradors. This bar had the feel of a downmarket chain. I could imagine Mother's response to a pub like this. She'd see it for what it was: a template designed by a bunch of branding gurus who never left head office. The strategically placed books gathering dust. Candles, vases and brightly coloured ornaments, probably all glued down for health and safety reasons. Chalk writing on blackboards informing us of the 'specials', which probably never changed. I could hear Mother's cynical voice in my head: 'Cookie-cutter design, as fake as the barmaid's tan'.

The charms on Sunny's bracelet jangled as I raised my hand to push my glasses back into place. The new safety clasp on the chain was fiddly to undo so I tugged the sleeve of my jacket down to cover it. It wouldn't do to raise awkward questions about who I was and how I'd come by the bracelet. I wouldn't want to upset anyone.

At the other end of the bar counter, the three staff were engaged in changing the whisky bottle on the optic: one actually doing the job, another dabbing ineffectually at the whisky they'd somehow spilt on the counter. And the third standing back from the others, hands on hips, her voice suggesting she found it amusing as she observed their struggles: 'Watch your elbow, Dan. You're close to the sherry.'

43

Along the wall, a series of laminated quotes suggested the landlord's efforts to stamp his personality on the venture: 'Let your smile change the world', 'Be a MaxiCAN not a MaxiCAN'T', 'Light tomorrow with today'. The choices shouted a blend of youthful zeal and charming naivety. I'd place a bet that the manager was the chap in his late twenties in the Instagram photos. Probably spent his spare time burning off energy, skateboarding or running marathons.

The advice-giver turned around and, obeying the edict to 'change the world', beamed a selfie-ready smile at me. I recognised her immediately from the photos on my wall. It was JayCee. Just as pretty and warm as the photos, but now with pink dreadlock extensions rather than the long blonde ones she'd favoured in my photo collection.

'Hi! Have you been waiting long?' she said, subconsciously rubbing a fading bruise on her arm. 'What can I get you?'

I shook my head. 'No, not long. A Coke please.'

She chatted about the weather as she squirted the fizzy liquid from the hose under the bar top. A delightful young woman, all bounce and enthusiasm.

'You're JayCee, aren't you?' I said. She nodded, smiling. I'd already concluded that she and Sunny were good friends from the photos and posts I'd seen online. 'Sunny often speaks about you.' I looked around the bar as if searching for her, then asked, 'Is she in today? I was really hoping to surprise her.'

The smile had disappeared. She set the glass down without looking at me, focusing on wiping a smear from the bar surface. 'We've not seen her for a while.'

'When will she be back? I'm happy to wait if she's popped out for a few hours. I've got her a belated birthday present.' I patted my handbag, implying a gift was inside.

'No, she's not here.' Her tone was flat, all bounce and warmth gone. 'We've not seen her for a couple of weeks.' The other two had drifted over; it seemed the bar staff had a tendency to coalesce.

'Is she on leave?' I asked. 'I spoke to her just before her birthday – we said we'd catch up properly when I got back from my holiday.'

JayCee glanced at the other two before she continued. 'We think she's in London. She went there for her birthday and hasn't come back yet. But she does that sometimes, goes off for a while.'

The blonde girl – the one with the bottled tan and the dishcloth – spoke for the first time. 'She got a new boyfriend . . .' she offered, her rising intonation implying an unstated question.

The lad called Dan nudged her in the ribs. 'Only one?' he said sarcastically.

'Don't be mean.'

He shrugged. 'I wasn't. Just saying it how it is.' I wasn't sure I liked him.

JayCee flashed a frown at them both and the banter stopped.

'She never mentioned any family here in England. Are you a friend?' she asked me.

'An old family friend, yes.' It was worrying that after their initial flurry of social media posts, they'd not taken

45

any steps to find her. 'It's odd that she didn't phone me if she was planning to move away.'

'She had to move out of the staff flat just before her birthday. Said she was moving in with some guy she'd known for a few months. Must've been while you were away.'

'Like I said. One too many dudes staying here with her overnight.' Dan looked pleased with himself. 'Rob chucked her out.'

Rob. He must be the skateboarding manager. I squirreled this information away with the other treasures they'd provided. You never knew what would be useful later.

'Yeah, but she wasn't worried about having to move out . . . just came into work like normal afterwards.' The blonde girl looked to her colleagues for verification. 'She never lets anything get to her. She just shouts and storms out and then an hour later it's all forgotten.'

'Yeah, but she might've had *another* row with Rob and not told us,' JayCee said. 'I know he wanted to put her on the books, make it legit, but she wanted to stay cash-in-hand. Maybe she decided she'd had enough this time . . . She'd said something about moving to London. . . . I guess that's where she's gone.'

'Wouldn't she have called you to tell you? You're her friends, she'd want to see you, keep in touch?'

'Yeah. We were, like, really cross when she didn't come in. You know what I mean? She should've called us. Rob went mental.' The blonde's diction was beginning to grate on me.

'You've not heard from her for a couple of weeks – have you told the police?' They looked from one to the other at the novelty of this idea. 'I mean, she could have had an accident or something.'

'Jeez. Do you think, like, something awful's happened?'

'I don't know. But I do think you should call the police and tell them what you know.'

They looked from one to the other like vulnerable children waiting for Mummy and Daddy to tell them what to do, unready to be thrust into this adult world of decision making.

'We wouldn't want to waste their time, though,' JayCee said. 'I mean, she's probably just decided to move on. Like I said, she was thinking of moving away.'

'You were the last ones to see her. You should report her as missing.'

'Do you think we should?' Dan asked.

'Yes, I think it would be a good idea.'

As I left the pub, all thoughts of lunch abandoned, Dan was already dialling the number. I hadn't given them my name.

Chapter 7

Now the police had Sunny's name, I judged it would take a day or two for the dots to be joined, before the inevitable rebooting of activity on social media as the news spread. They would add Sunny's details to the Missing Persons database, match the description to any un-named, unclaimed bodies. After the identification of Sunny, they would track down her relatives in Australia. I could only imagine the shock of that first contact and the deep pain of the terrible news . . .

My heart went out to them.

As the police beavered on with their work of finding the family, I put the day to good use, finding out all I could about Sunny, this girl I'd come to care about so much. While I'd achieved my goal of identifying Sunny and she would soon be reunited with her family, I was still curious about her. There was something that drew me to her story; this poor young woman who'd burned so brightly in her short life. I wanted to know more.

My first source was the photos JayCee had posted. Sunny had been tagged, so it was only one step to her profile page. I clicked the link, my heart pounding with the excitement of getting to know her and the thought of all I might find.

Her profile photo was a surprise: a stiletto heel crushing a vinyl record. She seemed to be going by the name Rusty Steel. Initially I assumed it was an alias, or possibly some modern reference linked to the cryptic profile image, easily decoded by her fellow millennials.

Her posts were intermittent; a flurry of activity then nothing for weeks. A handful of 'friends' and only following a few singers, none of whom were familiar to me. I searched back to February, when it seemed she'd first arrived in the UK.

'*So, hello London. Rusty here ready to show Britain what talent really means – LOL!*'

Underneath she'd placed an image of the *Britain's Got Talent* logo – a show that had never been on my TV screen for longer than the second it took to flick between channels. It looked like she was taking this quest for fame quite seriously: '*In rehearsals right now. Not ready to say more yet but (hopefully) you're gonna luv it!!*' There were four 'likes' and I made a note of the names. It seemed she was working in a restaurant at that time and a check of their website and social media confirmed my suspicion that these followers were her co-workers.

It struck me that there were no posts from her family. I wondered why her mum and dad hadn't commented; I'd have been encouraging my beautiful and passionate daughter in every way I could. Maybe they disapproved – thought she was wasting her time, dashing halfway round the world in search of recognition. Or maybe this was her secret, a dream she wanted to make real before she shared it with those who mattered.

One post showed a series of images of her on a small, bare stage under a banner reading 'Open Mic Night at The Railway – all welcome'. She looked stunning, her outfit designed to maximise attention rather than protect her from the chill of a February evening. Tight black shorts coupled with thigh-length boots over neon-blue tights, her sleeveless top tight and low-cut. I had to smile at her panache. Even if I'd *ever* had that level of confidence about my appearance, one cold look from Mother would have withered my enthusiasm. Her post declared the evening 'a huge success', with 'loads of interest' and requests for her details.

While Rusty Steel didn't blog regularly, there was a lot of information and it was easy to piece her movements together even with such sporadic posts. Key elements of her life and the people she met along the way; it was all there. Waitressing in a pub chain, then a few weeks in a coffee shop. Photos of her posing with different men, the named boyfriends coming and going, with no clear consistency in the type that attracted her or the reasons they split up. Around April she eventually settled at the Pheasant and Grape, where she 'found her crew': JayCee, Dan, Rob, Lola, John, Aki, Rick . . . the list went on. Eighteen 'friends' and many more likes for her posts. And links to songs about love.

I was pleased she'd found happiness.

Using my genealogy research skills, I collated all this information in month-by-month spreadsheets from the start of her time in England. Where she was, what she was up to, who she was with. Once I'd annotated all the photos with any names I could find, I printed everything out. Blu-tacked to my office walls, it created a visual timeline, just like you see in detective shows.

Sitting back to admire my progress, I was intrigued by the life of this tempestuous young woman; so different from anyone I'd ever known. She'd captured my curiosity – on the surface, carefree and happy; but what was driving this butterfly behaviour? Was she running from something – not wanting to grow up, avoiding responsibilities? Or was she looking for something she couldn't quite find, kicking over every stone just in case?

It seemed she was grabbing every opportunity, moving on when it didn't work out the way she wanted. Maybe I should learn from her: take a few risks, get out there and make things happen. And maybe she could've learned from me: a gentle hand on the tiller helping her channel her energies, steer her from harm. Someone who would care enough to always be there, whether she was full of fanciful dreams or impetuous behaviour. Help her to find what she wanted, whatever had been missing from her life.

It was easy to find the location of the restaurant where Sunny had worked when she first came to England, in a parallel street to the pub where she had performed. Shepherd's Bush, a lively shopping area.

The next morning, I travelled to London to continue my research. I wanted to see some of her haunts and maybe find some of the friends she'd made, hoping they would have memories of her to share. And, if appropriate, I would tell them the sad news. Better they hear it from me than to read about it online in a few days' time.

It ended up being quite a disappointment. There had been almost a complete turnover of staff at the restaurant since she left. Only the chef remained and he claimed not to remember her, even when I showed him a photo. However, he went quite red in the face and I wondered if there may have been something between them. Maybe an unrequited passion? Sunny had had more than her fair share of male admirers.

I had a bit more luck at the pub. It was an Australian-themed place, the needs of the young backpacking clientele met by Victoria beer, Ned wine, burgers and all-day brunch. Behind the bar, they had hung a huge upside-down map of the world – Australia at the top. Postcards from Sydney, Melbourne and Brisbane were tacked around its frame. In this environment, Sunny must've found an element of familiarity, somewhere she could feel at home.

It was a quiet period, just after the lunchtime rush, but I still felt slightly incongruous in these surroundings. Focused on my mission, I perched on a stall at the bar in order to engage the staff in seemingly casual chat. Having ordered their Beer and Burger Bargain, I pointed to the banner advertising the open mic nights.

'When's your next one?' I asked. 'I heard you get some good musicians.'

The young man laughed. 'Yeah. Sometimes. It's a bit pot luck.'

'I know someone who performed here a few times. She's a singer.'

'Oh, yeah? What's her name?'

'Sunny. But her stage name was Rusty Steel. Do you remember her?'

'Hard to forget. She almost lived here!'

'You knew her?' I was so thrilled I wanted to kiss him. 'Did she work here then?'

'No, but she was in all the time. Always talking about some bloke in the music business who was going to get her on *Britain's Got Talent*.'

'Oh, do you know his name?'

He shook his head. 'Nah. Just some dude who came and watched her one night. Sort of ageing rocker look. He gave her his card and she wouldn't stop banging on about it.'

'Do you know what happened? Did he help her?'

'Dunno,' the barman shrugged. 'He never came back.'

That evening I tried to distract myself with the Abbyss family, weaving the parts of their history together to create a seamless story. Usually this was the part I enjoyed the most, injecting the life into it, rounding out the characters with the odd fanciful fabrication:

'As a yeoman, John's day would've started at dawn. A quick wipe of his face with a damp cloth, before he donned his working clothes for his two-mile trudge across the fields . . .'

But this time it was harder to focus, my creativity had disappeared.

I couldn't wait any longer; I had to know if Sunny's family had been found. No one was going to tell me, so I resorted to my research sleuthing.

I opened the file on my pc and, one by one, dragged the pictures of Sunny and her friends into Google's 'reverse image search'. A useful tool I'd recently discovered, it 'does what it says on the can', enabling you to find other sites with the same photo.

And bingo, there it was. The shot of her with her colleagues from the pub was on a memorial page. Her dad had been busy.

This modern, very public way of mourning always seemed odd to me, but I didn't want to sit in judgement. People do strange things when they are in distress. He was no doubt devastated and needed a way to express his sadness. Probably a very sensible man most of the time. Ned Ryan, her dad, had headed his memorial 'A Tribute to Sonya Ryan: Ain't No Sunshine'. He'd embedded a link to a recording on the page and as my office filled with the wistfulness of Bill Withers' voice, a shiver went down my spine. It was the first time I'd ever *felt* the sadness of the lyrics.

The memorial page showed each stage of Sunny's life. In the first photo, a baby wrapped in a blanket lay cradled to the chest of an amiable-looking woman; a man stood behind them, one arm around her and the other hand resting on the shoulder of a young boy of eight or nine, their happiness beaming out from the screen. Beneath it, Sunny's dad had typed: *'Here's our little darling on the day we first met her. Three months old and bright as a button already, bringing sun into our lives from the get-go! Welcome to the family, Sonya Ryan.'* I paused to consider the unusual choice of phrasing: 'the day we first met her'. Then it clicked. I'd seen similar phrases in the past while doing my research – Sunny had been adopted by the Ryans.

Sunny's story played out in the images. A standard early childhood, it seemed: being pushed on the swing in her back garden, paddling in the sea under a grey British sky under the watchful eye of her older brother; Mum and/or Dad in every shot holding her hand or cuddling her. The mood changed abruptly before she reached her teens: *'Sunny coped bravely when her much-loved mum died. We planted this rose bush as a tribute to Mummy.'* In the photo, Sunny isn't much taller than the plant she's standing beside. Gripping a green can, she is watering the base of the shrub looking grimly determined. The headstone could be seen behind her, although I wasn't sure if I would be able to enhance the image enough to read the dates. She looked as if she was about ten years old. The lanky teenager standing to one side of the grave must be the brother.

I swallowed hard; the poor, poor child. Never knowing her birth mother, then losing the only mother she'd loved. She must've felt so lost and abandoned.

Subsequent photos showed Ned and Sunny boarding a flight: he had a fake smile plastered on, his hand resting on Sunny's shoulder; her face expressionless, the blankness of a child in shock. He took the children to live in Australia, his birth country apparently. Images of their house, detached, one storey, a pool in the back garden; of camping at sunset; of them on a boat in the bay, and of endless beaches. I studied their faces for clues – they both looked happy, which pleased me. She seemed so full of life, I could see how she came by the nickname Sunny; no wonder her dad looked so proud – who wouldn't be proud of a daughter like that?

In her late teens the images became more posed and moody: the supermodel pout, the haughty grandeur; Ned no longer appearing alongside, no longer deemed cool enough, I assumed. The brother seemed long gone – moved on for a job, leading his own life. There were some photos with friends but not many. It seemed that they moved house several times . . .

The final photo was the shot of Sunny and her friends in the pub. Beneath it, Ned announced the date he was coming over from Australia. He planned a cremation; the ashes to be interred with her mother's. Another rose bush planted.

My heart broke with the unfairness of it all. This poor man, losing his wife and then his daughter. Like me, he must feel so alone. But it seemed Sunny was drawing us together.

Chapter 8

It was a month since the accident and I was ready to go back to the bridge where it had happened. It was time to pay my respects to Sunny. I'd got to know her so well over the past couple of weeks, it felt like I was a relative kept up to date with annual round-robins, cards and letters. From her adoption by the Ryans at three months old, to her move to Australia, her growing up with Ned, to her recent travels in England – her story was coming into focus, but I still wanted to understand what drove her, find out what made her tick. And maybe I could find some clues as to how the accident happened.

I gave myself plenty of time for this journey back to the bridge, booking the night before at a local B&B. I arrived at lunchtime and had a ploughman's in the 'snug', an excuse to chat to the barmaid and pump her for information. I still wondered why Sunny had been in this area on the day of her birthday and wanted to piece it all together. What had she been doing?

From my research I already knew there was a small town, Gressingdon, on the other side of the A12. The barmaid informed me it was 'a magnet for tourists', who loved to travel on the local hopper train that connected to the London line. There was 'a pleasant walk' that would take me to the station and the little railway museum where they had some interesting local memorabilia. She rushed off in search of a map to show me, misinterpreting my 'I don't want to put you out' for politeness, rather than a lack of interest in walking and train museums. As her blood-red acrylic fingernail traced the route across fields, I scanned ahead looking for the pedestrian bridge that crossed the A-road. The place where Sunny fell. It was probably about twenty minutes' walk from here.

I tapped my finger on the map, indicating the bridge. 'I saw a police sign on the roadside a while ago when I passed this way. Something about an accident?'

She leaned in close to peer at the page, as if checking she was thinking about the same event, like they happened all the time. 'Yes, it was three or four weeks ago now, I think. Terrible thing. A woman died.'

'How awful,' I said. 'Did anyone round here know her?'

'No. Must've been a tourist. We get a lot of them round here.'

A dead end.

I drove round to Gressingdon later that afternoon to get my bearings. It was a quaint country town – the type you only found in the remoter parts of rural England – that remained unsullied by a skirt of modern housing. It sat in the sweet spot: accessible to transport links with its quaint station building, but just far enough from the A12 not to get constant traffic noise.

Wanting to check out the route to the pedestrian bridge in order to be ready for the next morning, I manoeuvred the car through the lanes leading from the main street. When the tarmac gave way to a dirt track, I realised I could go no further and had to carry out a complicated series of shunts backwards and forwards to turn the car around.

Back on the high street I located the town's flower shop. The florist helped me put together a beautiful bouquet: pale lemon and gold carnations, bright yellow and orange gerbera, mango calla lilies. Sunny's colours.

The woman took it back to the counter where she fussed with cellophane.

'Will there be anything else?' she asked, not raising her eyes from her task. She was doing that thing with scissors that makes the ribbon curl. 'A card maybe?' She added a gaudy satin-effect bow and smiled at the flowers, not at me.

A thought struck me. 'Do you sell helium balloons?' Maybe Sunny or the person who bought her the balloons had been in this very shop.

'We don't stock them this time of year. Only Valentine's and Halloween. I can order them for you.'

'You didn't handle a large order about a month ago, did you?'

She frowned, looking up at me for the first time. 'You're not from the press, are you? Here about that accident again?'

'No, I—'

Before I could formulate a reasoned response, she had interrupted me. 'That will be forty pounds. Cash or card?'

The next morning I felt strangely anxious, my stomach churning so much I only managed two slices of toast at breakfast. I'd left the flowers in the car overnight and their happy-sad scent welcomed me as I unlocked the vehicle. I planned to park as close as I could to the bridge, pay my tribute to Sunny and then make my way home. The ducks and cats would be missing me.

Getting out of the car, I cradled the bouquet like a much-loved child. Fiddling with the cellophane, coddling the flowers, an unbidden thought arose – Samantha. I'd planned to call my daughter Samantha.

I shivered, although I wasn't cold; not now, don't go there. Leave that in the past. Now is the time to focus on Sunny.

I breathed deeply – in for a count of seven, out for eleven – then walked towards the bridge. She'd taken this same path – the sun had been shining and she'd been here, laughing, with her birthday balloons. I hoped she'd enjoyed that last morning.

On the bridge I looked south, in the direction of my home. This was where she must've been just before she fell. The thought made me queasy and I clutched the rail for support. The sun was directly overhead and I was hot and flustered in my woollen jacket and scarf. I focused on my breathing until I was calm again.

60

'Misadventure'. What kind of an adventure could she have been having up here? There was little to excite the imagination once you'd left the postcard prettiness of the town. I looked to the far side of the bridge but whatever was there lay hidden by a mass of trees, the ash, beech and oak now losing their leaves. They must've looked magnificent a month ago in their autumnal glory.

I bent to place the flowers against the concrete base of the barrier, resting them in the shade so they might last a little longer. It seemed fitting to say a few words, but I'm not a religious woman and couldn't think of anything appropriate. I should've prepared.

Leaning over the safety barrier, I peered down to the road. The speed of the vehicles passing below made me light-headed and nauseous. Even if she'd been alive before she landed on my car, she wouldn't have stood a chance. It was just so sad. I started to cry. It was then I saw him – a young man at the side of the bridge, at the top of the steep embankment. I took off my glasses and wiped my eyes with the back of my hand. When I looked back he hadn't moved; he was standing stock-still as if mesmerised by the traffic zooming past, unaware of anything else.

My stomach churned as he took a step forward, turning sideways to ease himself down the slope towards the roadway. From where I was standing, I could see how dangerous this was – one foot wrong and he would end up cartwheeling into the path of the cars. Was he going to fling himself in front of a vehicle? I wanted to cry out 'No! Stop!' but didn't want to risk distracting him and cause him to fall.

I rushed back to the side of the bridge as quickly as I could and made my way through the bracken to where he'd been standing. Age, weight and general fitness were not on my side, and by the time I got there he was sitting partway down the slope, his back to me, head hanging. His forearms were resting on his denim-clad knees, his hands clutching some sort of artificial flowers, gripped so tight his knuckles were white.

Was he another colleague from the pub, someone I'd not seen when I visited?

My heart pounded as I edged forward. While it was potentially dangerous for both of us, I had to climb down there and speak to him. Luckily, once I'd started, the descent wasn't as terrifying as I'd imagined from the top. There were ridges in the dry earth where others had scrambled – the police no doubt, and before them, the graffiti artists who had tagged the sides of the bridge. As I got closer, he must've sensed movement as he looked over his shoulder. Our eyes met and my pulse raced – his photo was on my wall! Under *March* or *April*, I think – he was one of her many beaus. His cheeks were wet with tears, his nose running. He lifted his arm and wiped it across his face, the way a small child does. Frowning, he shuffled back from me, preparing to stand.

I put my hands out, palms up, in an attempt to signal I posed no threat. Although what harm he imagined a sixteen-stone, middle-aged woman could inflict on him, lord only knows. Losing my footing and tumbling us both into the traffic was the biggest risk.

He said nothing, just stared at me with the eyes of a cornered animal contemplating escape.

'I brought flowers,' I said. 'For Sunny.' I pointed to where the orange petals of the gerbera were just about visible between the vertical rails. He looked from me to the bridge several times, weighing me up, before turning to face the road again, his back tight with tension.

I waited for him to say something, but he remained silent. Balanced unsteadily on the slope, I was aware that an attack of cramp in this precarious position could be my undoing. Unable to maintain my stance and desperate to find out more, I lowered myself to sit near him, relieved that my ungainly efforts went unobserved. Once seated, as comfortably as possible on the forty-five-degree slope, I tried not to puff as I caught my breath. I tugged my skirt down over my knees, noticing a run in my tights where I must've caught them on the brambles.

Next to me he sat rigidly, staring out across the roadway to the trees beyond. Tears still tracked down his face to drip from his chin.

'Why did she come here?' he mumbled, almost to himself. His English lightly accented, the words difficult to catch, swept away by the noise of the passing cars.

'We may never know,' I said.

He gave the faintest of nods, lowering his head almost to his chest, the shaking of his shoulders signalling that he was crying hard. I shuffled slightly nearer to put a hand on his forearm, to let him know he was not alone.

Swept by a strong maternal concern, I had an urge to hug him but was uncertain how responsive he would be to such a gesture from a stranger. I gently rubbed his back as people do with babies.

We sat like that for some time.

Climbing back up the embankment later was not as easy, my knees and back having stiffened from perching on the slope. He went ahead, reaching down to take my hand to help, pointing to where I should put my feet. At the top we stood facing each other, both feeling exposed for the first time.

He had heavy brows, a Roman nose, his hair grown longer and unruly since the photos on my wall. Russian? Dmytro? That was one of the names she'd used in her posts.

'You were Sunny's boyfriend.' A calculated guess. Although, I realised, he may be one of many. He featured in more of the photos I'd found than any of the other men.

He nodded sadly. His hands fidgeted, unsure what to do with themselves. He had left the plastic flowers on the embankment, his own tribute to her.

'Will you come for a coffee with me?' I asked. 'I would love to talk with you.'

Chapter 9

We ended up in an anonymous chain on the high street in Gressingdon. A strong black coffee for him and a latte for me. He pulled out his wallet to try to give me the money and a picture of Sunny beamed at me from the inside.

'She looks beautiful,' I said, pointing to the image. I reached into my bag and pulled out my diary. Tucked in the back was a copy of a photo I'd printed from the net. I held it up so he could see it, trying to reassure him — I too have a photo of her. He took it in both hands, hungry to see her again.

'She was happy, always laughing,' I said.

He frowned, looked me up and down. 'Who are you? How did you know Sunny?'

I reached for the photo and placed it on the table between us. 'Sunny's real name is Sonya. I'm called Sonya, too. We're related.' *Oh, I said it. I'd actually said it aloud!*

I hadn't planned this, hadn't set out to deceive; it was a spontaneous response. My heart was thudding like rocks cascading down a mountain, but I felt strangely relieved, like I'd shared a huge secret I'd been carrying alone. I'd been imagining what it would be like to have a daughter like her since the moment I'd discovered Sunny was adopted. Playing with the idea, trying it on for size.

Imagining she could have been my Samantha.

'How can you be related?' He sat more upright in his seat, his frown deepening as his doleful green-brown eyes scanned my face. 'She lived in Australia with her family.'

'Yes. But I am a blood relative. Her real family.' He stared at me unsmiling. 'Sunny was adopted when she was a baby. She didn't know me until recently.' I spoke slowly, giving him time to take it in.

'I know she was adopted. She told me.'

'She came from Australia to find me. Sunny was . . .' I paused, suddenly aware of the significance of what I was about to say. There was no going back. 'Sunny was my daughter. I am her mother.'

'Sunny is your daughter?'

'Yes. I had to give her up. I would have kept her . . . but I didn't have the chance.'

His frown deepened. He appeared an intense young man, not given to lightness and levity.

'She told me about you,' I said. 'I wanted to meet you but I didn't know how to find you. I know she cared a lot about you.'

'She said this to you? You knew about me and Sunny?' He was biting at the skin by his thumb, his fingers callused, knuckles red. A labourer or tradesman then.

66

I nodded.

'So, why didn't she tell me anything about you?'

'She wanted her dad to know first.'

'Ned?' he said, a dark expression on his face. 'In Australia?'

'She wanted to tell him face-to-face, not on the phone or by email.' Once I started expanding on my imagined story, hearing myself say the words aloud to him, it seemed like it was true. Like I'd known her and we'd really had the conversations I'd been imagining these past weeks. 'She hadn't told anyone about me. You are the first of her friends and family that I have met.'

There was another silence while he processed this information. I had no idea how he would react. My stomach danced with nerves, concerned he could bolt at any moment, not wanting to lose him when I'd only just found him. It was clear from his behaviour that he had really cared about Sunny and I hoped he would want to talk to me, someone who also knew and loved her. Eventually he looked me directly in the eyes and said heavily, 'I am pleased to meet you, Sunny's mother, Sonya.'

'Likewise, Sunny's boyfriend, Dmytro.' That neatly summed up what we knew about each other. 'It's so sad that we had to meet like this.' I paused, took a sip of my latte, not wanting my curiosity to scare him off. 'I don't suppose you know what happened the day of the accident? It's all such a mystery.'

He kept his eyes averted. 'She said she was going to London . . . to London for a recording . . . She didn't

say how many days . . . I took her to the station . . .'
He petered to a halt.

'Yes. Everyone thought she was in London, even her friends at the Pheasant.'

So, he hadn't been with her when she fell. Had he bought her the balloons? Were they a gift sent by her colleagues at the pub? And why was she on the bridge? I had so many questions but they would have to wait; for now I needed to focus on getting to know him.

Our coffees grew cold as he drip-fed more of his story in answer to my gentle questions. He'd come from Ukraine several years ago on a tourist visa. But it didn't take much to put two and two together and work out that he must have overstayed and was probably working illegally. He was taking whatever work he could get, sending money home to his family. It was easy to sense how alone and lonely he was, with few friends here in this country, Sunny his only real friend. No wonder he'd suggested she move into his flat when she was thrown out of the accommodation at the pub.

Of course, I still had lots of questions, but it was far too soon to push harder on the events the day of the accident. I wondered why he wasn't going to London with her on her birthday, whether he knew about the other men in her life. So many avenues I wanted to explore but they would have to wait until I had won his trust.

The sky was now dark outside in that sudden countryside way, and the staff were wiping down tables around us.

'I will go now,' he said.

As he moved to get up, I reached over to stay him for a moment, needing to satisfy my curiosity on one last point. 'What happened to her belongings? Her clothes and things?'

'I have her things.'

'Would you let me collect them? To look after them until I can return them to Ned when he comes to the UK.'

I left it a couple of days before I rang Dmytro. 'Hi, it's Sonya. Sunny's mum.' It was amazing how natural, how right, it felt to say. 'I wondered when it would be convenient for me to come over. To collect Sunny's things.' An 'assumptive close', I believe it was called. I really wanted to see him again and I didn't want to risk him changing his mind.

'Tonight. I am here.' His voice sounded monotone, tired.

He gave me the address. It wasn't far from the pub where Sunny had worked, thirty minutes' drive for me. I arranged to meet him at six o'clock.

The flat itself was above a betting shop. Dmytro stepped back in the narrow passageway to let me in, but with the bike stashed in the hallway there wasn't room for me to squeeze through. He turned and led the way. The steep stairs were lit by a naked bulb adorned with cobwebs, the carpet threadbare on the treads.

Catching my breath after the climb, I took stock of the scene before me. I'd anticipated the flat would be uninviting, but this looked almost uninhabitable. The main room, a kitchen-cum-diner-cum-lounge, was strewn with the stuff of day-to-day life. Everything lay discarded where it had last been used. The sofa was buried under crumpled clothing, a mountain of dishes was piled up in the sink, and empty cigarette packets and stray pages from newspapers littered every surface. Incongruous among the grimness and clutter, a bright orange shagpile rug suggested an abandoned attempt at homeliness. I wondered if that had been Sunny's touch.

'Dmytro,' I said, shaking my head in dismay. I gesticulated to the mess. 'What's happened, love?'

He shrugged one shoulder, his eyes downcast. 'No one sees it but me.'

I pushed some of the clothing to one side and sat, cautiously, on the sofa. 'You aren't looking after yourself. Are you eating properly?'

'I eat bread. Beans.' The latter was evidenced in a small collection of empty cans next to the bin. Maybe he intended to recycle them. Funny the routines we hold onto when everything else falls apart.

'Do you have any milk? Shall we have a cup of tea?' I asked. From my hasty internet research, I understood that Ukrainians like tea almost as much as us Brits.

He washed up two mugs that had been lying in the sink with the dirty crockery. His movements were slow, as if everything was an effort. A fly buzzed against the window pane above the draining board but he ignored it.

'Have you been going to work?'

'Yes,' he said, without turning round. 'I go to work. I come home. I go to work . . .'

I wanted to ask him how I could help, if there was anything I could give him that would make things better, but what did I know about how to heal another's broken heart when I'd never managed it for myself?

He came over to the table and pushed aside a dirty plate to set the tea down, then slumped heavily on the chair opposite. I didn't speak, leaving the silence to give us both some space. The image of Mr Cool marched across the side of my mug and I guessed it had been a gift from Sunny. I could imagine her buying it. No doubt there was a matching Little Miss version somewhere in the sink. Little Miss Naughty, if her reputation at the pub was true. As I reached for the handle of the mug, I saw Dmytro's eyes fix on Sunny's bracelet around my wrist.

'Is that Sunny's?' His voice was accusing.

'Yes.' I held my arm up so the charms swung freely. My contacts had identified the original clasp as relatively common in the 1960s, neither antique nor valuable. 'The police gave it to me,' I said, which was true. 'After the accident.'

'I gave her that. The heart,' he said. He pointed to the charm.

My fingers found the small silver heart, embellished with a squirly letter S.

'S for Sunny,' he said. He reached forward and turned it over, showing a symbol like a jiggly capital A. I'd not

71

noticed it before. Cyrillic script, I guessed. He pointed to his chest. 'D. For Dmytro,' he said.

I took his hand in both of mine and he didn't pull away. 'Dmytro, I'm sure Sunny loved you very much.' I wanted to help him in any way I could, but knew I had to approach it carefully. 'I feel you are like family . . . almost like a son to me.' I paused. 'You have no one here, in this country. Please, let me be a friend to you.'

He looked away, but when his eyes eventually met mine, I swore I would never forget the heavy sadness in his face.

When we'd finished our tea, he gathered up Sunny's things. They didn't amount to much – a handbag covered in silver chains, a backpack that Dmytro filled with some clothes and a few odds and ends he located scattered around the flat. She had travelled light in the way of young people today. They were unencumbered by the need to own stuff when they could borrow it, or buy it cheaply, use and discard it. These millennials were a different breed to the post-war, make-do-and-mend culture of my generation.

Dmytro's flat was a case in point, there being no sign of a washing machine in the small kitchen. I guessed that he used a launderette, assuming they still existed. Before I left, I offered to take some of his washing for him. 'It's no trouble,' I said. He shrugged and I promised I would return in a few days.

It felt good to be able to do something for him, even if it was only a small gesture.

Back at home, I unpacked Sunny's things, planning to store them neatly until I could return them to her dad. I'd already cleared a space in the wardrobe in the spare room; I liked to keep everything shipshape, couldn't bear living in chaos. Folding the T-shirts and hanging up the skirts and jeans brought me a frisson of pleasure. Admiring the neatly organised piles and hangers, it was as if she was away at college or out for an evening and might return home any moment.

Other than the clothes and the usual wash-kit and make-up, the bag held the odds and ends of a back-packing life. I flicked through the tourists' guide to London, looking for places she'd ringed or any notes, but the only page with a folded-down corner was the map of Shepherd's Bush – the location of the open mic Australian bar. Her passport photo wasn't flat-tering, but then whose was? Disappointingly, there wasn't a mobile, diary or illicit letters to pique my imagination. There was just a notebook with a few pages of scrawled notes, song lyrics copied from the web, the address of a few websites. Her handwriting really was a mess. At the back there was a list of dates and numbers in wandering columns. It wasn't clear what they could refer to. I scanned that page into my laptop to think about later.

By the time I'd finished with the backpack and stashed it on top of the wardrobe, the washing machine had finished its spin cycle.

Downstairs I shook one of Dmytro's T-shirts to get the worst of the creases out before I placed it on a hanger to dry. The printed logo made no sense – *Oops Apocalypse*. A band or a film, I assumed. I'd look it up when I got a moment. Seeing his flat had opened my eyes a bit, the way he was existing rather than living, in contrast to Sunny, who seemed to grab every moment. It made me realise how long I'd put my own life on hold. All those dreams I'd had as a young woman, the plans that I'd had . . . I don't like to think about it, but all this emotional upheaval was taking me back there.

The year that Gran died, when *everything* had started to go wrong.

Hard to believe, but that was nearly thirty years ago. Where had the time gone?

Chapter 10

Gran, Dad, me and Mother. The four of us had lived here at The Old Vicarage for most of my childhood, since I was a toddler. When Gran died I was just turning twenty. I was broken-hearted at the loss of the person I loved most, my closest ally, my one champion.

Gran left the house and some money to me via some sort of trust, so I would inherit after Dad died. She'd never got on with Mother, saw her for what she was, a self-centred woman. Gran's ashes had barely been collected from the crematorium when Mother breezed through the house removing all evidence of the grandmother I'd loved. The oriental rugs replaced by fitted patterned carpets; wood panelling hidden behind damask wallpapers with heavy printed borders; the dark-wood furniture disposed of, in its place large puffy sofas, glass and brass tables, wicker chairs and lacquered orange-coloured wood. Behind her back, Dad called it Mother's 'florals and frills period', but he never openly objected to anything she suggested.

While Mother was distracted exploring the hang of a swag curtain, discovering the joys of arranging plastic flowers, I had what she alternately termed 'a bit of a breakdown', 'my difficult phase' or 'your funny period'.

There was nothing funny about it at all.

I was twenty when all this happened. It was when I'd just met Sam. My first-ever boyfriend. I'll never forget the excitement of those initial dates. The way he looked at me, like he really wanted to know everything about me. That feeling of being special. The slow move from hand-holding to hugging to kissing. I still remember how Sam smelt close up, his hair freshly washed with herbal shampoo; I could feel the downy bristles on his chin, soft against my cheek. His touch was warm, tentative, caring; my skin responded with goosebumps and yearning.

From the first date I loved him more than I ever thought possible.

Once I'd known Sam a year and was confident we were a serious couple, I plucked up the courage to take him home to meet the family. Mother put on her posh voice when he came round to tea, dusted off the best plates, forced Dad into a shirt and tie for the occasion. How impressed they'd been that I'd managed to catch a clean-cut young man – an electrical engineer, no less, 'working in the oil and gas industry'.

I'd just started a job I adored – training to be an archivist – and I thought 'this is it'. There we were: two young professionals at the start of our lives together, the future laid out. Happy ever after.

It was soon after that I realised I was pregnant. When I told Sam, I thought he'd be happy. I thought we'd start talking about a wedding, discuss names for the baby, plan for our little family. But a few weeks later he announced he was going to Saudi Arabia on a contract. He'd be away six months. It didn't need to be said, but it was clear this pregnancy was my responsibility and he assumed I'd get rid of our baby . . .

Even thinking about it now, so many years later, the tears well up; my insides churning and turning, heart racing, like when you shoot down the dip on a rollercoaster ride. And all I wanted, then and now, was someone to put their arm around me and gently rock the sadness away, just as Gran used to do.

The heaviest part of this secret was my appointment at Under 21, a local drop-in advice centre. It went without saying that I couldn't tell my family. Dad was plagued by business worries, the upcoming general election and his gout. And Mother . . . well, even if she hadn't been 'suffering with her nerves', years of experience had taught me it was easier never to involve her.

Although my story must've been a familiar one, the volunteer at the drop-in centre allowed me time, her questions gentle and caring. She encouraged me to go and see my doctor for an examination, gave me leaflets explaining options.

'You can change your mind at any time,' she said. 'Right up until the last moment.'

I'd nodded, staring at the leaflet in my lap: *A Woman's Choice*. This wasn't what I wanted, but what choice did

I have? There was no space in our narrow little lives for another problem.

'There's plenty of time to think. Is there a family member or friend you could talk to?' the lady said.

I shook my head, keeping my head down, eyes averted, the tears welling..

'Do you have someone who could go with you, if you chose to attend the clinic?' She reached for my hand, the way a mother would, her eyes searching for mine.

She correctly interpreted my silence. 'Don't worry, pet. Look, here's my number. You call me and let me know if you do decide to book an appointment and I'll come with you.'

She sat with me for a long time. Her name was Sue and she volunteered at the centre three days a week. That's all I knew about her. But I'm sure there is a place reserved for her in heaven.

I knew I could never go back there.

The following weeks were hell; the sickness, the stress of hiding everything from Mother, the mental turmoil. When I couldn't sleep at night, I'd lay in bed stroking my belly, rehearsing different scenarios. Ever practical, I thought of approaching the managers of the trust to see if they could release some of the cash Gran had left me. I could run away to a village where no one knew me and have the child alone. Then I imagined sending Sam a photo of me, our baby and our home, and he would be so excited he'd rush back to propose to me. Or in some versions of the fantasy, I would turn up in Saudi and find Sam. I pictured how he'd fall in love with us both, adoring our child at first sight. I saw the three of us travelling around the world together, happy to touch down and make a home wherever his contracts took him.

In all these daydreams, I knew how much I wanted my baby. She was always there at the forefront of my mind. I was sure she was a girl. My Samantha.

I would have to find a way to work out the rest.

But, in the end, the decision was made for me. I was four months gone when I was gripped by the most awful pains I'd ever felt. The amount of blood was shocking.

To be fair to Sam, he had written from Saudi – for a few months at least. His letters were full of news about the contractors' compound, raving enthusiastically about the weather and the pool. Praising the skills of the Filipino engineers working alongside them. The letters became thinner in both pages and content, until they petered out.

He never once asked about the child.

I think it was the following summer that Mother told me Sam was home. His mother had told the chemist; then the chemist mentioned it to Peggy, who of course rushed round to tell Mother. Apparently he was 'pleased to be back and waiting for his next contract'.

He hadn't written to tell me and I wondered if he planned to surprise me, but after a few days he still hadn't turned up at our door. So I bucked myself up, did my hair the way he liked it, put on a happy face and wandered around some of his old haunts, hoping to bump into him. Then one day I was queueing to pay in the newsagents when he strolled past the window, tugged along by the family dog. Plugged into a Walkman, flicking his fingers to whatever he was listening to, he paused while the dog peed up a lamp-post, giving me time to stare unseen. His thick black hair was longer than before, his eyes hidden behind dark glasses, face tanned. He was like a movie star and my heart fluttered. He lifted his hand to wave to someone and I automatically waved back, even though he wasn't looking in my direction.

A young woman about my age ran up to him, stood on tiptoe to kiss him on the lips.

A young woman I recognised.

From the shop doorway, I watched as they sauntered down the street, his arm around her waist, her staring up at him.

Hilary. She'd left school at sixteen to work in the chip shop.

Not long after that, I found myself strolling into the chippy. I remember it so clearly: Hilary turning to face me, her chin barely clearing the level of the high stainless-steel counter, she was so short.

'What can I get you?' she asked me, without any signs of recognition.

Hopefully she mistook my open-mouthed gawping for indecision as to whether to have cod or plaice. In reality I was shocked by her appearance, that Sam could have chosen this oily-haired, pimply little girl-woman over me. 'You're Hilary,' I said, eventually. 'We went to the same school.'

'Oh, yeah.' Her jaw worked like she was chewing gum. 'You're Jane.'

I didn't correct her.

I took to popping in on occasions, loitering to chat. I followed her one evening to find out where she lived. Sat on the bench down the road, watching to see if Sam turned up.

I did some odd things – left a red rose on the doorstep, sent her cards signed with the initial D and a kiss, posted her chocolates. In the chippy on one of my regular visits, she confided in me that she had a boyfriend *and* a secret admirer. I oo-ed and ah-ed and picked a bunch of wild flowers for her on the way home, another gift from the ardent D. I encouraged her to think it was the blond chap who called in for skate and chips on a Friday night – I'd heard his mate call him Den.

Of course, Mother found out. She discovered one of the letters in my bedroom, still on the roller of my typewriter. It was probably a good thing that it ended there. I'd moved things up a notch – Dennis was suggesting he and Hilary meet in the pub. I had a half-baked plan that I'd slip a note to Dennis too, contrive a meeting between them.

I don't know what I was thinking. Maybe I hoped Hilary would leave Sam for her new devotee, comparing the two and finding Sam wanting. Or that Sam would find a card or love letter and accuse her of two-timing him. I wasn't myself at the time – I was young and twisted with grief; losing Sam and our baby, losing Gran, losing dreams.

A few months later, there was an advert for staff in the window of the chip shop. I asked the manager where Hilary had gone, my hopes building that she'd moved away and Sam was now available.

She *had* moved away. With Sam. He'd taken her with him to Holland for his next contract.

After that I spent two years in my personal wilderness, battling a storm of loss and longing, struggling to find a way out. But one day the sky felt less heavy, the air less dense and Gran seemed to be looking down from heaven, telling me it was time to pull myself together. Soon after that, Dad found me another archiving job, working for someone he knew through the Rotary Club. And I settled into a routine. No shocks, no surprises, a steady nine to five, supper at six, reading or television until bedtime.

And things were going well. There was even talk of the company sponsoring me through college, potential for promotion. Then Dad had his first stroke. With Dad marooned, speechless, in his wheelchair, there was no buffer between me and Mother, no one to believe in me and help me fight my corner. I held out against her pressure for a while, but words like 'career', 'opportunity', 'dreams' were not part of her lexicon. I could find no way of explaining in terms that she could comprehend. She was like a toddler with her needs and demands. But, of course, she dressed it up nicely, pointing out how close I was to Dad, telling me it was what he would want – for me to stay home and be the one who looked after him.

At first we hired carers. But she played on my love and my guilt, saying Father felt abandoned when they left, sitting there in the evening, alone in this huge house with just the TV for company. So I cut back on overtime even though I wanted to save some money.

Then I negotiated shorter hours at work; by the fifth year, a job share. She never thought to revise her own schedule, limit *her* commitments. That woman invented 'me time'. Dad's illness and her demands took up more and more of my life until I was defeated. Before I knew it, my dream career had been whittled away one splinter at a time.

For a long while, I blamed Dad - for being ill; for having worshipped Mother so she believed she really was deserving of everyone's attention, every whim catered for. She was used to being the sun around which we all orbited, Dad under the greatest pull. Mother lit up the room for him and I was always hidden in her shadow. He saw her as the beautiful Aurora of Roman myth, bringing light to the day, seducing everyone with her charms. To my mind, the Buddhist sun idol Marici would've been more fitting: many faces to show the world, not all of them pleasant.

When he died, there was just the two of us, me and Mother, and I did whatever I needed to placate her. She married again a few years after Dad passed and the two of them moved down to Devon. When she'd drained the life out of the next chap with all her demands, she sold their house and moved to Spain with Georgio. The last time I actually saw her was five years ago when they flew into Heathrow for a brief stopover, en route to a holiday.

She'd asked me to meet them at the terminal, 'to have a catch up and a coffee', and I fell for it. A ruse to get me to help with the mountains of luggage before I drove them between airports in time for their next flight.

Chapter 11

'Thank you so much, Janice. That was really fascinating.' My nominated host led the WI audience in a short round of applause, before continuing, 'We have ten minutes for questions, then tea will be served – or wine for those not driving! And I believe Mrs Goodwin has provided some gluten-free treats for us tonight.' There were a few scattered claps for Mrs Goodwin. 'So, questions?' She looked at her watch to confirm the time; no doubt they had to be out of the hall on the dot of nine.

I had been so distracted by Sunny over the past month that I'd not given my preparation for the WI talk as much attention as I normally would. Luckily it had gone well. I'd felt strangely at ease, my style more expressive, my stories free-flowing.

I generally enjoyed the Q&A sessions nearly as much as the ancestry research, confident in my professional know-how. The first couple of questions were the easy ones to handle – 'what does "do" mean on the census?' (it's short for ditto); 'why are the adults' ages often wrong in the 1941 census?' (they aren't, they're rounded up or down). But my heart sank when I heard the start of the next question.

'This is one that will interest you.' A sure sign it wouldn't, but I smiled encouragingly. The speaker was a woman in her seventies. She continued, 'My great uncle, no I mean great great uncle, was supposedly married in Stepney in 1848 to a woman called Edith, or some say Edwina, Gibbs. But my nan found a letter in an old suitcase that said . . .' These personal questions required more diplomacy; they were usually convoluted, factually inaccurate and dull for everyone but the speaker. I waited politely for the woman to finish, while my host did some throat-clearing and checking of her watch.

'He sounds like an intriguing man. Quite a modern approach to relationships, some might think!' I censored a reference to Tinder that popped into my mind; mustn't risk offence. 'I'd love to hear more after the other questions have finished.' It was my usual practice to take these offline; they were easier to manage with a glass of wine in my hand. It never hurt to be courteous and, as Gran used to say, listening costs nothing. I'd won a few clients that way, at my previous talks.

After the questions, I circulated until I became trapped next to the tea urn by an elderly woman determined to give me chapter and verse of her family's experiences at the Somme. The degree of repetition suggested early-stage dementia. A hand touched my elbow.

'Cynthia, can I borrow Janice for a moment?' My rescuer was a smiling blonde woman, forty-ish, a little younger than me.

She handed me a large glass of red wine as she steered me away. 'I thought you might need this.' She chinked her own glass against mine. 'I'm Becky. Cheers!' She was quite short, barely reaching my shoulder, and had to look up at me. 'Great slides. Loved that old photo of the three generations on the beach, all wrapped up in their coats and hats. Classic!' Her smile was broad and genuine. 'And I thought your handling of the "Edith Gibbs" question was worth an award for diplomacy. Very clever – *an intriguing man*. Philanderer more like.'

'I'm glad you enjoyed it.' Mother hated this kind of small talk. *Vicarage chat*, she used to call it. Yet another thing I was good at and she'd despised me for. 'Are you part of the WI?' I asked.

'Not exactly. I tend to sit in sometimes if I'm around, but I'm really here to make sure they've got everything they need. I'm in charge of "venue hire".' Becky made speech marks around the phrase, but it didn't annoy me like it usually would. Her bubbly personality made me think of Sunny – it was just how I imagined her to be: relaxed and bouncy and fun to be around. 'I prefer this sort of thing to the kids' parties.' She gesticulated to the WI members. 'Less chance of sugar highs and unexpected accidents.'

'I don't know about that!' I nodded my head towards the cake table where a lady with a Zimmer was trying to balance a loaded plate and a cup of tea. Becky laughed and I felt a surge of warmth.

'Do you do a lot of talks? You're very good. I wouldn't have the confidence,' she said.

I noted her phrasing: the question, the compliment and the self-disclosure. But this wasn't some technique she'd learned to make friends, it seemed to come naturally to her.

'Mark Twain said there are only two types of speakers in the world – the nervous and the liars.' I was rewarded by another laugh.

'Sorry to interrupt.' The tone suggested the speaker wasn't. 'I just wanted to ask a question about the 1921 census.'

Becky beamed a charming smile at the older woman who had cut us short. 'Of course, Fay. I'll leave you two to chat.' Her tone was gracious. Becky took a swig of her wine then leaned towards me. Leaning closer, she whispered dramatically, winking at Fay, 'Don't be tempted to try the orange cake – it's made with polenta! Texture like the bottom of a parrot's cage.' She touched my arm, 'Great to meet you', and disappeared off.

The next day, I reviewed the pictures of Sunny that I'd saved, selecting three where Sunny was face-on to the camera. I cropped out the people and background, enlarged her image, and printed them on the Best Quality photo setting. The pictures fitted perfectly in the frames I'd bought, the gold surround setting off the copper-red tones in her hair nicely. I placed my favourite on the shelf above my desk. It felt good to have her there, like she was helping me in my ongoing search for her story.

With Ginger dozing on my lap, I looked up the websites Sunny had listed in her notebook. The first two weren't that interesting – a blogger giving advice to applicants for

Britain's Got Talent; then a web address Sunny had labelled 'Mary O'Brien!' which led me to a Wiki page on Dusty Springfield. The third was a YouTube channel. A click of the mouse and my hand flew to my mouth as Sunny appeared before me. It was heart-stopping to see her there on film. Like I was meeting her properly for the first time. I paused the recording to catch my breath. I wanted to savour this moment. Just like those meditation exercises where you take five minutes to eat one strawberry, this needed my full attention.

Initially, I muted the volume so I could concentrate on her image without distraction. She was perched on a stool in a student-type bedroom, talking directly to camera. Her frizzed-up auburn hair, her bright clothes, everything about her was big and bold; she seemed to take up more space than her slim physique warranted, her constant movements suggesting an excess of energy and confidence. I watched her in silence for a minute, enthralled, before returning to the start of the clip to put the sound on.

She had a strong Australian twang. In her excitement, her voice was unnecessarily loud.

'Hey dudes, I'm Rusty Steel.' She twirled a strand of her hair around her finger as she spoke; coquettish rather than nervous, her bright lipsticked smile proud. 'Welcome to my channel, Rusty does Dusty, my tribute to that sixties legend, the great Dusty Springfield.' Without any further announcement, she sprang up from the stool and launched into 'Little by Little', a song from a time before *either* of us was born.

Ginger attempted a duet. Her yowling started at the first note, almost as if she sought to drown out Sunny's voice. I had to laugh. To be honest, I wasn't sure who was more out of tune.

Sunny's gesticulations were full of drama. She mimed ripping her shirt with both hands as she sung about her torn emotions; she became Ophelia pulling at her hair to show her lover was driving her mad. During the chorus she swayed her hips energetically from side to side. It was quite exhausting to watch.

Sunny herself was pretty breathless at the end, as she sat back down on the stool. All that dancing and passion had taken it out of her. She leant forward towards the camera. Raising her left hand she made a beckoning gesture towards the viewer, drawing us in. Then, suddenly, she flipped her middle finger straight. 'For John, number one shit person!' she said. She laughed a loud false cackle, clapped her hands together and said, 'I reckon that's a wrap,' and the screen blacked out.

I wondered who John was that she was that angry with him and wanted the world to know. I watched this clip a few times, quite proud of her, giving it her all like that. There was something compelling about the recording – the fizzing energy, the self-belief.

'Rusty does Dusty, eh? What do we think of that?' I said to Ginger, snuggling her face next to mine. 'I'm guessing she ruled out *Sunny does Cher*!' I laughed at my own joke.

I watched the rest of her recordings with the affectionate indulgence of a loving parent. Sadly, her enthusiasm outweighed her talent, but maybe with some tuition she'd have made it. It made me wonder about the man who'd given her his business card. Why had he encouraged her ambitions to enter the TV talent show? She'd met him at the Australian bar at the open mic night. Is that why she'd told her friends at the pub that she was going to London? Was she planning to see him again?

I wrote 'John?' on a Post-it and added it to my wall.

Chapter 12

The next day I went to see Dmytro to return his
laundry. I'd phoned him when I got back from the WI
talk and he'd said he wasn't feeling well. By the time
I arrived that day he'd taken a turn for the worse. He
opened the front door wrapped in a blanket, his skin
ashen, the faint tang of stale sweat suggesting it had
been some time since he'd showered.

He laboured his way up the stairs to his flat, then slumped
on the sofa, coughing, his eyes red-rimmed and watery.
I put down my bag to place the back of my hand on his
forehead; he felt hot and clammy, but was shivering. It
didn't take Sherlock Holmes to deduce this was flu.

'Do you have any medicine?' I asked pointlessly. He
shook his head without looking up.

'I am not a child. I don't need a nanny—' he splut-
tered, before folding in on himself, overtaken by a
racking cough. The poor boy must've felt wretched.

I opened the fridge and found only a knob of mouldy
cheese, half a jar of strawberry jam and some marga-
rine. A quick check showed the shelves of the kitchen
cupboards were equally bare. He needed someone to
take charge, to look after him.

'Dmytro, I'm going to the shops to get you some food and medicine. Where are your keys so you don't have to come down and let me in when I get back?'

Still not recovered from his coughing fit, he waved vaguely towards his jacket, hanging on the back of the door.

'Are they in the pocket?' I had to pull out his beanie hat to find them, nestled at the bottom with half a packet of extra strong mints. I made a mental note that he liked mints. I'd buy him some when he was well again.

I returned laden. I'd bought the essentials he'd need – medicine, bread, milk – and the few treats I could find in the small parade of shops.

I slipped his set of keys back into his jacket pocket. While I was out, I'd got a spare set cut; they would be particularly useful if he ever wanted me to pop in and do something for him while he was at work.

He hadn't moved from the settee since I'd left.

'I think you'd be more comfortable if you could lie down. Would you prefer to be in here on the sofa or in your bedroom?'

He let me lead him into his room where I straightened the bedclothes for him. Leaving him to get undressed and under the duvet, I went to the kitchen to make him some hot chocolate, to take away the taste of the flu medicine. When I knocked on the door five minutes later, he coughed a response which I took to mean I could enter.

He had pulled the covers up tight around his neck. He looked so small and childlike laying there, my heart went out to him. It was cold in his room so I knew he'd appreciate the hot water bottle I'd just bought him and I tucked it in beside him. I supported his head to help him sip the medication from the spoon. He shook his head when I offered the hot chocolate, his sad dark eyes blinking.

'I'll sleep now . . .' he said and closed his eyes.

I shut the door to his room so I wouldn't disturb him.

It took me a while to get things shipshape, but by the time I sank down onto Dmytro's sofa with a cup of tea I was proud of my efforts. I admit, it was curiosity as well as cleanliness that drove some of my efforts. While I tidied, I took the chance to look for any signs of Sunny, clues that would help me understand her story. A jumper hung on the back of the bathroom door; a hair tie, entangled with long auburn hairs, in the cupboard above the sink; a fashion magazine under the coffee table, thick glasses doodled on the models' faces, fanged teeth or devil horns sprouting from their heads. I left them all where they lay.

It was like setting up a son in a new flat, making it homely for him. The place was aired, the washing-up done, surfaces cleaned and polished, the food and treats stashed in the cupboards. My work here complete, I looked back in on him to say goodnight and he stirred slightly. I was pleased to see he'd been sleeping. The flu medicine had worked its magic.

'I have to go soon,' I said. It was getting late and I'd not left food out for the ducks or cats. I put a mug of tea and some fresh water on the wooden chair that served as a bedside table. 'Can I get you anything to eat before I leave?' He shook his head. 'You must take more of this medicine at nine this evening. Every six hours, no more. Do you understand? It's important.' He nodded. 'I'll come back to see you tomorrow. Night night, sleep tight.'

'Sunny said that too,' he mumbled.

I kissed my fingertips and put them to his forehead. 'From both of us,' I said.

There was a missed call on my mobile. I pressed the series of icons to get to voicemail.

'Hi, I hope you don't mind me calling you. It's Becky. We met at the talk you gave. I got your number from the WI.' There had been no need for the explanation, I knew who she was immediately; you could hear her smile.

'Yardee yardee. Too long to explain on the phone but I've a favour to ask. I'll reward you with coffee, g'n't, a fry-up or whatever your poison, but call me when you can.' I couldn't help but warm to her; like Sunny, she had an energy about her.

It turned out she wanted to interview me for an article about family history for a local magazine.

'Is that your job?' I asked her when I phoned her back. 'I thought you managed the village hall bookings?'

'Since the divorce I've become the original Jack of All. I think they jazz it up these days by calling it a portfolio career.' I laughed at her self-deprecating humour. 'The village hall is a voluntary thing I started years ago. My boys had gone to Cubs there and they needed help organising the place. The three of them are bloody great hulks now, so that will tell you how long ago it was! It seems I'm part of the fixtures and fittings now.'

We arranged to meet up in a greasy spoon near where she lived.

It turned out she earns pin money from the occasional article, but her main income comes from photographing houses for one of those online estate agents.

'I write the descriptions too. *A beautifully presented cottage combining the charm of the period with the convenience of modern updates.*' She used her toast to mop up the bean juice. For such a petite woman she had a hearty appetite, which I found endearing. 'Those are the easy ones to write, but for the top-end properties they like something more emotionally evocative.'

I laughed. 'Yes, I've seen them: *When Jessica and Simon first set eyes on Primrose Mansion they knew it was the home for them. Jessica says that she fell in love with the grandeur of the sweeping tree-lined drive and could imagine their children playing in the orchard.*' My desk drawer was full of those quarterly mail-outs from estate agents, often accompanied by a letter informing me '*people are looking for a property like yours*', imploring me to go straight to Flog It & Sons when I was ready to sell. It was one of those things I fantasised about – moving out and being free of the weight of my adolescent experiences;

starting again somewhere else. But I wasn't sure I was brave enough. 'They can get quite flowery, can't they? It's the same for the family histories I research – some people want clear facts and others a poetic epic.'

'Gosh, I'd never thought about that. Nowt so queer as folk.' She pushed her plate away. 'I'm plain vanilla myself. You?'

'Bog standard; as it comes. No window dressing,' I said.

When we'd finished eating, she ordered two cappuccinos and started her interview. Her questions were intelligent and she was genuinely interested in my responses. By the time we left I'd somehow committed to showing her how to get started with her own family tree.

She was easy to like.

And she seemed to like me.

I made the mistake of telling Mother in our Sunday call. I hadn't meant to – my nascent friendship with Becky didn't feature on my conversational topic list. Recalling the conversation afterwards, it started to go downhill when Mother accused me of being profligate – me of all people! It was after I mentioned the amount I spent on duck food each month, so maybe that was where it went wrong. Next she accused me of not earning enough to 'waste money'. Strangely emboldened by recent events, I stood my ground: 'On the contrary, I'm working on some very interesting research, a *paid* assignment for a ninetieth birthday.' Before she could interrupt, I added that I was likely to get *even more* work following my *very successful* talk at the WI. On a roll, I described the *publicity interview* with Becky, elevating her to *a local journalist* and, before I knew it, I'd implied that she and I were now firm friends, working on her family tree together.

'Oh dear.' There was a pause which Mother allowed to hang for several beats too long. 'You know how you can get a bit . . . shall we say, obsessive. Just remember, if things go badly, I'm too far away to bail you out this time. You don't want another funny phase.'

Once again she was harking back to the initial cause of my breakdown after Gran died: Sam, Hilary. My baby that never was: Samantha. The series of events that changed everything for me, bleaching the joy from my world and making me live this particularly beige life I had come to inhabit.

Mother would never let me forget the mistakes I had made.

Chapter 13

It had been a long wait for Sunny's funeral, over six weeks since the accident. It had taken a couple of weeks to identify her. Then Ned had to come from Australia to make the arrangements, the complexity of which were no doubt compounded by a combination of police and coroner bureaucracy. But Ned had, at last, announced a date, time and place on the memorial page. Family flowers only, donations to Barnardo's.

I offered to take Dmytro, but he was clear about his feelings. 'Her soul is gone. There will be no last kisses,' was all he would say.

Dmytro's decision made me undecided about whether I should attend. Part of me felt it wasn't right, that it was wrong to intrude on Ned's grief. But another part of me desperately wanted to be there, to pay my respects to Sunny, to see things through to their logical end and – maybe – find closure. To achieve my mission and, literally, see her back with her family. As I sat at my desk dithering, a beam of sunlight fell on Sunny's picture and I took this as a message – I was meant to go. I kissed my fingertips and touched them to the photo. 'I'll be there for you, sweetheart.'

I planned to arrive at the crematorium early so I could watch people turning up and discreetly join the group. However, I was just leaving the house when I was disturbed by the sound of tyres on the gravel drive. It was too late to duck back inside and avoid this visitor; I'd just have to get rid of them as quickly as I could.

Flo, from the other end of the village, drove round the bend in her battered old automatic, pulled up in front of the house, reversed, then edged forward towards the privet, as if there were white parking lines she mustn't cross. I stayed where I was, watching impatiently but knowing that she was easily distracted and could shoot through the hedge into the ditch if she hit the wrong pedal. Once satisfied the car was well parked, she took so long to get out of the car that I walked over. I tapped on the window and she jumped dramatically, throwing the magazine she was holding in the air to join several that were already in the footwell. Clutching at her chest, she lowered the window to speak to me.

'Oh, I didn't see you there. I've got your copy of the *Village Voice* here somewhere, but they've got in a bit of a jumble. They were in house-order when I set off but I had to stop quite sharply for Meg on her horse at that narrow bit near the memorial and they all shot onto the floor.'

'Let me help.' I went round to the passenger side and opened the door.

'You look very smart. Where are you off to?' she asked.

I drew my new cashmere coat tight across me to hide most of my funeral garb, not wanting too many questions asked. 'Meeting a new client. He wants me to research his Huguenot ancestors in Spitalfield. I'm just leaving.'

'That sounds really interesting. Silk weavers, weren't they? I read a novel about them once. I think it had a blue cover. Do you know the one I mean? I think the author was called Bishop or something like that . . .'

Flo was one of those women who you couldn't hurry and at least while we were guessing author names and discussing Huguenot history, she wasn't interrogating me about why I was dressed so sombrely, in head to toe black.

By the time I'd helped her sort the magazines and Flo had retrieved my copy, I was fifteen minutes behind my schedule. I unlocked the front door and chucked the *Village Voice* on top of the pile of circulars on the hall sideboard.

At last ready to leave, I took a deep breath and felt for Sunny's bracelet where it was tucked deep in my coat pocket to give me confidence.

When I arrived at the crematorium, the only space I could find was at the far side of the car park. I hadn't dared to make up the lost time by driving faster; it was a car accident that had led to me being at this funeral. Scurrying across the gravel, I could see a small group of people gathered outside the doors of the crematorium. A glance at my watch told me I was five minutes late; these people must be waiting for the next service. I picked up pace – Sunny's memorial was already underway.

The usher held a finger to his lips as he opened the door to the chapel to let me in. The only noise I was making was panting which couldn't have been heard above 'My Way', which echoed round the room. It seemed the service had only just started, so I had a moment to take stock while I caught my breath. The room was barely half full, as I'd expected, given that most of her friends and family were in Australia. People were still standing, their backs towards me. A handful of older people I assumed to be her English family were wearing black; the younger generation were less sombre, although thankfully not in jeans and hoodies.

I slipped into the last row, unacknowledged by a grim-faced man at the other end of the pew. It was a small overheated room and I was still struggling to shrug off my new cashmere coat when Sinatra finished and they all sat down. I was so hot and flustered I could barely focus for the first few minutes and without thinking started fanning myself with the Order of Service, the nearest thing to hand. Even though no one saw, a wave of embarrassment passed through me as I registered what I'd just done. Smoothing the paper out carefully, I said a silent 'sorry' to Sunny's smiling image on my lap, although I doubted that she would've cared about decorum.

Fidgeting uncomfortably in my seat, my stomach churned anxiously. I shouldn't have come. I should have taken that morning's delay as a sign. I don't belong here. But my self-admonishment was interrupted as the celebrant finished his introductions and called on Sunny's dad, Ned, to speak.

Ned walked to the front and stood in silence, composing himself. Before today I had wondered if Ned really looked like his photos, or whether he'd chosen the most flattering ones to put online, like people on dating websites. He wasn't as tall as I'd imagined. Broader, chunky in a solid kind of way. He looked nothing like Sunny, but why should he – they weren't related by birth. He looked smart in his suit, the creases from the packaging still evident in his new shirt. I'd guess he was in his early sixties. His hair was white, slightly receding, giving him an air of sophistication that disappeared as soon as he opened his mouth. His accent was reminiscent of Sunny's on her video clip. I warmed to him immediately.

'Thank you for coming today.' He paused to look around the room. My heart pounded as he looked briefly in my direction, my fingers tightening around Sunny's bracelet in my pocket. I needed to find a way to give it back to him, but hadn't worked out how.

'We all knew Sonya as Sunny. Some of you knew her better than others. I just want to say a few things about her. Firstly, and most importantly, she wouldn't want your tears. She earned her nickname from the first day we met her. Sunny by name and by nature.'

Reading from a creased sheet of A4, his hand shook but his voice was fairly steady. He paused for a beat between each statement as if he could only manage a few words at a time.

'The other thing that sums up Sunny was her sense of adventure. When she was a little kid, we had to have eyes in the back of our heads because she was always up to something. Her ambition was to be Spiderman so she'd be allowed to climb anything without us telling her to get down. She was into everything and left a trail of destruction behind her wherever she went. As she got older nothing changed! She was reckless, full of crazy ideas and never planned anything as there was always something more exciting around the corner. Why concentrate on one thing when you could do half a dozen at the same time? I used to tell her "slow down, take a breath" but she couldn't be told anything.' A man sitting next to JayCee nodded in agreement and JayCee nudged him in the ribs. A work colleague, I assumed.

This was exactly how I'd imagined Sunny: a force of nature, tearing a path through life, not stopping for anyone. I sat straight in my seat, eager to hear more.

'Yes, sometime she drove me mad. Her hair would block up the plug holes. She didn't get Monty Python; she hated my Oasis albums. She used to sing loudly in the mornings.' The pub people laughed at this one. From the fact he didn't go on to mention her recent musical ambitions, I guessed it was her secret. 'She cheated at Scrabble – she played the Aussie slang edition before it was actually invented!'

'But, of course, none of this mattered . . . There was so much about her to love. She always woke up smiling. She made the smallest thing fun and would always find an excuse to celebrate, particularly birthdays . . .' At the mention of birthdays it seemed there was a collective intake of breath, everyone thinking back to the date she died. He stopped, closed his eyes and took a deep breath before he could continue. It was so brave of him. He could've got the celebrant to read his eulogy but he wanted to honour her himself.

He choked up on the last few words. 'She was my darling baby girl, my ray of sunshine. I reckon she was the best daughter anyone could've asked for . . . better than I deserved. More than anything, I wish . . .' He breathed in deeply, held his breath for a few seconds, eyes closed, and we were all transfixed; waiting with bated breath to hear *what* he wished.

'I wish I could turn the clock back.'

The silence was broken by the clatter of the chapel door behind me. The man who had been sitting at the far end of the pew was gone. Probably one of her lovers wanting to pay his respects and leave without having to face her family.

Chapter 14

I don't know how we all got through the rest of the service. They should have issued trigger warnings as we came in. We filed out to 'Bring me Sunshine', which, while apt for the event, didn't match our moods or the cloudy skies above.

The English side of the family formed a small knot around Ned, making small talk; 'lovely service', that kind of thing. One of them – the mother's sister, Jemima, according to the Order of Service – had read a poem after the Moment for Reflection. It was something about falling leaves, which seemed particularly ill-chosen given the manner of Sunny's death. I watched them from a distance, trying to work out the relationships, who was with who, signs of animosity or warmth. But none of them appeared at ease with each other, the men shaking hands formally, the hugs brief and awkward. The miles and years that they'd been apart coming between them.

Not wanting to get into conversation with any of the family members in case I was interrogated, I went to the courtyard to admire the floral tributes. The messages themselves were standard fare, *Always in our thoughts,*

Sorry for your loss, so nothing to learn there. But I took a few strategically angled photos, ensuring I caught the names of some key people, like her godmother. It might be useful to have a list of relatives if I needed to get in touch to return something of Sunny's.

As others came over to look at the flowers, I moved out of the way to stand under the trees, scanning the mourners for JayCee's pink hair. I recognised the bar staff, but there were a number of people I assumed were pub regulars standing near her. In contrast to the family, they were relaxed, their faces animated as they chatted. Curious to see what I could find out, I wandered over to say hello, uncertain whether JayCee would recognise me.

'Hi, JayCee,' I said. 'Dan, Rob.' They were standing next to her so I nodded to include them. Over the years I've learned that if you use someone's name, they will assume they should know you too.

'Oh, hi. I didn't see you in the service,' JayCee said.

'I was at the back.'

'Are you coming to the wake? Sunny's dad's staying at the pub and he decided to hold it there,' JayCee said.

The blonde girl interjected: 'He's paid for all the food and drink!' Her surprise made me smile – you could hardly have a whip round, could you? But this was probably the first time she'd been involved in the behind-the-scenes organisation of a funeral.

The two lads nudged each other and drifted off to join a cluster of locals in one of those fierce and pointless debates about football.

'We're leaving soon,' JayCee said. 'Rob's got room in his car if you need a lift.'

The wake. I was intrigued, but what if someone asked who I was? '*A friend of the family*,' I'd say; but which member of the family exactly? No, I must keep my resolve. Pay my respects and leave.

'No, but thank you,' I said. The blonde girl had trailed after the lads and JayCee was already looking over my shoulder for an excuse to escape back to the other youngsters. 'I'm just going to have a few words with Ned and then I'm off too.'

JayCee glanced towards him. 'He'll be pleased to see you again. He's ever so nice but he doesn't know anyone local.'

I touched her arm gently, a signal I was leaving. 'Thank you for being such a great friend to Sunny. She always used to talk about you.'

'That's nice . . . We got really close when we shared the apartment. It was fun. We were like sisters then.'

'I bet you're not as messy though!' Anecdotes in Ned's memorial speech had backed up the impression I'd got from Dmytro's flat. Sunny was not one of life's cleaning obsessives.

'No, she won that award for sure.'

'Before I go, there was something I wanted to ask you.' An expression flashed across her face, too quick for me to interpret before the sad smile was back in place. She raised her eyebrows, waiting.

'Sunny mentioned someone called John. She seemed angry with him but wouldn't talk about it. Do you know who he is?'

JayCee's expression turned stony. She nodded her head towards the group of men that her colleagues had joined. 'He's that tosser,' she said.

I recognised his face, but from where exactly I couldn't say. He stood with his legs strangely wide apart, hips thrust forward as if posing; his trousers tight, his jacket unfitted, sleeves rolled up at the wrists. The sun-damaged, wrinkled skin and too-long hair suggested a faded rock star. The type that expected an audience even when he wasn't performing. The star of his own show.

'And that's his wife, LeeAnn. She's lovely. I don't know why she puts up with him.' She pointed to an anorexic-looking woman in a smart steel-grey dress, a matching jacket over her arm. There was an aura of sadness about her, dark patches under her eyes. She was turned slightly away, staring off into the middle distance, her fingers fiddling nervously with a pair of sunglasses, which made me think of Lady Macbeth wringing her unclean hands.

'He led Sunny on, then dumped her and Sunny went a bit mental. She said she was going to tell LeeAnn. But I think they got back together again – Sunny told me he was arranging something for her birthday.' JayCee shrugged, implying she didn't know for sure. 'Sunny kept arguing with him in front of everyone. That's why Rob made her move out of the pub. *Bad for business.*'

'Ah, I see.'

It seemed the poor love had a knack for attracting the wrong sort of men. The fling with John had clearly overlapped with loyal Dmytro, who she'd been seeing for several months at that point. His flat must've been a convenient place to go when she was thrown out of the pub. What tangled webs . . .

A thought struck me – maybe John was the man who gave her the business card. Had Sunny followed him here from London? 'Is he a musician? Does he have a record label?'

JayCee shrugged a what-do-I-know. 'He was in a band once and he's been on TV. He's a flash bastard, that's all I can say. I tried to warn her.'

But as Ned had said during the service, she wouldn't be told.

We said our goodbyes and I was surprised when JayCee hugged me. It felt genuine. Like we'd made some sort of connection through Sunny. They'd clearly been great friends.

People were beginning to disperse to their cars. As I walked across the gravel towards Ned, I planned this to be the final part of the journey. Keep it simple, offer my sincere condolences, shake his hand and leave. Closure.

Just as I went to speak to Ned, he was distracted by one of the cousins. I stepped slightly to one side to give them some privacy. The man clasped Ned in a bear hug before releasing him just as suddenly, turning on his heel to leave. A piece of paper Ned had been holding fluttered to the ground and I bent to retrieve it. Then things happened so quickly, like a beautifully choreographed routine. Afterwards I wished I had a recording so I could watch in slow motion – our hands almost touching as Ned reached down at the same time, mine pale beside his. Sunny's face beaming up between us, *In loving memory of Sonya Ryan.* Ned glancing sideways at me, a double-take, the sharp intake of breath.

He straightened up, his hand to his mouth.

'Oh my god,' he said. 'Your hair . . . I . . . the colour in the sunlight . . . so like Sunny's . . . it took my breath away . . .'

There was a break in the clouds and the sun was now high above us. He closed his eyes for a moment, steadying himself, and I felt so sad for him.

'Sorry. Quite a shock,' he said.

Unthinking, I put my hand on his forearm. 'Do you need to sit down? Can I get you some water?'

He opened his eyes and placed his hand on top of mine. His palm felt warm and dry. 'No, no. I'm fine . . .' He paused, swallowed his emotion. 'Thanks. It was a surprise, that's all.'

I handed him the Order of Service that I'd picked up. 'I'm really sorry for your loss,' I said. 'It was a beautiful service.'

The clouds had vanished completely as I got into my car. Inside the vehicle it felt warm; I lowered the window to let some air in, watching the other cars leave for the wake. Sitting there, I tried to compose my thoughts, my fingers playing with Sunny's bracelet on my lap. I couldn't shake the idea that the exchange with Ned was another sign. My head knew it was illogical – and maybe it was the heightened emotion of the day, but it felt as if Sunny had wanted Ned and I to meet. To connect.

Like she wanted me to ease his pain. But how? What could I possibly do that could help him?

Chapter 15

Sitting at my desk staring at Sunny's picture, my fingers played over each charm on her bracelet as I wrestled with my conscience.

It was hard to accept, but I knew what I had to do. I had achieved my original goal: I'd played my part in helping the police identify Sunny and brought her back to her dad. I'd not abandoned her. Now it was time to let go, move on and back to my 'real' life: my calls to Mother, my genealogy assignments, maybe develop my friendship with Becky and branch out into the world a bit more. I could join the WI, sign up for piano lessons. Join a choir.

I had a plan.

But I needed to see Ned one final time to return Sunny's bracelet and I had to think this through carefully – what I wanted to say when I met him. And what I wouldn't say.

As I saw it, I now had two options to close the circle and help him find peace.

As a pretext, I could say I was a recent friend of Sunny's – maybe something about her singing. I could say we met in a choir or in a music class. *'I didn't know her well but we'd hit it off.'* That would make sense. She'd told me she wanted to make it big, shown me her private YouTube channel. When her bracelet broke, I offered to get the clasp fixed for her. I could tell Ned I admired her, have a brief chat, return the bracelet and leave. Disappear from his life and close this whole saga.

Or, I could tell him that my life changed on 16th September, just as Sunny's ended. I could tell him my part in it all. Tell him the truth and seek his understanding that both our lives changed that day.

Before the funeral, Ned had been staying at the Pheasant and Grape. Several times I found the phone in my hand, toying with the idea of calling to ask JayCee whether Ned was still there, or if they could tell me where he had moved on to. Each time I put the phone down again without dialling, debating whether it was the right thing to do. But in the end, I decided *what will be will be.* I will just go there to see. If he is there, we will speak. If he is not, it wasn't meant to happen.

I drove to the pub pondering the simultaneous realities of Schrödinger's Cat.

He wasn't there.

I didn't know what I felt. Disappointment? Relief that the decision was out of my hands?

I took another quick look around the pub to check, but there was no sign of him. A casual enquiry to a barmaid I didn't recognise confirmed that it was JayCee's night off. Having driven such a long way, I decided to stay for a drink and something to eat. It had been another day when I'd forgotten to have lunch, I'd been so distracted. That was it, another decision made. I would eat, then leave.

An hour later I was ready to head for home. I nipped into the ladies first, a habit I'd been taught by Gran, who had instilled in me her fear of *getting caught short*. Something to do with an air-raid shelter and a communal po.

I checked my watch as I washed my hands. It was still relatively early. There was a good documentary on catch-up or, if I was so minded, I could pull together the material for the Abbyss family that I needed to deliver in the next few weeks before the great aunt's ninetieth birthday. The hot-air dryer failed on all counts and I wiped my hands on my trousers to dry them as I came back to the bar.

And there he was.

In the snug across the other side of the pub was Ned, a full pint of beer in front of him, suggesting he'd only just sat down. Decision remade.

He looked up as I approached and gave me a faint nod of acknowledgement. His appearance had changed since I'd seen him at the church. Then he'd somehow pulled himself together, spruced himself up to give Sunny his best. Now his sweatshirt was stained, the bags under his eyes dark from lack of sleep, a cold sore nestled in the corner of his mouth. I felt a little overdressed and was glad I'd not topped up my lipstick in the loos.

'We met at the funeral,' I said. 'May I speak with you?'

'Yes, of course. I recognise you, your hair.' He gestured to the empty chair across from him, a signal for me to join him. He half stood up to shake hands and I hoped he didn't notice how much mine was shaking. 'Can I get you a drink?'

'I'm fine for now, thank you. I just wanted to have a word. I won't keep you.'

He sat back down again. 'Did you work here with Sunny?'

I gave a politician's answer. 'I didn't know her very long, but we hit it off from the start.'

'She made a big impact on people in a short space of time. A bit like Vegemite – it was an all or nothing thing: people adored her or didn't get her.' I had the impression he'd used that line to describe Sunny before.

'I wanted to return this to you.' I took the small jewellery box from my handbag and placed it on the table, halfway between us. Even having made the decision, I didn't want to part with it. He stared at the box, frowning as if it was a cryptic 3D puzzle he had to fathom.

When he made no move to open it, I felt the need to say something more. 'Sunny's bracelet. I was with her when the clasp broke.' My planned speech. 'I got it fixed for her. I thought you might like to have it back.'

He reached for the box, his fingers trembling slightly as he opened the lid.

'I never thought I'd see this again. Figured she must've lost it on her travels. She was always losing things.' He lifted the bracelet from the cotton wool where I'd carefully placed it the night before. The charms jangled as he held it up, the silver glinted in the light. I was pleased I'd cleaned and polished it.

He found the acorn charm and held it between his thumb and forefinger. 'I bought her this for her four-teenth birthday. *From little acorns mighty oaks* . . . She had so much energy and passion. I had such hopes . . .' He held his breath, trying to contain his emotion, but he was on the edge of tears, averting his eyes as his fingers continued to work round the charms like they were rosary beads.

He wouldn't want me to see him like this. 'I'm sorry, I didn't mean to upset you.' My voice was shaking with unexpected emotion, mirror neurons fired up in the face of his grief. I thought I was bringing part of Sunny back to him, that it would make him happy. 'I'm really sorry. I should go.' I'd got it so wrong.

I pushed my chair back to stand and he looked up, his brows creased in sadness, his face pale. He placed his hand on my forearm to stay me and I shivered at his touch.

'Don't go. Please stay. It really helps . . . to have company . . . to talk to people who knew her.' His fingers worried the charms on the bracelet as he spoke. There was something fascinating about them, like doll's house ornaments or Monopoly counters, miniature versions of the real thing.

I nodded towards the bracelet. 'It's a lovely way to mark events.'

He stopped at a tiny ballet shoe. 'Her mum bought her this one when she started learning. She loved dancing when she was young but she got too tall. A real performer.'

I smiled, thinking of her YouTube videos; she was certainly that. He passed over a number of the charms without comment – a treble clef, the heart from Dmytro, a single pearl – before stopping at the teddy bear clutching the small blue stone.

'Sapphire. Her birth stone,' I said. Although Gran would've said she was far from typical of that star sign.

He glanced up at me and his smile turned to a frown as he reached across the table towards me. For a moment I thought he was going to touch my hair and my reflex was to pull back, but he reached for the chain around my neck which I'd not realised had fallen outside my blouse. The thin silver chain I had bought last week. A chain that held half a heart, its edges jagged as if torn in two. Its matching half now in Ned's hand, on Sunny's bracelet, where I'd had the jeweller place it.

My way of keeping a connection with her once I'd returned the bracelet to her dad.

I had spent so much time researching Sunny and daydreaming about my relationship with her that it sometimes felt as good as true. Like we'd actually met and spent time together, getting to know each other. Somehow my permanent mourning of my never-to-be daughter, Samantha, had become entwined with imaginings of Sunny. I'd so often thought about how my daughter would have been. A daughter I would love, like Ned loved Sunny – without expectations or demands that she be anything other than what she was.

Sammy/Sunny, we would have talked about everything. She'd have got back late at night, keen to tell me her gossip. We'd have shared jokes and secrets and recipes. She'd have bought me sentimental keepsakes and special gifts, like this necklace . . .

It's my only defence for saying what I said when, once again, he asked me how I knew Sunny. It was just there in the forefront of my mind, the lie I'd told Dmytro. I'd imagined it so often, it felt so real, that it may as well have been the truth. And I *so* wanted to make Ned happy again; to give him a way back to Sunny. Where was the harm?

'How did you know her?' He demanded.

'We're related.'

He shook his head, frowning hard as he tried to comprehend what I'd said. 'D'you mean you're from her birth family?'

'Yes.'

'How?' His stare was intense. 'How are you related?'

'I'm Sonya. I'm her mother.'

Ned held up a hand as if to stop me saying anything further; like he needed time to process what I'd said before he heard any more. 'No. I don't see how . . .' He ran his hand through his hair, leaving tufts sticking out at rakish angles, dishevelled and vulnerable. 'How did you track her down? When did you get in touch with her? She never showed any interest in finding her birth family.'

'She found *me* actually. It was through one those DNA sites. You know, where you send a sample off to be analysed.' They were a relatively recent development and I'd investigated them to see if they could be a useful tool for my genealogy assignments. 'I did mine a while ago. Just out of interest to discover more about my heritage.'

'I don't get it. How does that link you to Sunny?'

'She sent a sample off earlier this year sometime. The site sends me an email whenever it finds someone who shares some patterns in the DNA. Usually they're fairly remote connections – third or fourth cousins, that kind of thing. So it was a bit of a shock when Sonya's name popped up. More than I had ever dared to hope for.'

His head bobbed up-down, up-down, like one of those nodding dog toys I had as a child. He was still trying to take it in. 'Sunny sent off a DNA sample? She was trying to find her birth family?'

'Yes. She said she wanted to find me.'

'Did the two of you meet up? Did you see her?'

'Yes. Many times since she arrived here in England.' I lifted the necklace with its half-heart charm, pointed to the matching one on the bracelet. 'She bought these for us both. We became very close.'

He looked at the floor, head down, his fisted hand to his mouth, rocking slightly as he thought. Uncomfortable staring at him, I lowered my eyes to the table where he'd placed Sunny's bracelet. I wanted to reach for it, to reclaim it, but had to content myself with clutching the torn-heart charm on my necklace. I waited for him to say something. When he did, it was as if he was speaking to himself, mumbling his thoughts aloud, and I had to lean forward to hear.

'She didn't tell me.'

I should leave, before he accuses me of lying. This was not what I'd intended. I should have stuck to my plan. 'I don't want anything from you. I just wanted to give you Sunny's bracelet. It meant a lot to her and I thought you'd like to have it back.'

'Are there other family? Did she meet anyone else?'

'No. There's only me and some distant relatives I never see.' He looked so distraught it was clear I was making things worse for him. 'I'm sorry. I shouldn't have come. It was completely inappropriate to drop this on you when you are mourning her. I just thought . . .' I paused lost for words. What did I think? That I could make him happy by helping him keep Sunny's memory alive? That maybe together we could find some sort of meaning for all that had happened? That this was what Sunny would have wanted?

'It kind of makes sense,' he said, almost to himself. 'It all happened so quickly, her just up and leaving for England. There was no chance to talk about anything.'

I'd been right – he didn't know about her quest for fame and fortune on *Britain's Got Talent*.

He straightened in his chair. 'I've got so many questions. I don't know where to start . . . I'd like to talk with you. But not now. I need time to think. Could we meet again? Tomorrow?'

We arranged to meet the next evening outside the pub and drive somewhere quiet to talk.

That gave me twenty-four hours to make decisions.

Chapter 16

I'd been taking a risk, lying to Ned like that. For all I knew, Sunny may have already been in touch with a whole extended family . . . but I doubted it. There was no mention of it at the funeral, no floral tribute marked 'love Mum'. The few mourners were all from the English side of the family or the pub. And there were no name and contact details in Sunny's notebook, no mention of her birth mum among the online posts about *Britain's Got Talent* and her gigs.

As soon as I'd discovered Sunny was adopted from Ned's online tribute, I'd tried to research her birth family. But that sort of thing wasn't easy.

Closed adoptions . . .

They were still common in the 1980s and '90s, neither the birth nor adoptive parents knowing anything of each other. So I knew it was probable the Ryans hadn't been told anything of baby Sonya's origins. But the law had changed since: an adopted child could get their birth parents' details when they turned eighteen. And blood relatives could register their willingness to be contacted if the adopted child wished to find them. But it didn't appear Sunny had bothered.

My curiosity led me to research what I could. Based on the assumption that the Ryans hadn't changed her first name when they adopted her at three months of age, I'd searched the records for all babies called Sonya born in the UK on 16 September 1992. There were six in the right quarter, right year. I'd ordered birth certificates for each, on the off chance there might be something obvious to point towards adoption, like the father's name being missing. When the certificates had arrived, a quick glance had allowed me to discard the obvious no's. And then I had my likely candidate.

If Sunny's birth name was Sonya, it seemed a possible birth mother was a Deborah Wicks. The named father, Robert Davis, was registered at a different address.

If Ned asked for my full name, this was my best alias. It felt awful to tell an outright lie but now I'd embarked on this course, what could I do? I was Deborah Wicks, known to everyone by my middle name, Sonya. Sunny's birth mother.

But even as I came up with this plan, part of me knew this was absolute madness.

It's not that I set out to be deceitful. My stories were never developed with a nasty intent; I wasn't after money or revenge or anything. I just wanted to make people happy.

Gran had always loved the stories we spun together. Encouraging me to embellish, we'd bounce off each other as we danced with the truth. Reminiscing, she would ask me if I remembered a particular trip to the seaside or circus or farm, but I would have been too

123

young to have laid down any particular memory of my own. However, by the time I'd reached my teens, I'd heard her anecdotes and seen the family photos often enough that I could piece together the jigsaw to help her relive it yet again.

'It was a hot one that day in Cornwall. Do you remember?' I'd prompt.

'You fairly ran into that sea with all your clothes on, you little tyke!' Gran would say.

'I was so excited. You told me there were mermaids there!'

'Who's to say there wasn't? You found a huge shell—'

'And you told me it was part of a mermaid's bikini! You let me bury your legs in the sand . . . I gave you a beautiful tail.'

'You tried to put seaweed in my hair.'

'But you said, "What mermaid has green hair?"'

Borrowing from various sources, I'd embroider the story until the memory became crystal clear. My memories, her memories, a fabrication, what did it matter? The stories grew a life of their own in each repetition.

I'd defy anyone to tell me there was harm in that.

The next evening, Ned and I ended up sitting on a park bench facing the river. I'd met him at the pub and suggested I drive us somewhere quiet. This was the only place I could think of where we could have a private conversation without bar staff or waiters constantly interrupting to ask if they could get us anything.

The bleakness of the coming months was already pressing in, the November air damp and chilly, the fallen leaves congealed in unsightly muddy clumps. Small grey-white moths clustered around the street lamp above our heads where I hoped they'd stay. I turned up the collar of my coat as I waited for Ned to speak, my stomach fluttering.

'This looks like a nice place. Did you come here with Sunny?' he said.

Not one of the questions I'd anticipated.

'Once,' I said. My pulse was racing, my jittering nerves causing my leg to twitch and I crossed my legs tightly to stop it.

'I want to thank you,' Ned said. 'For being there for her when she was all alone . . . For accepting her when she came to find you. Not everyone would do that.'

'Everything's changed since Sunny came into my life,' I said. I felt I should say more. 'I wanted her to tell you that she'd found me, but she wanted to do it face-to-face. She didn't want to hurt you.'

'She said that?' I couldn't read his expression in the shadows, but his tone sounded relieved.

I'd done the right thing. This was going to be all right.

'There's something I wanted to ask you.' His tone suggested this was important and I realised I was holding my breath in anticipation. 'About the accident. Do you know much about what happened? Have the police spoken to you? Are you in touch with the Family Liaison Officer?'

'I . . .' My mind went blank. I felt frozen to my bones and must have shivered because Ned touched my shoulder, concerned, and I flinched.

'I'm sorry,' he said. 'Maybe it's too cold to be out here for very long? But there's so much to discuss.' He looked at his watch. 'I was just wondering, did the police tell you anything? Have they told you about the inquest?'

Police. Inquest. I closed my eyes to help me calm down, to give me a chance to think, which Ned again misinterpreted.

'Oh, I'm so sorry. I've upset you. I just—'

'No, it's okay.' *Get a grip. Focus.*

'It's just that I'm trying to piece it all together. I wondered if the police had said anything that might help me work out what happened.'

'I'm not in touch with the police. I was on holiday when . . . when the accident happened. I knew nothing about it for weeks. When I went to the pub to see her, that's when I realised she was missing. The only information I have is from the newspapers.'

He nodded. 'They say it was just a stupid accident. The post-mortem showed no defensive wounds, so apparently there's no grounds for suspicion. But what the hell was she doing on that bloody bridge? She must have been meeting someone.'

'I don't know. It doesn't make much sense.'

'There's going to be an inquest. They've already appointed a coroner's officer to start the investigation. I'll probably stay here in the UK until they sort out a date.' He took a deep breath before continuing. 'You know, they said she'd been drinking already that morning. Started her birthday celebrations early.' He swallowed hard. 'The police think she was climbing on the side of the bridge, lost her balance and fell . . . I guess it's possible. She could be daft like that.' He shrugged. 'I feel so sorry for that woman. The one in the car she landed on. It's lucky she wasn't killed too.'

My heart started thudding hard in my chest, my pulse galloping. The next step would be hyperventilating and a full-blown panic attack. I tried to slow my breathing, unable to take my eyes from his face, searching for clues as to what he may know; instead noticing the creases round his eyes, registering he looked a bit like an actor I couldn't place; that his cold sore looked worse, spreading along his lip; my brain dancing off at tangents.

Oblivious to my reaction, wrapped up in his thoughts, Ned continued where he'd left off. 'The driver was knocked unconscious in the crash apparently. The poor woman, just going about her normal day . . .'

I had to respond, say something. 'So, the driver . . . the woman . . . she didn't see anything?' My voice sounded weak and shaky.

'No, the police said she's a victim, not a witness.'

'Were there any other witnesses?' I had to know. 'Has anyone come forward with information?'

He shook his head sadly. 'Not much of any use. Some people said they saw the accident happen in their rear-view mirror. They think they saw a man on the bridge but couldn't be sure.'

The man in the red hat.

Ned picked the flaking paint off the arm of the bench as he talked, running his nail deep into the ridges in the wood. 'You know, I was always scared for her – waiting for something awful to happen like this. She had no fear.' He was struggling to hold back his emotion and turned his head away.

I sat in silence, my hands clasped together so tightly in my lap that my fingers were turning white, the only outward sign of my anxious state. The cold was making my nose run, the emotions raised by talking about Sunny and the awful accident making it hard to control myself. I sniffed noisily.

'I thought she'd fall off her surfboard far out to sea and drown. Or some drunken larrikin would take a corner too fast with her in the passenger seat. I told her time and again "don't take unnecessary risks", but you know what she'd do? Hum the theme tune from *Jaws* and walk out. But they say no one was to blame – it was just a stupid bloody accident. But surely someone must've have been with her? Or she was waiting for someone? I can't get it straight in my head.'

'Me neither. It doesn't seem to make much sense.'

'Well, we're not going to find our answers sitting here freezing to death. Let's head back.'

Find our answers. He needs me. He needs me to help him find the truth.

Walking back to my car, he asked me if Sunny had any siblings, if I'd stayed in touch with her birth father. An image of Sam flashed into my mind and surprising us both, I started to cry.

I wish. I want.

'I'm sorry. I—' I turned away from him, trying to pull myself together.

'There's no need to apologise. I shouldn't have asked out of the blue like that.'

'No. The man . . . He . . . I never married, after I lost her . . .' I stuttered to a halt. This truth was far too painful.

'It's okay. We don't need to talk about it.'

'Sorry,' I mumbled, wiping my eyes. 'It wasn't a good time in my life.'

Driving back, he didn't ask many more questions after that, just wanted to talk about Sunny; and I wanted to listen, to learn about her. Ned seemed uncomplicated, almost naive. I imagined how shocked he must've been by some of Sunny's behaviour and wondered how much she had actually told him.

The information I volunteered he took at face value; I felt close to her the minute I saw her (true); she had made lots of friends since she'd been in the UK (true); and we both loved to sing for an audience (less true – although I was in a choir once upon a time). He said she must've inherited her voice from my side of the Wicks family, along with her height and colouring.

People hear what they want to hear, see what they expect to see.

When he asked me if we could meet again, what could I say but yes?

As he was about to get out of my car, he started hunting for something in his pocket.

'Sonya, I'd like you to take this back.' It was the box holding Sunny's bracelet. 'Sunny would have wanted you to have it.'

Another sign. That was when I knew for sure – all this was meant to happen. He had said it – it was what Sunny would have wanted.

Chapter 17

I'd not seen Dmytro since before the funeral so drove up to visit him later that week. He was grateful for the stew I'd made him; knowing his pride, I told him I'd had too much lamb for one person and didn't want to freeze it. Other than half a carton of milk, there didn't appear to be anything in his fridge. The place was becoming a tip again, all my good work tidying undone, but my heart went out to him. He seemed very low and unfocused, still stuck in the work-sleep-work cycle, with nothing else to distract him from his grief.

But I had a plan. An article I'd seen in that font of wisdom the *Daily Mail* had suggested that 'socialising and a sense of purpose' were good for depression. While I was boiling the kettle, I launched my opening gambit.

'I'll shoot off after we've had the tea. I've seen some bookshelves on sale – ex showroom stock. My neighbour was going to collect them for me but he's put his back out. He was trying to dig up a tree root. At his age! I want to pop in and see if I can get the shop to deliver.' Dmytro didn't respond, a mere nod of acknowledgement, so I ploughed on in a conversational tone, 'Anyway, if they deliver next week, I'll just have to leave them in the boxes in the hallway. I doubt I'll be able to lift them myself. But at least I'll have them.'

He flicked his sad dark eyes towards me without lifting his head. 'I could help you collect them.'

'Oh, I wasn't hinting.' He was hooked and I had to make sure I didn't lose the catch. 'But if you could, I'd be really grateful.'

It was arranged. I was to pick him up so we could drive to the store to collect the flat-pack furniture. 'You are very kind, Dmytro. It's such a relief. My house is a difficult place to find and the delivery drivers always get lost. None of the houses have numbers and I share a postcode with three other houses spread out over half a mile. I'll throw in a lunch. How about that?'

'There is no need for lunch. I said I would help.'

Driving home, I made plans. As Sunny's boyfriend, he would have been welcome at my home any time. We would have been a happy little family, the three of us, and I wanted to give him a sense of that. I would research Ukrainian traditional dishes and see if there was anything within my skill range. Comfort food was what we both needed.

It was my Sunday call with Mother that made me think harder about the situation. Unexpectedly, she had asked me if I had any plans for the coming week, no doubt expecting the answer 'no'.

Stupidly I volunteered too much information. 'A friend is coming over to help me with my new book-shelves. I said I'd cook us a meal.'

'That woman? The one that interviewed you?' Mother clearly didn't remember Becky's name, but at least she recalled that I had a new friend.

'No, a young man who—'

'A young man?'

'Yes, he—'

'How do you know this young man?'

'He helps Becky out with the village hall. Odd jobs and things.'

She drew in a deep breath. 'A friend you say . . . This young man is a friend . . .'

'Yes, Mother. A friend though Becky. Everything is fine.' All that childhood practice at lying was coming in handy.

'I hope you're right. We don't want you getting *giddy* again. Running away with your ideas.'

'I am not remotely giddy, Mother. You can rest assured.'

After I hung up the phone, I had to admit to myself that maybe I had been a little *giddy* and not thought this through fully. Other than the visit from the police, I could count on one hand the number of people who'd crossed the threshold of The Old Vicarage this year, and that included the delivery man who'd lugged a heavy parcel of research books into the hall for me last month. I'd tried to give him a chocolate bar as a thank you, but he told me he was diabetic. Dmytro would be the first visitor since the police, so there were some housekeeping issues to deal with. While I kept a clean and tidy house, a quick once-over was in order. I grabbed a pen and paper to make a list of To Do's as I went round.

I started in the hallway. The jumble of coats hanging by the front door and my worn old wellingtons could be moved somewhere else. The circulars and freepost lay on the sideboard, waiting for the pile to grow high enough for the move to recycling. Last month's copy of the *Village Voice* was under a charity circular for the Salvation Army and a leaflet about an autumn sale. Stapled to the cover of the church magazine was a hand-scribbled note: *Janice, could you help sell poppies this year? I can't do your end of the village. Tom.'* Feeling guilty, I realised that I'd not got back to him, but there was something else about the note that niggled at me. I reread it several times before it struck me.

Janice.

Dmytro knew me as Sonya.

Oh, goodness. I'd invited him to my home. Once he knows where I live, he could look the house up online and find out my real name from the council tax records. My brain bounced back and forth, sallying from 'why would he do that?', to running through all the other ways he could find out who I really am. There were methods of tracking down information about people; I knew that only too well from years of genealogy and family research.

What *had* I done?

I needed to make a plan, come up with a story.

Okay. This was *not* my house.

I was house-sitting for the owner who lives abroad. That would explain some of the disrepair. And I could lock some of the downstairs rooms that I don't want Dmytro to see, tell him these were rooms that the owner was keeping private. And, just to be sure, I'd unscrew the name plate from the gatepost. It would be hard to research a house with no name.

Relieved to have a simple solution, I breathed more easily. But I must be more careful and *think* before I embarked on any other reckless ideas, even if they were intended to help others.

Planning the meal for us cheered me up again, imagining what Dmytro might enjoy, researching ingredients and recipes. The day before he came, I sliced vegetables and prepared the main dish. The first course was borsht, the hot beetroot soup recipe followed to the letter to make it as authentic as I could. The chicken Kiev was far easier. And, to keep things simple, I decided to serve it with mash, peeling the potatoes in readiness, then leaving them in water in the fridge. I wanted everything to be just right.

It was only when Dmytro and I entered the furniture shop that it struck me – I'd done it again! When I'd reserved the bookcase by phone, I'd used my real name. I could feel a fluster coming on, which was only a couple of steps from a panic attack. *Keep calm. Breathe.* As we entered the store, I looked around for ideas to distract Dmytro, to enable me to sort out the purchase without him by my side. The Bargain Buys area was at the back of the building, the shop-soiled old stock hidden behind the rows of new sofas, tables and sideboards that made up the main display. Spotting a row of shiny new bookcases, a plan formed.

'While I go and pay, could you be a love and pop over there and find out the price of the new stock?' I pointed in the direction. 'I'd love to know how much I've saved. I'll meet you back here in a few minutes.'

I scurried to the pay desk and congratulated myself on my quick thinking.

As I tapped my code in to the credit card machine, I asked the assistant, 'Where do we collect the units?'

'They'll be packaged up ready at the warehouse entrance.' He handed my card and the receipt back to me. 'Thank you, Ms Thomason. Just give your name to the warehouse supervisor.'

My name.

Oh gosh, I hadn't thought this through at all.

Dmytro knows me as Sonya Wicks. Who can Janice Thomason be? I walked slowly back to Dmytro, my brain churning. He was perched on the edge of a chintz sofa, shoulders slumped, staring at the floor. This was no time for me to be drawn into his sadness – I had to concentrate on my story. I paused by a gateleg table, pretended to inspect its folding mechanism to give me time to think.

Who could Janice Thomason be if I was Sonya Wicks?

The householder! What a perfect solution. Janice owns the house but works abroad. I, Sonya, am the house-sitter.

I'm buying the bookcase for the woman who owns the house . . . She'd asked me to replace any broken furniture . . . and order things in her name . . . so that she has the guarantees . . .

Pleased by my quick thinking, I strode towards Dmytro with new-found confidence and a smile on my face.

On the journey to my house, I enlarged on the invented story of how I came to be looking after the property for this woman, which, of course, he accepted without question.

'It's a big place and can get quite draughty in winter, but it soon heats up with a nice log fire.'

'Does your neighbour chop the logs for you? How is his back now?'

It took me a split second to recall my previous story of the fabricated helpful neighbour, but I bounced back. 'No, that would be too much to ask of him at his age. I buy the logs from a local farm.'

I made a mental note to develop some sort of method to help me keep track of what I said, when and to whom. Maybe a colour-coded spreadsheet . . .

★

After a cup of tea, Dmytro set to unpacking and rebuilding the bookshelves with a degree of energy I'd not seen in him before. I left him while I went to heat the soup and put the potatoes on to boil. Popping my head round the door to give him a five-minute warning to be ready for lunch, I found him balanced on a chair, screwing up the sagging curtain rail, a task that hadn't even been on my radar. He was such a thoughtful young man.

Over our lunch I asked him about his homeland. I was keen to find out more about Sunny, but didn't want to leap in too fast. It took some coaching but he slowly shared his story: his mother was Ukrainian, his father Russian, and they had lived in Pripyat before he was born and had to evacuate after the Chernobyl accident. Shocked, I resolved to find out more about this history.

'They left everything behind,' he said. 'It was very sad for my mother to lose her home like that.'

'How awful. How did they cope?'

His shrug suggested this was too hard a question to answer in words. 'My father found new work but it was not well paid. This is why I came here – to earn good money. To send money home. And I like it here now.'

He told me his parents now live on the outskirts of Kiev, where he was born and grew up.

'Did you visit the cathedrals?' I asked. 'I'd love to go to the Golden Gates.'

He snorted a sarcastic laugh. 'You live near London. Have you been to the Tower? The Queen's palace? No, when I was at home I was too busy studying.'

'What did you study?'

'Science. I worked in a lab at a college as a technician.'

'It sounds like a good job.'

'Yes, I loved it. But the money wasn't good. When I came here, I thought I'd be able to get the same job but it was hard. But I make enough money now to live, and to send some home. Maybe one day soon I'll find a good job again.'

He told me about his family, his fourteen-year-old sister who hoped to be a doctor. How his mother was saving the money he sent for her future. And I thought what a perfect partner he must've been for Sunny, this kind, intelligent, loving young man.

'How did you meet Sunny?' I asked him.

'She didn't tell you?'

Apparently he'd bumped into her by the fridges in a corner store. Literally bumped into her. And she'd dropped everything she was carrying.

I could imagine it. Sunny dashing through the shop, in too much of a rush to pick up a basket. Tacking up and down the aisles, grabbing anything that took her fancy – a boxed pizza, iced buns to share with the others, a magazine, a carton of milk. Stopping to get beers, her shoulder shrugged to balance her rucksack and wedge the fridge door open, while she rummaged within for the cans. Dmytro approaching, distracted by a call on his mobile, knocking the door of the fridge with his wire basket and setting the whole chain in motion . . .

He told me that he'd stopped to help her, and she'd immediately engaged him in her shopping project. I could see him retrieving the things she'd dropped, her loading more goods on top, Dmytro disappearing behind a pile of packets and tins.

Of course, he'd offered to help her carry it all home.

There was a Guinness advert once, involving a domino-cascade of objects, each perfectly placed so that as one fell, it toppled the next. Suitcases, wrecked cars, flaming bales of hay, crutches – a chain of unrelated items crashing into each other and flowing like a river down the path of the village where they were filming. Life is like that sometimes. A touch of a wire shopping basket on a fridge cabinet door and look where we end up.

The rest of the afternoon went well. The only tricky moment occurred when Ginger nonchalantly strolled in to join us as we were finishing dinner.

'You have a cat?' Dmytro asked. He reached out to stroke her and she arched her back towards him. He picked her up and ran his finger along her throat, making her purr.

'Not really. They're feral cats from the farm in the village. There are two of them. They're meant to live in the barns and catch rats. But they prefer it here.'

'I like cats. They're independent. They come and go when they want.' He tipped his head on one side to look up at me. 'Sunny hated them.'

'Yes, I know.' I stopped myself from saying more in case I dug a hole for myself, waiting for him to say something, hoping he would tell me why.

'Hmm. You have two cats? So it's not genetic then, her allergy?' he asked.

An allergy. 'No, not my side of the family anyway.'

He placed Ginger on the floor and we both watched as she stretched each back leg in turn, then sat down to clean herself. 'They've a cat in the betting shop, downstairs from my flat,' Dmytro said. 'It brushed against Sunny once. She was sneezing and scratching all evening.'

'Yes, she told me about that. That's why I always locked the cats out of the house if she was visiting. And I vacuumed everywhere just before she arrived. You can't be too careful with that kind of allergy.'

A narrow escape. But another useful piece of information to add to my files.

Chapter 18

I was sitting at my desk staring at my email inbox.

I had never had a complaint about my professional work before. The feeling was akin to bringing home a bad school report, ripe with the teacher's sarcasm – 'Janice still seems to believe young girls should be seen and not heard, contributing nothing to class discussions'; 'Janice doesn't seem to realise that Goal Defence is an active role in netball and she cannot just block the other side by getting in the way'. It wouldn't be allowed now. There'd be angry parents demonstrating outside the school gates.

Mother's voice echoed down the years: 'You've let yourself down.' And indeed I had, but not just me: Mr Abbyss and his great aunt, whose ninetieth birthday was in three days' time. I opened my diary, as if that might give me a different answer, but it was there in my own handwriting. There really was no excuse. I had failed to deliver by 21st November as promised. The work was now days overdue.

Glyn Abbyss' email was, thankfully, reasonably courteous, although understandably cross: 'huge disappointment' . . . 'need to find some resolution' . . . 'not at all what we expected'. I was that girl in white knee-high socks again; already heading off to stand in the corner to contemplate my sins before I was allowed back to join the responsible, hardworking, reliable children who always remembered their gym kit.

I felt sick.

I tried to be rational. There was still time. Just about. If I worked through the night to pull things together, I could get the file to the printers by tomorrow morning. He charged more for a rush job but I'd lose money on this project anyway. To salvage what I could of my reputation I intended to give Glyn Abbyss a huge fee reduction. Damage limitation. I had to stop him writing a bad review online. My thoughts were tumbling one over another, my hands shaking, and I felt on the verge of panic.

When the phone rang and I heard Becky's voice, I surprised both of us by bursting into tears.

'Oh my god. What on earth's happened, hon? Are you okay?' The care in her voice set me off again.

I spoke between sniffs and gulps. 'Sorry. Sorry. A work problem. I missed a deadline. I've let people down.'

'Oh, Jan. Come on, it can't be that bad.'

'I'll be okay. I think I can fix it if I work right through the night. This isn't like me.'

None of this was like me. I didn't let my clients down. I didn't talk openly to other people. And I didn't cry in front of comparative strangers. But I had.

'What can I do to help? There must be something.'

By the time Becky hung up, she'd decided she was 'popping round' that evening with some food for me, so I could work straight through. She'd offered to help me with paperwork and typing (an impressive sixty-five words a minute apparently), which, while very kind and potentially helpful, had to be avoided at all costs. I couldn't have her in my office where she'd see my wall plastered with all my information about Sunny. I wasn't ready to share that – yet.

I thanked her profusely, trying to think of something nice I could do for her – maybe send her some flowers tomorrow. I wasn't used to spontaneous kindness and it felt warm and reassuring but also somehow discomforting. It was usually the other way round. Gran used to say it was the Virgo in me – we find it easy to give but hard to receive, apparently. Like to play the hero.

It felt strange that Becky was coming to my house. Even though we'd seen each other a couple of times and had the occasional phone call about her family tree, I wasn't yet accustomed to the to-and-fro of friendship. Yes, there were people I knew well enough in the village who would stop for a chat, professional contacts in the world of genealogy, clients who kept in touch, but no one who 'popped round', unbidden, caring enough to put themselves out for me on a damp autumn night.

Since my earlier breakdown, after events with Sam and Hilary, I'd been cautious about who I allowed into my life. Mother had thought it was for the best, after I had befriended another person and got 'overly involved'.

It had started when I'd spotted an article about one of my favourite teachers, Mrs Harrison, in the local paper. I'd not seen her for years. In the newspaper photograph, she was at a residents' party in a care home. She had a jaunty Easter bonnet balanced on her thatch of grey-black hair, a knitted yellow chick in her hand, and there was a member of staff grinning beside her. But Mrs Harrison's face was expressionless, like she was above these indignities, mentally back in her classroom considering someone's homework, her red pen poised for praise or critical comment.

I started visiting her. She had early-onset dementia and thought I was her daughter so, not wanting to upset her, I played along. In truth, I probably encouraged the fantasy a bit. She smiled so brightly every time she greeted me, stroking my hand and cuddling me. The staff got to know me, my weekly visits being more regular than those of any of her trio of elderly friends who turned up en masse for cake whenever there was cause for celebration. I left my details so the staff could reach me should Mrs H need anything brought in. It gave me great pleasure to take her small treats, a bottle of Guinness, a warm cardigan, some lavender talc. We built up quite a relationship over the ten months I visited and everyone in the home knew me.

Needless to say, Mother didn't take it very well when an agency carer phoned to leave a message for me: 'Can you tell Janice that "mum" has taken a turn for the worse. Can she come in as soon as possible?'

That took a bit of explaining.

After that, at Mother's suggestion, the scope of my life shrunk to something I could control, without what Mother spitefully called my 'delusions and deceits'. Just routine and plans and no surprises. For me or for her.

But since Mother moved abroad with Georgio, I no longer felt her critical presence looming. It's fair to say I'd kicked out a bit through my forties. I'd extended my family history hobby to set up my little business, had the odd organised holiday tour abroad, joined a few clubs. But there had always been something missing. Since the accident and finding Sunny, I realised you only have one life and this is it. No one could make it work but me. It was time to take chances, to embrace opportunities, to make friends.

To live.

To love.

And all these events with Sunny had helped me see that.

I ran a clean tissue over Sunny's picture to remove the specks of dust that had settled, then touched a kiss to my fingertips and placed them on her forehead. I stretched, then started my email with new-found confidence that this would be all right. That *everything* would be all right.

Dear Glyn,

I apologise profusely for the late arrival of the Abbyss Family Research Book and any inconvenience this may cause. Since I took the commission there has

been an unexpected death in my family. I should
have contacted you to advise you that a delay was
inevitable. Please take my assurance that the Abbyss
family history will arrive by registered post on the 27th
in time for your great aunt's birthday on the 28th. In
recognition of the unintended upset this has caused
you, I would like to waive the second half of the fee
which was due to be paid on completion.
  Yours sincerely
  Janice Thomason

I pressed the send button and took a deep sigh, before reaching for the Abbyss files to get started, one ear open for Becky's arrival.

Hearing Becky's car pull up, I rushed downstairs to meet her.

Normally I would have hoovered, made a bit of an effort, but in the circumstances, I knew Becky wouldn't be concerned. She blew in as soon as the door opened, a carrier bag swinging in the crook of her arm and a tower of Tupperware boxes stabilised by her chin.

'Can you just grab this one? Oh, no. Hang on. It's all . . .'

One of the containers crashed to the parquet floor and the hallway filled with the appetising aroma of beef stew. A yellow Post-it declaring '2 mins at 900' floated in the gravy and there was a half-second's silence as we looked from the floor to each other and then – I don't know why – both burst out laughing.

'Oops,' she said, which set us both off again.

It took us a while to clear up, Fred wanting to help by eating what he could, Becky constantly apologising about how she was meant to be saving me time not making more work. But, down on our hands and knees together, mopping up the mess, I felt really happy.

This is what it's like to have friends.

Chapter 19

Geed up after my successful lunch with Dmytro and the visit from Becky, I wanted to extend the hand of friendship to Ned. Neither of us understood the events on the day of the accident and I wanted to know more about Sunny.

When he'd asked if we could meet up again and said we should find somewhere private, I couldn't think of a good excuse not to invite him to my house. But still cautious about giving out my address, I phoned him and said I'd book one of the local cabs to pick him up.

'This place I'm house-sitting is off the main road and so difficult for people to find.'

Once he'd rung off, I phoned an anonymous cab company in the local town to give them detailed instructions to locate the property and where to pick him up. And this time I remembered to book in the name of Sonya Wicks.

Ned arrived with a bottle of wine and some flowers, which was thoughtful of him. I thought it best if we pace ourselves so went to put the kettle on. When I came back to the lounge he was holding the framed photo of Sunny that I'd placed on the bookshelf earlier. He put it back, pretending to attend to the alignment of the frame with the shelf edge to hide the fact he was blinking rapidly, rubbing at his eyes with the back of his hand.

'I've not seen this one before,' he said, trying to smile. 'She was a diva when it came to having her picture taken. Even when she was little.'

'You must have lots of photos,' I said. A statement of the obvious but I didn't want to say anything that might upset him more. He was so vulnerable, so alone and sad.

'Paula – my wife – used to stick them all in albums before she died. One for every year.'

I nodded encouragingly.

'I had to go through them all to find photos for the memorial page . . . It was one of the loneliest things I've ever done.' He turned away from me, his shoulders tight with grief, his head bowed. And I could taste the salt of my own tears, recalling the sad photo of Ned and the two children at Paula's grave, imagining how painful that must have been.

He searched his pockets for a hanky and I discreetly put the box of tissues next to him, just like a professional counsellor, taking one for myself.

'I'm sorry, Sonya,' Ned said, noticing my tears. 'Coming here, upsetting you too. I just have no one I can talk to about her. No one who understands.'

'I know,' I said quietly. 'It's the same for me.'

'People mean well . . . but the things they say. A woman came up to me in the pub last week and you know what she told me? She understood how I felt because her dog died last year. Her *dog*.'

'I remember when my gran died. I was heartbroken and a neighbour said "at least you still have your mother". Which . . . well . . . it didn't help.' I stopped myself from saying more, conscious this was personal territory that I may not wish to explore with Ned. 'I suppose they don't know what to say.'

Ned held his head in his hands, rubbing his forehead. 'I guess you're right.' He sighed a long drawn-out breath. 'It's all so hard though.'

'There's no manual for us to follow. We just have to work it out as we go. We're doing the best we can.'

I poured tea, giving myself something to do and allowing Ned a few seconds' space.

'Thanks,' he said taking the cup, his hand shaking slightly, the liquid slopping from side-to-side. I'd brought in a plate of chocolate digestives but neither of us had the appetite.

Ned looked around, taking in his surroundings, and I was pleased I'd spruced the place up, added some brighter colours. The sort of thing Sunny would have helped me choose.

'Did Sunny come here to visit you?' he asked, his voice still subdued.

When we'd met previously in the park, I'd given only the sketchiest of outlines about how Sunny had found me. I'd described how the DNA site had identified that we were relatives, sharing 48 per cent of our DNA (a detail I'd obtained from one of my genealogy client projects).

I'd told him that we'd exchanged emails via the profiling site initially, how thrilled I'd been to find out she was actually in England and we could meet up face-to-face.

Of course, since that conversation in the park with Ned, I'd imagined that first meeting with Sunny down to the smallest detail. I had created such a clear image, it was as if it had actually happened, the feelings my own. As if my Samantha had actually existed, or Sunny was Sammy, it all muddled together in my head. I knew exactly how it felt – an overwhelming combination of shock, excitement and an immediate surge of love for this striking young woman, the daughter I thought I'd lost.

'Yes, she came here all the time,' I said. 'The first time, I asked her if she might prefer somewhere more public, like a cafe. Neutral territory. But I think she was curious to see where I lived.'

'Nosey more like! It must've been so emotional, to meet her, after all these years.'

'Yes, I'm not sure who was more nervous,' I said. 'We hugged for a long time, I remember that.'

'What was your first impression of her? Did she seem . . . happy?'

I nodded, reassuring him. Every parent wants their child to be happy. What's that saying? You can only be as happy as your saddest child.

'The first thing I noticed was her smile. It was so warm. We couldn't speak at first, just stood there grinning at each other.' He placed his cup on the table, leaning towards me, more interested in my portrait of Sunny than lukewarm tea. 'Of course, she commented on our hair colour. Obviously I have to dye mine now but the colour . . . hers was the exact same shade. I told her we were a family of redheads, inherited our dad's colouring . . . Her grandfather by birth.'

'Do you have photos of your family? I'd love to see them.'

'They're in storage while I'm living here but I'll dig some out for next time we meet.'

'What did you talk about? Tell me from the beginning. Don't miss anything out.' He was hungry for details.

'You know how these things are, everything happens so fast and afterwards you wish you could replay it and savour every moment. Let's see . . . She sat where you are now. She was wearing a short summer dress – lime green, like the cushion behind you – high sandals, bright orange platforms they were. Big hooped earrings.' The portrait I was painting combined elements from different photos I'd collected. I could see her as I spoke, right there before my eyes.

'And of course, her bracelet. She always wore that.' I looked down to the chain on my wrist and touched the acorn charm, the one he'd bought her for her fourteenth. He'd done his best by her. 'You raised her to be an amazing young woman. She was always so full of energy and ideas. She was a real credit to you.'

'Did she say anything about why she came to England? Was it because she wanted to see you?'

'No, she didn't do the DNA test until she was in London. I suppose being here made her wonder about her English roots.'

'Oh.' He looked down at his hands, slightly crest-fallen. 'Yes, that makes sense.'

'She told me she was here to enter *Britain's Got Talent*. You've seen her recordings. She had huge ambitions.'

He frowned. 'Recordings?'

'Online. Rusty does Dusty. You haven't seen them?' His expression answered my question. 'She only made the videos this summer . . . I guess she wasn't ready to send you the link until she'd polished them up.'

'Can you show me? I'd like to see them.'

I clicked through on my phone. 'Anyone Who Had a Heart'. Seventeen views, all of them me. Tapping the start icon, I passed the phone to Ned just as the recording of Sunny announced, 'Rusty Steel here. Welcome to my channel – Rusty does Dusty.'

There was a sharp intake of breath and Ned went pale, the shock of seeing her for the first time, after all those months when he thought he'd never see her again.

'I didn't know,' he said. He held one hand to his mouth as he watched, his breathing shallow. When the clip finished, he blinked away tears, then screwed his eyes shut, rubbing his face with both hands. 'Oh god,' he said. 'I should've been there for her.'

The website automatically moved on to the next clip, 'Rusty Steel here . . .'

'I'm sorry. I should've thought . . .' I said. 'Maybe we should stop it playing? Leave it to watch another time.'

'No. I need to see her. I want to watch.'

'I'll get you some water.' I thought it best to give him some privacy.

154

I waited in the kitchen until the final song finished before making my way back with two glasses of water.

'Thank you.' He took the glass, his hand slightly trembling. 'Do you know this John bloke?'

'He sometimes goes to the Pheasant. I think that's how she knew him.' It didn't seem appropriate to tell Ned of his daughter's affair with a married man. 'He'd been in the music business and she hoped he would support her career.'

'It seems there's so much I don't know about my own daughter . . .'

'She was an independent, twenty-six-year-old woman, "finding herself" by travelling the world.' I laughed gently, kept my tone soft. 'Did you tell your parents everything you were doing when you were that age? I certainly didn't.' To be honest, I didn't have to; I never made a move without Mother's approval.

'I guess not . . .' He gazed out of the window, not focusing on anything in particular. 'I just wish I could rewind time . . .'

Later, returning from the kitchen with two glasses of wine, I found Ned looking at my books. I'd always been an avid reader. They looked good on the shelving unit Dmytro had built for me, their battered spines a jolly mix of hues contributing to the character of the room.

Ned ran his finger along the top row, his head turned sideways to read the titles. 'Wow, quite a collection. Reminds me of my wife, Paula. She couldn't pass a bookshop without going in.'

I'd arranged them by colour and by theme: historical, foreign, classics . . . He took a sip of his wine. 'There must be hundreds here. Which is your favourite?'

He was obviously a literary man and my heart warmed to him even more. I knew exactly where my most treasured book was on the shelves. I pulled out a hardback, the purple dustcover tatty and ripped, the artwork all sixties' psychedelic swirls.

'*I Want*,' he said, reading the title. He turned the book over to read the blurb on the back cover but there wasn't one, just a photo of the writers. I didn't need to look at it to see the image – the lost look in the eyes of Nell Dunn, the secure bear-like presence of Adrian Henri, her co-author. Both hippy rather than hipster.

I'd treasured this book since I was seventeen. It had belonged to Mrs Harrison, my teacher, the gentle soul who succumbed to dementia. She had brought in a pile of records and books she no longer wanted and offered them to us. Most of my classmates turned their noses up at her rejects. There was no Bowie or Rolling Stones, no Philip Roth or Douglas Adams. It was a motley selection but, feeling sorry for her, struggling in with this box of gifts for us and no takers, I feigned interest to make her happy. I ended up taking most of the assortment, I think, my LP collection almost doubled – that's how I discovered Fleetwood Mac. And among the pile of poetry books was this. The story of two lovers spread over the course of fifty years, it's not a conventional romance – there is no happy ever after. But it touched me in a way I can't explain.

Seeing Ned standing beside me, reading the quotes I'd underlined, I felt exposed. Like I'd shared a precious secret part of me with a stranger who'd only asked for directions to the bus station. Don't ask me, I thought, don't ask me who or where or when, because I once thought I had that kind of love, but I was wrong. But I want, oh yes, I want.

'Would you trust me enough to let me borrow it?' he asked.

I felt a huge surge of warmth towards him. 'Of course,' I said.

When his taxi arrived later, he said he'd had a lovely evening and asked if we might meet again. I said yes. We were becoming friends, it seemed. And just like Dmytro, he needed my support right now. The three of us drawn together through Sunny. He kissed me on the cheek in that European way that all people seem to follow these days and, unfamiliar with the sequence, I assumed it was just the one cheek and it turned out to be two and our noses bumped. I didn't need to look in the mirror to see I was flushed, but Ned seemed unfazed.

Later, tidying up the glasses, I found my book lying on the side table. He must have forgotten it after all that wine.

Chapter 20

Sunny's notebook was wedged open with a corner of my keyboard as I tried to copy her writing. So typical of Sunny, it was overdone and flamboyant, all large letters and loops; a mix of lower and upper case that bore no relation to convention. I'd been practising for half an hour, but the sheer lack of consistency made it almost impossible to master. I was endeavouring to make a realistic copy and failing badly.

I'd made the mistake of embellishing my stories for Ned a little too much. In describing the first time I met Sunny, I told him she'd taken loads of photos of us. And, when he asked if I had any copies, I stupidly said yes. But as if that wasn't bad enough, I didn't leave it there – I said she'd printed one for me and written me a loving message on the back. Of course, he'd asked to see it. I'd managed to distract him with an anecdote about her allergy and the cats, and by the time he left he'd had a lot of wine, so I was hoping he wouldn't remember. But, in case he did, I needed to be prepared.

I berated myself as I tore up my latest attempt at Sunny's writing. The trouble is, I never knew when to stop. I never set out to fib. Just like when someone asked if you liked their new haircut/painting/house — the intent in one's response is not deception but to be nice, to make the person feel good. My stories were always intended to make people happy. I wasn't a liar but a magician, producing a dove from my sleeve right before their eyes. No one cared how it was done, they just wanted to believe it had happened. In many ways, forging Sunny's message was no different from the parent who crafts a note from Santa, or scatters glitter around the hearth to be found on Christmas morning. It was all about keeping the fantasy alive.

In the end, I kept the handwritten message short: *So glad I found you!!! All my love S xxx*. The photo was the easier part, my skills with editing software good enough for the task. All I had to do was take a selfie with my new red hair then blend my image with one of Sunny. Once it was done, I wondered why I'd not created one before and set about finding others that might be edited together and look good in a frame.

I dabbed a little of the perfume I'd found in Sunny's bag on the back of the photo. I didn't usually wear scent myself but I made a note of the brand to buy some more when I was next near a chemist.

Becky had invited me round for dinner. When I arrived, the TV was on quietly in the kitchen where she was preparing our meal. She didn't seem to be watching it, so I assumed it was for company, although she made no move to turn it off now I was there. I so rarely go into other people's homes that it always strikes me how differently people live.

Becky opened the bottle of Merlot I'd brought – 'Buyers Choice' from Waitrose – and poured us both a glass. She smacked her lips as she took the first sip, 'Hmmm, yum.'

I perched opposite her at the breakfast bar while she chopped something that looked like some sort of greens, but she informed me was pak choi. A Christmas advert played for one of the superstores and her head popped up like a meerkat.

'Don't you just love this one? I did it at karaoke last week.' She sang along with the tune, marginally out of key but still better than Sunny. 'Oh I Oh I Oh I Oh I . . .'

'I don't think I know it. Maybe if I heard a bit more, I'd recognise it.'

'So my rendition wasn't enough!' She laughed and fiddled with her iPhone, the volume drowning out the TV. 'Ed Sheeran – you must know it.'

I restrained myself from commenting that I knew neither the singer nor the song. The room filled with the introductory beat which I recognised from the ad. 'Wait for the chorus and join in. You can be my backing singer!' I was sucked in by her energy and playfulness, in awe of the lack of self-consciousness which allowed her – a forty-something-year-old woman – to dance around the kitchen singing at the top of her voice about sleeping with someone she'd met in a bar. 'I'm in love with your bodeeee.'

A tall young man wandered into the kitchen and she tried, unsuccessfully, to engage him in the performance, dancing around him like he was a maypole.

'Knock it off, Mum,' he said, taking a beer from the fridge. 'That song is so crap.'

'Jan, this is Jordan, my middle son. Jordan meet Jan. He's home from university. Takes after his dad – he's the one with the brains.' Her voice was proud and there was love in her eyes as she gazed up at him.

I wanted to ask what he was studying, show an interest, but I wasn't sure of the protocol for meeting the son of a new friend. By the time I'd struggled to get up from the bar stool intending to shake hands, he'd given me a thumbs-up and was heading towards the door.

'You're lucky it was me and not André,' he said over his shoulder.

Becky snorted a tight little laugh. She immediately turned off the iPhone.

'André?' I said, once I could make myself heard without shouting.

'My youngest, just turned seventeen. All teenage angst and disapproval. Need I say more?'

Another Christmas jingle played in the background but this time she didn't join in, her balloon deflated. I found these adverts incredibly trying. Who were these lucky people who could conjure up a group of family and friends who *actually* relished spending Christmas together? Did it exist in real life?

'Have you got any plans for Christmas, Jan?'

'No, I . . .' She'd caught me unawares. I hadn't

161

prepared a cover story yet, what with Christmas being over three weeks away. Given her enthusiastic expression, it didn't seem appropriate to launch into a list of all the things I find difficult about it. Mince tarts for one.

'You must come and join me and the boys – we always have a houseful of waifs and strays.' She was rummaging in a cupboard for something and didn't notice my face darken. Is that how she saw me – someone wandering the streets with no one to care for me?

She emerged with a 'ta dah!', wok in hand, and returned to her theme, her eyes sparkling with excitement like a child. 'I just love it – the cooking, the games, the decorations. Tyrone works at B&Q so I asked him to get us a tree next week and if André will move his motorbike, I can get the tinsel and stuff out of the garage. We have such a laugh on Christmas Day. I cook loads of food; you'll have such a great time. Much better than being on your own.'

She looked up for the first time and I didn't need to say a word before she started to apologise. 'Me and my big mouth. I didn't mean it like that – I wasn't implying you have no one to see or anything—' I cut her off, forcing a smile to my lips.

'No, I'm sure you didn't mean that.' Although we both knew that it was the truth. She topped up my wine glass; a *don't be cross/please stay* gesture.

She rebounded quickly. 'It would just be such fun to have you here. There's usually loads of people popping in and out – friends of the boys, their dad and his mate, a couple of neighbours.' She wasn't selling it. I couldn't see where exactly I would fit into this motley collection of people. Between the maiden aunt and the elderly deaf man from next door, I feared.

I took a sip of wine, a non-verbal sign that I wasn't mad at her, not looking to pick a fight. An idea hit me that made my smile genuine. 'Thanks, I would love to come, but I'm probably celebrating with a couple of friends. I'm just waiting for confirmation.'

Relief danced on her face. She really wanted me to like her; maybe she genuinely valued our nascent friendship. I found her always-on, upbeat personality intriguing. Like Sunny, it was a quality to be admired, and she was someone I could learn from as I tried to embrace life.

'New Year then. You'll come to our New Year's Eve party? You can't turn me down twice,' she said.

Becky's Christmas invite had sparked a thought – why not ask Ned and Dmytro to spend Christmas with me? I could treat us all to a hotel lunch. It would save them being alone at such a painful time and provide a chance for them to meet each other and talk about Sunny together. Before I broached the subject with them, I made a booking: a table for three at my sixth choice of hotel. There wasn't much available and I had to accept a cancellation; apparently I should have booked in September. As I paid the deposit, they set about managing my expectations. It was really a table for two so would be a little cramped, it was near the kitchens, and we could only stay two hours. All the same, I felt quite excited when I hung up the phone.

Dmytro took some convincing.

'How can I meet Sunny's dad? Who would you say I am?'

'Sunny's boyfriend.' I couldn't see why he was throwing up objections.

'He'll have too many questions.'

'Like what? He'll just want to know more about you.'

'He'll want to ask me about what happened on her birthday. Why I wasn't with her. Why she was on the bridge. Who gave her the balloons if it wasn't me?'

'Why would he expect you to know? We're all in the dark. Anyone could have bought them for her. Possibly someone at the pub arranged for the balloons as a surprise.'

He raised his eyebrows cynically. Shook his head. 'You know, she told me she was going to London.'

'Yes, everyone thought that.'

'She was meeting another man.'

'You can't know that. You weren't there. Don't torture yourself.'

Eventually I convinced him that no one would want to discuss the day of the accident over Christmas lunch. We would be coming together to remember the good times with Sunny and share our memories.

'I think Sunny would've wanted us all to be together and it would seem strange if you don't join us. It would mean a lot to me to have you there.'

He conceded that he'd think about it and let me know. He sent me a text later that evening to say yes. He's a good lad. I knew he wouldn't let me down.

Chapter 21

The day after I'd seen Dmytro, it was an unusually crisp, bright morning and Ned called me to suggest we go for a walk together. It turned out to be a longer, more arduous walk than I'd imagined, Ned striding at quite a pace, insisting on deviating from the route to climb every hillock in case there was 'a great view' (more fields).

In between these diversions, we shared anecdotes of Sunny. I mentioned her cat allergy again, recapped how she'd started sneezing when she first visited my house. He told me she'd demanded a pet so they got her a snake, but she soon lost interest. On the flatter sections, where I didn't need to gasp between words, I chatted more, telling him how she and I had signed up for a local choir: 'We only went once – we brought the average age down by twenty years between us!' He was intrigued by her dreams of a singing career, asking me for information on what she had planned, what she had done. I told him about her 'Open Mic Night' performances; how I would travel to London to sit in the front row with my glass of warm Chardonnay cheering her on. My visit to the Australian-themed bar where she'd performed furnished me with a vivid description. Ned said he was sorry to have missed it, wished she'd sent him the recordings. We both agreed she was a great performer, if not the best singer.

He was calmer and more relaxed than he'd seemed in ages. Maybe exercise and fresh air were as beneficial as the health and happiness gurus claimed.

We'd been going at least an hour when I spotted a fallen tree and – rather breathlessly – suggested we sit for a while and take in the view (fields with sheep). I took out one of my bars of Cadbury's and passed it to Ned who snapped off a row and handed it back. Reluctantly I rationed myself too, when really I wanted to wolf down both slabs after all the exertion. While Ned poked around under the bark of the tree like a kid looking for insects, I snuck an extra couple of squares before tucking the rest of the bar deep in the holdall out of temptation's way.

Not finding anything of interest, he sat down beside me.

'Are you going back to Australia for Christmas?' I asked, hoping my tone was suitably casual.

He shrugged. 'Yes, I guess so.'

Oh, that was not what I'd hoped. I'd assumed he'd stay here in the UK until the inquest, which was likely to be sometime in January. I tried to hide my disappointment. 'I expect you have friends and family who want to see you.'

'Yes.' He paused, eyes down and it felt as if he was unable to look at me for some reason. 'I've had a lot of invitations. People have been very kind.'

'That's nice.'

'They've all been very kind,' Ned repeated, raising his head to stare out at the horizon where grey smoke belched from the incinerator at the rubbish dump, recently rebadged the local 'Waste-to-Energy Eco Park'.

He was going home to be with all his friends and – other than when he made his fleeting visit to the UK for the inquest – I would probably never see him again. He didn't really need me at all. He had all these other people waiting in the wings to support him. I bit my bottom lip, disappointed at the thought of him leaving so soon, having no one to share Sunny with – a gnawing in my chest.

'And you?' Ned asked. 'You must have family and friends you want to see? People you spend Christmas with?'

He really had no idea about my life, but why should he?

'I was invited to go for lunch with a friend, but I don't think I could cope with a large gathering at the moment.'

Ned had lapsed into silence beside me. The thought of him leaving, just as we were getting to know each other, made me want to go home and mope. Put on some melancholy music, sit in my dressing gown with a tub of ice-cream. I contemplated wallowing songs, creating an imaginary playlist: 'Alone Again Naturally', 'Memories', 'Are you Lonesome Tonight?' . . .

'I think you're right,' he said. I had no idea what he was talking about.

'Sorry?'

'I don't think I can cope with it all – a big group, someone else's family.' He ran his thumbnail along the ridges in the bark. 'I'm not sure what would be worse – being with people who don't know about Sunny, or with friends who know and keep checking I'm okay. Giving me those special caring looks. I don't think I can face it.'

'So, what will you do? Stay at your house in Sydney on your own?'

'I doubt they'd let me get away with that.' He snorted a hollow laugh, working the piece of bark lose absent-mindedly. 'Maybe I should just save the cash and stay here. It wouldn't be so bad if the weather stays like this . . .'

I laughed. 'I wouldn't put money on it.'

Could he be serious?

We walked back towards the car in silence, a direct route this time with me in charge of the map. Ned was lost in thought. As I unlocked the car, he took a deep breath and announced, 'I don't think I can face going home for Christmas. Everything's still too raw. I'm not ready to face people. You know what it's like.'

'Oh, yes,' I said, pretending to search for something in the holdall while I decided how to propose my idea.

Here goes, if I don't say it now, I never will. 'I've been thinking. If you're sure you're not going home, and you've nothing else planned, maybe we could have Christmas lunch together, rather than both of us being on our own? I just hate the thought of you spending it alone when you'd usually have been with Sunny. It just seems so sad.'

I realised I was wringing my woollen beret in my hands and tucked it back in the holdall. 'That is, unless you prefer to be on your own, of course. Not that you can really. Be alone, that is, not staying in the pub with all those people around.' I was wittering on.

Some moments passed before he said quietly, 'Thank you . . . I'd like that. Yes, thank you.'

Back at the Pheasant, before he could get out of the car, I broached the subject of Dmytro. 'There's someone else we might invite to join us at Christmas, but only if you don't mind. A young man who was close to Sunny. If it's too much, you can meet him another time.'

Ned sat up straighter in the passenger seat and turned towards me. I had his full attention. 'Someone from the pub?'

'No. You've not met him yet. His name is Dmytro. To be honest, I've not known him that long myself. Sunny was always chatting about him, but she never brought him round.'

Ned listened intently as I told him how I'd met Dmytro at the roadside memorial a month after the accident, after Sunny had been identified. How distraught we both were, how we had come together in our loss.

'He's been quite ill with depression, not coping well since . . .' I couldn't bring myself to say *her death*. 'He's been lost without her.'

'What's he like, this Dmytro?'

'He's a loving, intelligent, thoughtful man.' I twisted the charm bracelet around on my wrist to show Ned the heart Dmytro had had inscribed with their initials. 'He bought her this. He adored her and was really good for her. I think she was beginning to settle down a bit. Just before I went on holiday, she told me she planned to move in with him.'

I took a photo of Dmytro and Sunny from my bag, one he'd given me. Dmytro's face was bright with love, not the pallor he'd assumed since her death. Sunny was laughing – all teeth and hair – her hand caressing the side of his face as she held his cheek to hers. It was a tender moment, no doubt posed by Sunny. I passed it across to Ned, letting the picture do the talking.

He stared at it in silence, his thumb stroking Sunny's hair as if she were there.

'I'd like to meet him,' he said eventually. He passed the picture back to me. 'Was he serious about her?'

'Yes. From his perspective, they were a couple. They'd been together about six months. But Sunny . . . well, you know what she was like. She cared about him, but you know she loved attention.'

'Do you mean she was cheating on him?'

'I don't know. Dmytro suspects she was meeting another man on the day of her birthday. It's the only thing that makes sense. The people at the pub thought she was spending her birthday with a friend. And she told Dmytro she was going to London for a few days to see someone about her music. Dmytro dropped her off at the station, so why didn't she just get on the train? Why go to the bridge? Maybe she *was* meeting another man.'

'I bet it was the man they saw leaving the bridge.' His voice carried an edge of anger. 'Probably a married guy who had to disappear ASAP. Otherwise, why wouldn't he have done something to help her? If he wasn't to blame for the accident, why wouldn't he have contacted the police so they could identify her? The bastard.'

He glanced towards me, looking for answers I couldn't give.

'I thought that too initially, but I've been over it so many times. Was she with someone and they argued? Was she waiting to meet someone and she just fell?' I kept my voice quiet and calm. 'We don't know what happened. A friend could have met her at the station and given her the balloons, then she missed the train and she was just passing time wandering around on the bridge. She could've climbed up for a better view of something and fallen. Realistically we have so little to go on. The man they saw on the bridge may have been nothing to do with it.'

Ned's gaze flitted back to the windscreen and the darkening winter sky. He was silent for a minute or so. 'You remind me of Paula,' he said eventually.

I held my breath, unsure if this was a good or bad thing, to be compared to his wife.

'She always had a sense of perspective, didn't jump to conclusions.' He turned to me, sadness heavy on his face. 'She kept me balanced, helped me to see reason. I still miss her. She was a good woman . . .'

Overwhelmed by this validation – *I reminded him of Paula, I too was a good woman* – and suddenly exhausted by everything, I felt the unexpected pricking of tears. Covering my face with my hands, I rested my forehead against the steering wheel, not wanting him to see my unexplained distress. I heard him shift towards me in the passenger seat. Mumbling soothing meaningless words as one would to a child, he gently patted my back and a tingle ran through me as I shivered, my skin prickling with goosebumps. And I understood all that had been missing in my life.

Someone who cared, someone to care about.

Chapter 22

'Penny informs me you're not helping with the free Christmas Lunch Service this year.'

Mother was not happy. It always amazed me how much displeasure she could convey down a phone line. A talent I should master for dealing with my broadband provider.

I'd been helping out with the seasonal free lunches for longer than I could remember. Initially I was assigned to Preparation, hidden in the kitchen peeling mountains of potatoes and chopping the vegetables ready for the Cooking Team – a grand name for Mrs Piper and Jean-from-the-cafe, wearing jolly aprons and Santa hats. When the organisers had recognised my helpfulness and my skills at small talk, I was promoted to Dishing Up and then Waitressing. To be honest, I quite enjoyed helping out and it broke up what would otherwise have been a long day of TV repeats.

'Of course,' Mother continued, 'I had to pretend I already knew what my daughter is up to on Christmas Day. But, as usual, I'm the last to know.'

'Sorry, it was a bit of a last-minute plan.' I'd prepared my story. 'I've been invited to have lunch with Becky and her family.' I launched into a description of Becky's family, who, as far as I could tell, were as nice as I painted them to be. The only difference in my version was that Becky was still living with Nelson, rather than having an extended trial separation. 'He's a very successful dentist in Harley Street. He's worked on lots of famous people.' This was true. I'd looked him up.

'You ought to get him to take a look at your teeth. I suppose we should've got you braces like your father suggested, but I wasn't to know how snaggle-toothed you'd turn out.'

I refused to be baited. 'Anyway, Becky's a good cook and I'm looking forward to it.'

'Don't forget to take a gift for the hostess.'

'I've already got that in hand.' I hadn't.

'Oh, really? And what have you bought?'

The newly acquired bottle of Sunny's favourite scent stood before me on the desk.

'Some perfume.'

'Well, I just hope it's not one of those overpowering ones that will put you off your dinner. I was at the Robinsons' for drinks the other day and I swear she'd sprayed herself with fly spray. "Early signs," I said to Georgio. "She's losing it."'

I listened with half an ear while doodling a note to myself to select a small gift for Dmytro and Ned, a gesture of my affection for them. A warm hat for Ned, a pair of leather gloves for Dmytro. Wrapping up my new family ready for winter.

I was looking forward to our little gathering. The first of many, I hoped.

As the day for the lunch with Ned and Dmytro approached, excitement and anxiety juggled for top billing in my guts. When I'd proposed the idea, I'd been visualising a jolly experience, the three of us laughing and joking together, dressed up in our finery and enjoying good food and relaxed chat, as we whiled away a pleasant couple of hours. Each time I thought of it, it was like being enveloped in a warm comforting hug. The day would be our own version of one of those Christmas adverts; our self-styled family group drawn together through Sunny.

But as the reality of it hit me, I began to worry. What if the two men didn't get on? What if it turned out like that childhood Christmas when there was a row about some clumsily spilt gravy and everyone stomped off home early? What would be worse – if the men argue or if there is an awkward silence? And what if I say the wrong thing, or we all get too maudlin about Sunny?

To calm myself down, I made a list of my concerns and set about trying to address each in turn. I knew silence would be the most difficult thing for me to handle. Social awkwardness made me babble and I couldn't risk that – who knows what I might blurt out. I would play to my strengths: thorough research, organisation and curiosity about others. After all, 'Failing to prepare is preparing to fail,' as Dad used to say.

A few hours of brainstorming helped me fashion a number of conversation starters, which I categorised under headings: anecdotes, interesting facts, traditions and generic questions. To show interest, I fashioned some intelligent questions specific to their countries: I was particularly keen to know about the Ukrainian tradition of putting spiders' webs on Christmas trees – there had to be a story behind that which could keep us going for ten minutes. And then there were a dozen generic questions I could pull out of the hat: favourite Christmas food, the country where you would love to spend Christmas if you could, best or worst present ever. (I was sure I'd win that one with my example of Mother's gift of a dictionary of antonyms and synonyms. Nothing intrinsically wrong with that, but I was only ten years old at the time and had been hoping for a Barbie doll.)

I would need to keep my wits about me, but with my preparation I was sure we would all have a lovely time.

Of course, on Christmas morning I woke early, the excitement too much. I was up and showered by five, already perusing my options for outfits; all ironed and laid out in one of the spare rooms. Two dresses, a calf-length skirt with a sparkly top, and a smart trouser suit with a soft waterfall-lapelled jacket. All brand new. There was plenty of time to try each outfit on again and work out which felt right. I was striving to look smart but not overdressed; 'effortlessly sophisticated' as one of the Sunday style magazines had described it.

In the end, I paired the trouser suit jacket with one of the dresses and took a photo to email to Mother later – proof of my new social life.

I was a few minutes early to pick up Ned from the Pheasant, so pulled into a parking spot where I could see the pub door. When he emerged, five minutes later than we'd agreed, he was talking on his mobile, moving the phone from one hand to the other as he struggled into his jacket. He was lost in his conversation and I was able to study him unobserved. His face was animated but he didn't look happy. There was a conflict in his body language; at one point a frustrated shrug, his free hand raised like the 'duh' emoji; then a hand to his chest suggesting sincerity or pleading. It was as if he were a marionette being worked by two different puppeteers.

Spotting me waiting, he waved and pointed to the phone, turning his back to me to say his goodbyes. By the time he walked towards the car, he had a smile clicked into place.

'Family?' I said, trying to sound casual rather than nosey.

'A friend.' He turned away to reach for his seat belt. 'So, we're meeting this Dmytro at the restaurant?'

We met in the reception area of the hotel restaurant. I spotted Dmytro, half hidden behind a large over-decorated Christmas tree, every inch of it covered with something sparkling. He was sitting rigidly on the edge of one of the sofas, looking as if he was about to be called into a doctor's surgery for an unpleasant procedure.

I was pleased to see he'd had made an effort with his appearance. His hair was cut neatly and, underneath his leather jacket, he was wearing a crisp white shirt – probably new as it was not one that I had ever laundered for him. I felt so proud of him, all shiny and polished for his first meeting with Ned. He stood up as we approached.

'Ned, this is Dmytro,' I said. 'Dmytro, this is Ned.'

They shook hands, Ned patting Dmytro on the back in a familiar, matey kind of way, as if they were old friends meeting in the pub. 'Good to meet you.'

'I am pleased to meet you.' Like his posture, Dmytro's delivery was robotic. 'I am Dmytro Petrovych Antonenko.'

'Wow, that's a bit of a mouthful.

Thankfully a receptionist interrupted to take our coats before Ned could say anything further, but luckily Dmytro didn't seem to take offence.

'Hey, no one told me the dress code! Look at you two all glammed up.' Ned gestured to his jeans and casual shoes, his fake bonhomie radiating to all corners of the reception area.

We'd barely got seated at our table when Ned launched straight in with his beer order, while the waitress was still handing out the menus. 'Dmytro, you look like a beer kind of dude. What will you have?'

I passed Dmytro the drinks menu and ordered a Coke while he made his mind up.

'So, how did you and Sunny meet?' Ned was straight in there. One had to admire his directness.

'In a shop.' Dmytro was monosyllabic in his response. This wasn't going to work if he carried on like that.

To get the conversation flowing, I embarked on the story Dmytro had told me before, adding a few embellishments from Sunny's perspective, so it sounded as if she had also shared the anecdote with me. 'The carton split as it hit the floor and there was milk splashed all up their legs, but Dmytro didn't make a fuss' . . . 'At the cash desk she bought him a bar of chocolate to say thanks' . . . 'He carried everything home for her on the bus – she said he was a proper gentleman.' I spoke quickly, enthusiastic in my storytelling, scared to pause in case Dmytro contradicted me or, worse, there was a silence.

'You were dating a while then?' Ned said to Dmytro.

I'd told him this already. Was he checking the truth of what I'd said, or testing Dmytro?

'Six months,' Dmytro said.

'March, they met in March,' I added, unnecessarily.

Ned's forced joviality abated while we waited for food and there was an uncomfortable silence. I became unpleasantly aware of the smell of cabbage drifting from the kitchens behind our table and the draft from the overhead air-conditioning unit which occasionally dripped water onto the carpet next to me. Shuffling my chair sideways to avoid it, I glanced around the other tables, trying to assess how our little group compared to others – did we stand out as a motley collection of oddballs? For every table of people wreathed in smiles, making animated conversation, there seemed to be another where a sulky teenager played with their phone or a fussy eater pushed food around their plate. An older woman at a table on the far side of the room seemed to be staring at us. She may have been left out of the chat or been too hard of hearing to take part, but she was definitely not engaging with those on her table. She adjusted her glasses, then placed her elbows on the table, chin resting on her interlaced fingers, a cross 'I'm waiting' expression on her face. It was one of Mother's gestures and gave me such heebie-jeebies that I had to look away quickly.

On our table, Ned had wrecked the hotel's Christmas display, pushing the centrepiece to one side to make room for his beer glass, standing it directly on the white linen cloth rather than the reindeer table mats. He was picking at the decoration on his cracker, separating the plastic holly from the ribbon, inadvertently transferring glitter to his cheek. I wanted to brush it off. I toyed with the idea of mentioning it and sharing the anecdote I'd read online: 'Ten people at a table doing craft projects. One of them is working with glitter. How many of the projects have glitter on them?' But Ned was fairly literal and would probably answer 'one'.

I was still thinking how to phrase it so he would understand the joke about the transmission of glitter to everything nearby, when he said, 'Looks like we're expecting quite a feast.' He was pointing to the array of utensils, now jumbled up next to his table mat where he'd been fiddling with them.

'Hopefully', I said, although at that moment I really needed a drink to calm my nerves rather than the Special Xmas Feast the hotel was offering. I launched into one of my prepared topics. 'Sunny said that in Australia, Christmas would usually involve a prawn *barbie* on the beach.' My voice sounded false, too upbeat, and I'd put a strange intonation on the word *barbie*. I needed to dial back a notch. 'I hope the hotel's prawn cocktail doesn't disappoint!'

'Christmas barbie prawns, ace! Shame Sunny would never eat them. Not after that food poisoning. She must've told you about that?'

Not having a ready answer, I busied myself straightening my napkin on my lap. Why on earth would I have discussed that with her? 'So many people have food intolerances these days.' Now I sounded prim.

'She was ill for a week,' Ned said.

I couldn't think of a sensible response so mumbled, 'Poor girl.'

There was a silence; metaphorical balls of dead tumbleweed blowing across the desert of our table.

'So, Sonya tells me you're from the Ukraine?' Ned said.

'From Ukraine, yes.' I wasn't sure whether Ned had picked up on Dmytro's subtle correction.

'What's your profession?'

'In Ukraine I help with science research, at a college.'

'And what brings you to England? Better jobs? Better women?'

'I'm working so I can send money to my family at home.'

'His sister wants to go to college too. Dmytro is helping her save up,' I interjected, but Ned ploughed on.

'What work do you do here?'

'Now, in winter, I do building work. Summer, I help on farms, picking fruit, packing eggs. That kind of thing.'

'How'd you get a visa for that?'

Dmytro flashed a look at me. I leapt in to help. 'Our immigration rules are different. We're desperate for the labour, skilled and unskilled. We get a lot of young people coming over specifically to work – or working on their travels, like Sunny.' I wondered if he realised she'd been paid cash-in-hand and how he'd have felt about that. Desperate to change the subject from the cash economy, I said, 'Ned used to be a sports physiotherapist. He's building a private physio practice now that he's semi-retired.'

'You like sport? Do you like football?' Dmytro asked, latching onto the word sport. 'I support West Ham. The Hammers.'

'Now you're talking.' Ned warmed up. 'Let me tell you about Aussie rules footy.'

As the first course was served, he was trying to describe a game that sounded like a free-for-all cross between rugby and soccer to a bamboozled Dmytro.

Chapter 23

Buoyed up by the success of our lunch, I left the two men chatting and finishing their drinks while I nipped back to reception to pay the bill. A woman in a strappy party frock was ahead of me at the reception desk, her two children behind her, arguing over who had the best cracker gift.

'It's not fair! Dad gave Phoebe the ring and I wanted it. He never even asked me.' The child tugged on her mother's arm while the accused Phoebe flaunted her pink plastic cracker ring by waving her hand in her sister's face.

The woman ignored them both, chatting with the receptionist about a cheese and wine event the hotel was running in January. She was one of those 'me first' people, oblivious to the scene behind her: the-child-that-wasn't-Phoebe now slumped on the floor with her legs out, blocking the space between the desk and the sofa.

'Excuse me,' I said to the child and, hearing an adult voice, the woman at last turned around.

'I'm sorry. What have you two done now!' She sounded well spoken in a slightly put on way. She reached down and grabbed the arm of the child on the floor, pulling her to standing.

'It's no problem,' I said and the woman looked up at me.

'Gosh! I recognise you. Weren't we at school together?' she said, the accent slipping.

My pulse raced. 'No, I think you've mistaken me for someone else.' Face-to-face, I knew exactly who she was. Melanie, the leader of the 'in' crowd of girls who used to mock me all through secondary school. They used to call me Mouse (among other things) and make squeaky noises in the corridors when I passed.

'I'd recognise you anywhere. We did domestic science together, didn't we?' She was right. They'd swapped my sugar for salt once when we were making cakes and Mother thought I'd done it deliberately to make her ill.

It turned out Melanie was a woman with an amazing memory and she warmed to her theme as if I was a topic on *Mastermind*. 'Janice, isn't it? You've not changed a bit – well, apart from your hair. It suits you like that. You used to have more of a bowl cut.'

'Thanks. You look great. I love your frock.'

'This old thing.' She was done up to the nines, hair in a fancy up-do with curled tendrils artfully arranged. The two girls were mini-mes, although their hair had become a bit dishevelled during the ring tussle. Melanie looked behind me, towards the dining room. 'You here with your family?'

Oh no, I couldn't let her meet Ned and Dmytro.

I gave a slight nod and spoke directly to the girls, to distract the inquisition. 'And how old are you?'

'They're ten. Non-identical twins.' As if reading my thoughts, she added, 'I was enjoying my career too much to start a family any younger. Are you still living in the area? We only come back for visits to relatives. We're in Cheltenham now.'

I was urgently looking for an excuse to get away from her, but as I stepped towards the cashier, she just carried on talking. I listened with half an ear, worrying that Ned or Dmytro could wander through at any moment to see what was keeping me. As their mother droned on with her life story, the girls started an intense but silent fight beside her, one trying to wrestle the ring from her sister's finger.

When one of them bumped her leg, Melanie's attention was drawn. 'Go and wait in the car with your dad,' she said, pushing them in the direction of the door. The children dealt with, she fiddled in a tiny clutch bag, looking for something. At that moment, Dmytro appeared behind her and my pulse raced as he paused to let the children pass, staring in my direction. I turned away towards the cashier. Hoping he wouldn't come and speak to me, and ask how I knew this woman, I spoke to the cashier: 'Can I pay the bill for table twelve please?'

'The Wicks booking? Three people?' the cashier asked.

'Yes.' I handed over my credit card without checking the bill, no energy to tally the number of beers and

Cokes. If Dmytro came over now he'd see my real name on the card.

'Oh, I mustn't hold you up,' Melanie said, without making any move to leave. What was wrong with the woman that she couldn't read my body language. I felt I might faint. Dmytro had walked past without a word, heading for the gents' toilet. I had to get rid of her before he returned.

'Yes, I must get back to my friends.' I put my hand out formally to shake hands goodbye. Melanie clasped my hand in both of hers, somehow managing to transfer a business card in the process, *Wedding Wonders – making every moment of your Special Day one to remember.* 'It's lovely to bump into you. We must keep in touch.' She glanced at my ring-free left hand. 'And if you hear of anyone who needs some advice, you'll know where to come.'

I was losing my peripheral vision by this point and from past experience recognised the signs that I was about to faint. I held it together until she had reached the door and then collapsed onto the sofa, lowering my head to get the blood flowing. By the time Dmytro returned, the cashier had fetched me a glass of water and I was feeling less dizzy.

'What is wrong?' Dmytro asked. 'You are very pale.'

'I came over a bit heady.'

'It's a bit hot in here and madam felt a little faint,' the reception chap said.

'Come and sit outside. It will clear your head.' Dmytro took my arm, helping me stand.

The receptionist tried to take my other arm. 'Yes, a good idea. There's a bench near the front door by the entrance to the car park.'

I sat back down, determined not to move. I couldn't risk Melanie spotting me being escorted from the building as her car pulled out of the hotel car park. Lord knows what might follow if she decided she needed to get involved!

'I'm fine for a moment here, thanks. Maybe you could fetch Ned and we'll get our coats?'

As we said goodbye to Dmytro, Ned embraced him in a bear hug. 'Hey, Mytro. Do you want to catch up for a beer sometime?'

Dmytro nodded. 'That would be good.' They'd hit it off.

Once we were in the car, I relaxed slightly. Despite my rollercoaster emotions, it had been a risk worth taking after all.

'He seems a nice bloke,' Ned said, fiddling with the heating controls on the dashboard. I'd have to remember to change them back once he got out. 'Not her usual type.'

'He was good for her,' I said. 'She was starting to settle down.'

We both lapsed into silence after that, each with our memories of Sunny and recent events.

I was exhausted by the time we pulled into the car park at the Pheasant. But there was one more emotional challenge to face: the rucksack that Dmytro had given me back in October was in the car boot. It was packed with Sunny's belongings, bar a few small things I'd kept for sentimental reasons, all ready for me to hand over to Ned. Now that he knew about Dmytro, I could explain how I came to have it.

As Ned got out of the car, I said, 'Can you wait a moment? I've something to give you.'

I held the rucksack at arm's length, not comfortable standing too close to Ned in case he was overcome with emotion and I forgot myself and tried to hug him. 'Dmytro asked me to give you this – a few bits and pieces Sunny left at his flat.'

'Thank you,' Ned said, taking the bag carefully like the precious gift it was, clasping it tightly as if I might try to snatch it back. 'This means so much to me.' He turned his head away for a moment, swallowing hard. 'Thank you,' he said again quietly. 'Thank you for everything.'

As soon as I got home, I kicked off my shoes and poured myself a large glass of wine. I lit the wood burner and sat in the darkening room, staring at the flames. I was just drifting off when my mobile rang: Ned's number.

'I hope I'm not disturbing you.'

'No. I'm just sitting by the fire daydreaming.'

'Sounds good. There's something I wanted to ask you.'

I steeled myself, uncertain if I was alert enough to answer sensibly, half asleep after a couple of wines.

'I want to scatter Sunny's ashes. I was thinking New Year's Day. Will you come with me?'

'I . . .' I was lost for words. That wasn't what I had expected. I had no idea what the right response was.

'If you need time to think about it, you can let me know during the week.'

'Whe—'

'I want her to be somewhere that feels right. I thought the churchyard where my wife is buried – of course, only if you're okay with that?'

I found my voice. 'But wouldn't her brother Matt want to be involved? He missed the funeral . . . And her friends in Australia? Aren't you taking her home?'

There was a silence before he said, 'I think she belongs here.'

I wasn't at all sure what to say, what *I* wanted, what was *right*. But I knew I couldn't let him do this alone. He needed me there.

'I don't need to think about it. I'd like to be there with you.'

'You're her mum, you belong there – with us.' He paused and I could hear the dull thud of music from somewhere in the pub. 'It would have been really tough going through all this without you. You don't know what a comfort you've been.'

Chapter 24

Before we could take Sunny to her final resting place, there was the small matter of New Year's Eve to get through. After I'd rejected Becky's Christmas lunch invitation, she'd insisted I join them for her party. 'Bring a friend,' she'd said, but much as I would have loved to have Ned by my side for companionship, that clearly wasn't possible. If I was to have both Ned and Becky in my life, I needed to keep my two identities as Jan and Sonya totally separate.

On the day of the party, Becky was in a panic about the arrangements – something to do with fridge space, the 'dessert canapés' and the closing time of the confectioner's. She climbed down off the metaphorical ledge when I told her there was plenty of room in my fridge. I said I'd collect the desserts before four o'clock when the shop shut. 'You're a hero!' she gushed, which made me feel good.

The shop – at the posher end of the high street in the next town – reminded me of those TV ads, the ones where the camera zooms in on the Master Confectioner earnestly stirring toffee, or delicately adding a final topping to a hand-made artisan chocolate creation.

Waiting for an assistant to respond to the ting-a-ling of the overhanging doorbell, I contemplated their salted fudge traybakes. That was more like it.

A young woman's voice asked, 'Can I help you?' and my hand shot to my mouth in shock as I looked up to see a pale face scattered with freckles and a halo of red curly hair. It was as if Sunny were there with me. I had to hold myself back from reaching out to touch her to see if she was real.

'Oh,' I said. 'Sorry. You remind me of someone.' On a second look, she was probably younger than Sunny. 'You could be sisters.'

The name on her badge said Alice.

Her smile was warm. Not as broad as Sunny's, but just as genuine. 'Does she live round here? Your friend?'

'She's my goddaughter. No, sadly she lives abroad. Australia.'

'That's possibly lucky for me. It's meant to be bad luck to meet your doppelganger. How can I help you?'

Furnished with the details of the order, she fetched several trays of mini desserts from the back room, lining them up on the counter. I watched her every move, my skin prickling with goosebumps.

'Is that your car outside? I can help you carry them,' she said. Her voice was gentle, calming. Much softer than Sunny's.

She balanced the trays with a practised hand while I held the shop door open and unlocked my car. 'Looks like quite a party you're having,' she said, passing me one platter at a time.

'It's my friend's party, not mine. I'm off to get my glad rags on after this. Are you doing anything nice tonight?'

'Quiet night in, just me and my little girl. It's quite tiring being on your feet all day but I wanted the extra shift.'

She turned to leave. 'Have a lovely evening,' she said.

'Wait,' I said. I pressed a ten-pound note into her hand. 'Please buy yourself a treat to see in the New Year.' I got in the car quickly, before she could try to hand it back or I accidentally hugged her.

I phoned Mother just before I left for Becky's party. Thankfully she was distracted by her own arrangements for the evening and didn't ask me how I was seeing in the New Year. My ready-made alibi was unnecessary – beside me, the TV page had been folded open with possible programmes highlighted.

It ended up being an interesting party and I learned a lot.

There was something mesmerising about Becky. I watched her surreptitiously over the course of the evening; from 'canapés to carriages' as her invitation had stated. From the outset she was the genial, charming host, welcoming people with a broad grin and a hug, sharing a personal joke, gushing over any token gift. I noticed how she placed her hand on a forearm, stood on tiptoe to kiss a cheek, praised a frock, a necklace or an aftershave. 'Well, look at you! You've scrubbed up surprisingly well. They're looking for a new James Bond, you know. Stand aside Idris Elba!', 'OMG. Those earrings. Santa smiled on someone; they are gorgeous.'

She introduced me to her eldest son, Tyrone, a stunning young man who reminded me of the actor Will Smith. 'And here's Della. They're off to a party with their friends.' Becky threw her arm around Tyrone's girlfriend as she introduced her, hugging her like a daughter, and a pang of jealousy tugged at me. 'I thought you'd have gone by now?' Becky said to Tyrone.

'We're waiting for Steve. We're giving him a lift.'

'Well, if I don't see you before you go, have fun! Jan, come and meet Bob. I told him about your genealogy work and he was intrigued.'

I was impressed when I first saw him, but Bob turned out to be easier on the eye than the ear. One of those people who close their eyes when they speak; he talked non-stop, answering his own questions and laughing heartily at his own puns. I took the opportunity to watch the goings-on in the rest of the room and that was when I spotted the arrival of the young policeman. The one who had come to interview me after the accident.

He seemed to be looking for someone and I immediately ducked behind Bob, my heart racing, guiltily assuming it was something to do with me. *Think rationally and calm down.* He wasn't in uniform, which suggested he was probably a guest rather than here on police matters. A friend of the family. Just as I am. *It's okay. Tonight I am Janice and there are no lies, no pretences.*

I heard Becky's voice: 'Steve, hi! Tyrone's in the garden, setting up the fireworks for later. Get yourself a drink.'

As Bob droned on about his exercise routine, I pondered my options. I could stay hidden in the corner here behind Bob's muscular bulk, or wander to another room, keeping an eye out for Policeman Steve so I could avoid him; or . . . I could go and speak to him, see if they are doing any further investigation. Before I'd weighed the pros and cons, my curiosity had launched me across the room with no more than a 'sorry, someone I know has arrived' to Boring Bob.

'Hi, I don't suppose you remember me, but we met after an accident. Back in September. You came to interview me in the hospital. You were very kind.'

'In hospital? Did you have a car crash?' He stared at my face, frowning as he tried to place me. Of course, I didn't have red hair then.

'Sort of. A young woman fell from a bridge and landed on my car.'

'Yes, of course! I remember. The Jane Doe. No one reported her missing for several weeks.'

'That's right. It was very sad.'

'Sonya Ryan, that was her name! Her father came over from Australia to identify her.'

'That must've been awful for him.'

'Yeah, pretty grim.'

'Did he have any idea what might have happened? Why she was on the bridge?'

Policeman Steve shook his head. 'No. Said he'd not spoken to her since she left Australia. He didn't even know she was in England. Obviously he was really shaken up.'

Interesting. I mentally filed that information away. 'Are you still investigating what happened?'

'No. It was just some sort of accident. Misadventure.'

It didn't seem I was going to get any more useful information from him. I looked at my watch. 'Gosh, I'm so rude! You haven't even got a drink yet. I've taken up enough of your time – you're here to enjoy the party, not talk about the day job.'

'No problem. Anytime.'

I might take him at his word on that. I still had his number in my mobile.

I'd not told Becky about the accident and, while there was nothing to hide about my part in it, it was a conversation I didn't want to get into with her that evening, so I returned to join Boring Bob in the corner where he was nursing an empty glass.

'Sorry about that. I just had to catch that young man. You were telling me about your circuit training.' Policeman Steve left with Tyrone and his girlfriend half an hour later, so I didn't need to avoid him for long.

I stayed until the New Year chimes, when I gave Bob a sisterly kiss on the cheek, joined in 'Auld Lang Syne', and made my escape during the oohing and aahing at the fireworks.

Checking my mobile when I got home, I found a missed call and a message from Ned. His voice was unnaturally loud as he strained to make himself heard above the celebrations in the Pheasant where he was still staying.

'Sonya? Sonya? Can you hear me?'

I imagined him cupping his hand round the receiver, the phone tight to his ear. 'Come On Eileen,' screeched a nearby female voice. There was a pause when he must've stepped outside as the background noise softened, although he didn't seem to have noticed as he still shouted 'Sonya? Are you there? Sonya?' His ears must've been ringing from the din. 'Oh, it's the answerphone. Sorry not to speak to you. It's just gone midnight and I wanted to wish you a happy New Year. Thanks for everything. I couldn't have done this without you.'

I tapped 2 to save.

In turn, I left a message for Dmytro. 'Shchaslyvoho Novoho roku,' I said. I'd been practising for days using Google Translate and, if nothing else, I thought my poor efforts may make him laugh. 'Happy New Year, Dmytro. See you soon.'

Setting aside Boring Bob, it had been an interesting start to the New Year: discovering that Ned hadn't spoken to Sunny since she'd left Australia; that he hadn't even known she was in England. Had they fallen out? Was that her real reason for leaving home so suddenly?

Chapter 25

The 'Garden of Rest' where we'd interred Father's ashes was a characterless municipal establishment, the cremation plots in tidy rows, equally spaced in the manicured grass. Everyone boxed in, numbered and neatly labelled with the same font, 'By order of the sexton', a controlled arrangement which I felt would have won his approval.

The cemetery where Ned's wife was buried felt different. Here things were a little more relaxed. Not in a lax way, no rubbish strewn around or football shirts tied to the memorial benches. But the wild plants were allowed free rein, the headstones reflected personalities and memories, the footpaths tracked off in different directions from the main pathways with no signs proclaiming 'Keep off the grass'. This was definitely where Sunny belonged.

As we walked to the grave, I carried the flowers while Ned clasped the urn of Sunny's ashes to his chest. I'd tucked a few gardening implements in the back of the car in case we needed to tidy up, anticipating the demise of the rose bush that he and Sunny had planted twenty years ago. But, as it turned out, there was not so much as a stump to show where it had been.

'We could plant another in the spring,' Ned said.

I felt a surge of warmth at the 'we' and the thought that he planned to still be here, with me, Dmytro and Sunny, for the next few months.

'An orange rose would be nice,' I said. 'She loved orange. It was her colour.'

Ned brushed moss from the headstone. He ran his fingers over the engraved lettering, his lips moving in a whispered message to his dead wife. A pang of guilt rose in my chest as if I was intruding. I took a step back to a respectful distance, turned away, just as I would have done if Paula had been there in person.

Ned unscrewed the lid of the dark plastic urn of Sunny's ashes and laid it on the ground. He took my hands and placed them on the urn alongside his and I held my breath, conscious of a strange dancing feeling in my guts. Together we gently shook the contents free. Watching Sunny's bracelet rise and fall with the movement of my arm, goosebumps crept over my flesh and I was overwhelmed by an emotion that I couldn't place.

'We miss you, our darling girl, and we always will,' Ned said.

Tears rolled down my face and I turned my head away, my chest tight. I looked towards the treetops, watching them bend to forces beyond their control as the wind battered them this way and that. I counted my breaths – in for seven, out for eleven – repeat, repeat, until I'd calmed down.

★

Back in the car we sat for a moment, each with our own thoughts. A heavy drizzle had started and rain trickled down the windscreen. Before I'd counted seventy drips, the sky had darkened and the light rain turned to a sudden downpour. The atmosphere between us seemed to have changed; the silence now felt uneasy like something needed to be said, but no one was willing to go there. I couldn't find an easy way to raise the issue that was top of mind, and had to refrain from breaking the silence with trite phrases like 'This wasn't in the weather forecast', 'At least it will be good for the garden'. You could certainly rely on me for small talk.

Ned was staring across the grass towards the pond, his fingers drumming out a pattern on his thigh, a subconscious habit when he was lost in thought. He looked drawn, his skin no longer the warm tan he'd had when he first arrived. I guessed he still wasn't sleeping.

'Will you have another service when you get home?' I launched in gently. 'So her brother Matt and her friends can pay their respects?'

'Her friends maybe, but not Matt. He's actually here in the UK.'

That was a surprise. 'Here? She never mentioned seeing him.'

'They haven't spoken for years. He calls her the Cuckoo.'

I couldn't imagine this. Why would he reject his sister? 'Whatever happened? Why did they fall out?'

'Sunny wasn't an easy child. I loved her to bits but she didn't make it easy. She's always been jealous . . . possessive of anyone she loved.'

It sounded like there was more to be said. I gave an encouraging nod, a sign of support.

'Growing up she was so jealous of Matt. If he came to me or Paula for a cuddle, as soon as she could walk, she'd push him away. We'd make it a game, all of us in one big hug, but she always preferred it when he wasn't around and she had us to herself.' Ned looked at me directly for the first time since he'd started his explanation. 'We really loved them both in the same way, Sonya, but I think she always felt that bit different because she was adopted.'

He wanted me to know he'd done his best, done a good job looking after her on my behalf. Unable to think what to say, I just nodded.

'Were they ever close? When was it they stopped speaking?'

'It was around the time she started at high school, it got worse. It started with small things . . . Matt's stuff going missing and him blaming her for it. Generally, it would turn up days later and not where he'd left it – I just assumed he was careless. When he was revising for his high school certificate, it started to get more serious. First his English course notes disappeared, but it got worse. He'd hoped to get in to study art at RMIT – his teachers thought he stood a chance and he was so fired up, he worked on his art portfolio for months at every spare moment . . . Then he found his sketches out on the porch, soaked through with rain. Sunny claimed she'd taken them out there to show someone and forgotten about it . . .'

'Do you think she was doing this out of jealousy?'

He nodded. 'She didn't have any friends at school. Matt had a whole bunch of mates who were in and out of the house all the time. But she was ten years younger than them . . . She used to play pranks to get attention. But she went too far. Much too far. She got one of Matt's friends in trouble with the police . . .'

He sighed again. 'It changed everything. He refused to speak to her after that and moved out as soon as he could afford to . . . We were never close afterwards. He thought I'd taken her side, let her get away with too much, and I'm not sure he's forgiven me, even now.' He shook his head. 'But she was only young and so insecure beneath that tough surface. We were all just getting over losing Paula and I was doing my best. But I still wonder if I should have handled it differently, been firmer with her . . . Of course, I made her apologise each time. I stopped her pocket money, grounded her for a month, but she had nowhere to go anyway.'

She had nowhere to go, no friends, always looking for love. It sounded so familiar. She and I, so similar.

'You did what you thought was right, and that's all any of us can do,' I said. 'You tried to do right by both children, I'm sure.'

Finally, he lifted his gaze to mine. 'Thank you. That means a lot to me,' he said. 'I'm so glad she found you, Sonya. That you were there for her, when she reached out.'

★

Later that evening I ran through the events of the day and considered how close we'd become, given all we had shared over the months. I felt sad for Ned; it sounded like he'd done his best but the Ryans were clearly not a close family after he lost his wife. No wonder he needed my support.

But there remained that nagging question: what made Sunny leave Australia so suddenly? There must have been an incident that triggered her leaving and I planned to find out what it was. I just needed to pick my moment. Meanwhile, I ordered his wife's death certificate, to confirm that she didn't die of anything suspicious. Just to be on the safe side.

Chapter 26

Over the following weeks I made sure I kept close to Ned. After our emotional experiences of New Year's Day I had an affection for him, but it was edged with curiosity that there was more to him than I knew. On one of our walks, I broached the subject of Sunny leaving.

'What you were telling me about Sunny and her brother. It sounds like she was quite a handful. Did she grow out of it as she matured?'

'Not really. She was never easy to live with.'

'She was still at home with you before she went travelling, wasn't she? I've been wondering why she left Australia so suddenly. I know she wanted to enter the music competition but was there anything else behind it?'

'She just needed space. She'd take off for a while if something upset her but always came back in a week or so.'

He wasn't getting out of it that easily. 'But what upset her enough to leave the country? And why come to the UK? She didn't get in touch with me for a while; was she trying to make contact with her brother?'

'God no! The antipathy was mutual.'

'So, what did happen?'

He cleared his throat before speaking. 'I started seeing someone she didn't approve of. I said I'd break it off but she upped and left.' His eyes took on that vacant hundred-yard stare, like you see in the photos of traumatised soldiers. 'She never gave me a chance to explain.'

He strode on ahead of me, unable or unwilling to discuss it further.

But this issue was like a wobbly tooth and I knew I couldn't leave it alone.

The bulb blew as I turned on the kitchen lights.

'Have you got a spare?' Ned asked, coming into the room behind me.

'In that cupboard, on the top shelf,' I said.

I could reach them myself, but Gran always told me that men like to be seen as indispensable. I filled the kettle by the light from the hallway, while he made man's work out of changing the bulb: moving the table, balancing on a chair. It made me smile, the warm contentment I experienced watching him do this small job for me. A quiet domestic moment shared between us, a glimpse of what happy family life could be like.

I tried to sound casual as I asked, 'When are you planning on going home?' It was stupid to let myself grow too fond of him, start building my hopes and dreams, ignoring the realities of the situation – that he would, probably, one day return home. Like someone on death row, I just wanted to know how long I had.

'They still reckon the inquest will be sometime this coming month. I'll stay until then.'

The inquest. With all that was happening day to day, I'd not given much thought to the impending inquest. I started fussing with the mugs and kettle, keeping my back to him. As Janice, I'd provided a written statement to the police last September. I hadn't actually witnessed the events so had nothing material to add – my statement was deemed 'non-controversial'. Back then they had assured me that it was unlikely I would be called to attend the coroner's court. And that young policeman, Steve, hadn't mentioned anything about it at the New Year's Eve party. However, I couldn't get the word *unlikely* out of my mind.

'Would you like to come with me, to the court?' he asked, unaware of the change in my mood. 'I don't know how it works, but once they know you're family I'm sure you could come.'

My hand shook and I missed the cup, pouring boiling water on the countertop.

'No,' I said. It came out a bit more abruptly than I'd intended, but the horror of my two worlds colliding at Sunny's inquest was too much. I watched the spilt water pool on the fake marble surface, my right hand tightly gripping the handle of the kettle as I willed it to stop shaking. 'No. I'm sorry. It would be far too upsetting. I just couldn't.'

'I'm sorry, Sonya. Of course, I wasn't thinking.' He appeared beside me, the dishcloth in his hand. 'I can see I've upset you. Sit down. I'll finish the coffee.'

I sat at the kitchen table as instructed. *Oh my God, I'd not anticipated this. What if I were called to the court as Janice? Would I be able to stop Ned going? Would I be able to get out of it myself?*

'They say it's likely to be a verdict of misadventure, just a stupid bloody accident.' Ned was wiping a teaspoon on the dishcloth rather than washing it. 'There's no way it was suicide; she wouldn't do that. They've got to rule that out for starters. Do you think you and Dmytro should write statements for the coroner? You know, to say she was really happy when you last spoke to her? I mean, you guys were really close to her. That would help, surely?'

My brain whirred, unable to formulate a sensible response but I was momentarily saved as my mobile started to ring, the muffled ringtone from the depths of my handbag announcing Becky. One problem replaced with another. I'd missed her earlier catch-up call and hadn't had time to call her back. Much as I'd love to have introduced Ned and Becky – the people I cared most about in the world – they each knew a different side of me and I couldn't reconcile the two.

My handbag was out of reach, the other side of the room, under the vegetable rack where I'd tucked it earlier. 'It can go to voicemail,' I said, my mouth dry with panic at the thought of my two worlds colliding.

Ned had put down the dishcloth and was already passing me the bag. I should've pretended to struggle to find the mobile, pulled out half a dozen other things first, looked at the number and claimed it was a cold caller. But I was too het up to think.

'Hi,' I said, holding the phone so tight against my ear it hurt.

'Hey, Jan.' Becky sounded upbeat. Her voice seemed to boom even louder than usual when she was excited. With projection like that she could've been a secondary school teacher. 'How do you fancy a day's shopping tomorrow? There's a 50 per cent sale on at Becket and Harris.'

'I can't talk now,' I said, trying to sound normal. 'I'm with a friend.'

I could almost hear her eyebrows rise at the other end of the line. 'A friend?' she said laughing, putting the words in inverted commas. 'Are you two-timing me? Call me later – if you get a chance! Mwah!' She was in one of her frivolous moods and I was lucky that she let me cut the call short without an inquisition.

'Sorry,' I said to Ned. I turned the phone to silent, then switched it off – belt and braces – tucking it deep in my handbag.

He waved his hand. 'No worries.'

Not for him maybe, but for me the problems seemed to be coming thick and fast.

'Anyway,' Ned continued as if nothing had happened, 'I'll stay for the next month at least but I need to move out of the pub. Maybe you could help me find somewhere on a short-term let? You must have lots of local contacts.'

I stared at him, trying to grasp what he was talking about. Did he mean my neighbours? I'd told him I didn't know anyone local, that I'd only been house-sitting here for the past six months.

'What's the name of the company? I could look at their website and see what they've got on their books but I don't know the towns like you do,' he said.

That made it clearer. Weeks ago, when Ned had asked me what I did for a living, I'd appropriated one of Becky's jobs. As far as Ned was concerned, I was a property photographer, subcontracting to online estate agencies.

'Yes, of course, I can help,' I mumbled, rubbing my forehead, as I tried to process this new challenge. 'I thought you liked being there, at the pub.'

He continued, 'It was great there at first, being with Sunny's friends, people who knew her. But I think it's time to move on. They've hired a new barmaid to replace Sunny. Seems a nice girl . . . Kiwi.'

'I'm sorry, Ned, that must be hard.' He put the coffee down in front of me and I realised I couldn't hold it together much longer. 'I think I have a migraine coming on. Would you mind if we skip coffee and call it a day? I can make some calls tomorrow and maybe we can arrange to see a few places later in the week.'

As soon as he'd left, I went straight to my computer to research inquests. I downloaded a number of documents and ploughed my way through them, highlighting relevant points.

There were two that were spectacularly helpful.

'Attending the Coroner's' Court informed me that all witness statements would be provided '*to the family and*

208

any other interested parties' prior to the inquest. I devoured the rest of the information then took out my special folder, where I filed all my important notes. 'Ned will see the witness statements', I wrote, underlining it in red. I jotted down my thoughts as they occurred to me. 1) Is my statement deemed a *witness statement*? How do I find out without drawing attention to myself? Could I ask Policeman Steve? 2) Ned has no way of connecting Janice Thomason to me. 3) If Ned receives all the statements in advance, maybe he won't want to attend court.

I referred to my next source: 'If you have been called to court but do not wish to attend' – a very literal title for a document that lived up to its promise.

I wrote 'You can ask to be excused', then added: 1) You have to contact the office in writing and explain your reasons. 2) The reasons need to be *serious* – is depression/anxiety serious enough? 3) If on medical grounds, a letter must be provided by your doctor.

It was some years now since my last mental health issues – the medication and psychiatrist had definitely helped. But over the past few months, since losing Sunny, the tears and the moments of panic could suggest I was losing control again. Maybe I should consider going back to see Doctor Sathanandan if I was summoned to attend the court.

It seemed there was no point worrying about the inquest. I could deal with it when I knew more specifics. Meanwhile, I still had to do some research into short-term lets and warn Dmytro of Ned's plan for us to provide statements about Sunny's state of mind.

Chapter 27

My breakfast the next morning was interrupted by a follow-up call from Becky. When she was on a mission, she was not easily distracted and she'd been out last weekend when I'd phoned her so we'd not talked for a while.

'I thought we could go shopping together this afternoon. I saw just the outfit for you in the department store. Trust me, you'll love it!'

While Becky described a red jacket – 'sort of crumply, like crushed silk but not quite' – and an actress who looked a bit like me – 'you know the one, she was in that *No Offence*' – I contemplated whether I had time to eat another mouthful of cornflakes before I needed to say anything and had just succumbed to a spoonful when she concluded, 'So, would two o'clock work for you?'

Buying a red-crumply-not-quite-silk jacket hadn't been high on my agenda but I could do with picking her brains about short-term letting companies for Ned. And, as I heard the eagerness in her voice, I realised how much I'd missed spending time with her over the past couple of weeks. I pushed semi-chewed cereal to the side of my mouth. 'Great.'

I could call Dmytro later.

★

It was hot on the fourth floor of the department store. Too many overexcited menopausal women, jostling for bargains in 'Ladies fashions – ageless style'. The jacket had sold out but, in her enthusiasm, Becky selected half a dozen items she thought would suit me. I limited myself to two: a pair of heels and a low-cut navy frock, similar to the style Becky had worn at her party. Perfect if Ned ever suggested a dinner out – flattering but not too 'shouty'. I didn't try it on, preferring the privacy of my own bedroom to the squash of a sticky changing room, delicately perfumed by the odours of the last lady-who-lunched. While Becky disappeared into the fitting rooms, barely visible behind an armload of outfits, I joined the queue at the tills.

'Special occasion?' the assistant asked. She folded the dress around several sheets of tissue, with complete disregard for global warming.

'My daughter's over from Australia. We're going for dinner and a show in London,' I found myself saying. The assistant had already seen *Phantom* herself and assured me we'd love it.

Outside the shop I steeled myself for a long wait for Becky. I'd whiled away almost ten minutes people-watching when, across the courtyard, I spotted the red-headed girl from the confectioners emerging from the 99p shop. She was pushing a toddler in a buggy, the child clutching a blue rabbit in one small hand and tugging at the Velcro on her sparkly trainer with the other. I was pleased to see the baby didn't have a dummy.

Alice, that was the young woman's name.

She stopped to look in the window of a bookshop and I stepped sideways to get a better view of her. Her hair was the same colour as Sunny's and just as wild, springing out at all angles from her headband. Perhaps she wasn't as tall as Sunny and she was certainly more graceful and fluid in her movements – in the videos Sunny was like a giraffe calf, all long limbs that needed concentration to control.

The baby seemed contented as Alice browsed, keeping herself busy by working her trainer loose and attempting to chew the ear off the bunny. Her hair was sparse but had a slight auburn tinge. Alice exchanged a few words with another woman with a young child, but I was too far away to hear what was said. She spun the pushchair round to head back the way she had come and I watched her until she was out of sight.

We got back to Becky's an hour later. Once all our shopping treasures were strewn around Becky's living room for inspection, Becky kicked off her shoes and flopped down on the sofa next to me.

'What happened between you and your husband?' I asked. 'He seems so nice.' Nelson. I'd met him at the New Year's Eve party but he left before midnight. They seemed to be on good terms. 'Why did you split up?'

Becky shrugged. 'We decided we should live apart when Jordan was fifteen. Nelson was working long hours in London and his dentist business was really taking off. It was all just too much stress.'

'But he seems to get on so well with you and the boys.'

'Oh, yes, he loves us all, but we just grew apart, I guess. We get on much better now we're not living together.'

I cock my head to one side, encouraging her to say more.

'You can imagine, with the three boys and him in the house – well, I guess there was too much testosterone. He couldn't stand all the arguments. It's constant with teenagers. Either sulks or backchat. The terrible twos and the teens are such hard work – you need to be a therapist, prison warder and Zen master rolled into one.' She flung her head back against the cushions and stretched. 'You did the right thing not having kids.'

People shouldn't assume.

I placed one of the cushions on my lap – purple and green, one of the ones she'd covered herself. She really was a master of all trades; she'd done a good job. 'I did have a child.' My voice was quieter than normal.

Next to me, Becky sat up straight, staring at me. 'What? What happened?'

'Thirty years ago. I had a daughter . . . Her name was Samantha . . . But . . . I called her Sunny because she was always smiling.' I'd not planned this and, not having steeled myself, it felt as raw as ever.

'Oh, Jan.' She looked aghast, one hand to her chest, her lips parted in an O of shock. 'I've put my foot in it again. I am so sorry. I didn't know.'

'It's okay. How could you know? I don't usually tell people.' I fiddled with the pink tassel she'd sewn to the braid, her stitches small and neat. 'It was a long while ago.'

'Oh gosh. What happened to her?'

'It's a long story. Some other time.' I was suddenly very tired. 'I had to give her up for adoption when she was young. I believe she's in Australia.'

'Can you track her down, through the adoption agency?'

'I've tried, but unless she wants to find me there's nothing more I can do.'

'That must be heart-breaking – not knowing where she is or if she's okay.'

'It is hard.' My voice was flat. I was running on my reserve tank. 'But I choose to imagine her happy, enjoying life. She may even have a child of her own now. A little redhead, carrying on the line.'

'You are so brave. Here's me always wittering on about my problems and you never mention your own worries.'

'That's what friends are for. To listen, to be there.'

She shuffled closer and leant her head against my shoulder. 'Jan, you're an angel. A perfect bloody angel.'

'I think it's the Virgo in me!' I said to the top of her blonde head.

Chapter 28

I'd told Becky a family member was looking for a place to rent for a few weeks and asked her how best to find somewhere. Apparently it was too short a period to get a proper rental and she was surprised I'd not heard of the organisations that let out rooms, or whole houses, for people while they went on holiday. It seemed a very trusting arrangement to me and I wondered about the insurance.

I guessed Ned would want something at the budget end to save on cash and there wasn't a lot of choice of properties in the area between here and the pub. But even so, I'd not expected that the places I'd chosen for him to view would turn out to be such disasters. The first place I took him to see was a sizeable flat, but it smelt of dogs with an undercurrent of something even nastier, probably coming from the stained hall carpet. Another, badged as a studio flat, was actually an en-suite room in a shared house, the communal kitchen boasting a fridge covered with passive–aggressive labels like a student hall of residence – 'Stop knocking on my door to ask about butter – buy your own'; 'Please respect my vegan shelf' – all pinned up with jolly fridge magnets.

The third house looked more promising, a tree-lined road with a neat front garden. But the scourge of Residents Only Parking meant that, by the time I'd found somewhere to park and we'd hiked the half mile back, we were marginally late. The owner of the place had left an envelope taped to the front door. The note inside was written in tiny but precise block capitals: 'SINCE YOU WERE NOT ON TIME, I HAVE HAD TO LEAVE FOR MY CLARINET LESSON. PLEASE COME BACK IN 90 MINUTES.'

'It's just how I imagine Hannibal Lecter would write,' Ned said.

'Did he play clarinet too?' I joked.

'Hmm, not in the film, but you never know. He got up to some odd things in his private life.'

'Narrow escape!'

I think we were both relieved to return to the car and be on our way.

Back at my house I invited him in for a coffee before I ran him back to the pub. He checked his watch.

'Another time maybe? There's a match on this afternoon. I'll get a cab back and get out of your hair.'

I was enjoying his company. 'You can watch it here if you like.'

He wasn't one to argue, anything for an easy life. He settled himself in the lounge and I made our drinks to a background of pre-match interviews.

While watching the game, he gave a running commentary, wincing at certain saves, cheering others.

But, even if I'd been interested in football, I couldn't have concentrated on the match. It was as much as I could do not to watch him, unable to control the surge of warmth and affection I felt sitting there, the two of us together in my lounge.

'Ned, you don't have to rent a place. You could move in here.' The words were out of my mouth before I'd consciously formed the thought. 'There's enough room. Why don't you stay here for the next month or so, until you go home? That is, if you want to, of course.' I started burbling, 'I mean, you might not want to. You might want your privacy and—'

'I hope you don't think I've been hinting?' he interrupted me.

'No, not at all. It just struck me as a good idea. Save you a few pounds.'

'Are you sure? Wouldn't I be in the way?' he asked, a trace of a frown on his brow. 'The bloke who owns this place wouldn't mind?'

'It's a big house and it would only be for a few weeks. Seriously, it would be a pleasure.'

'Well, thanks, Sonya. If that's okay with you, it'd be great. One less thing to worry about. We ought to celebrate with a bevvy!'

He stood and, as he bent towards me, steadying himself on the arm of the sofa, it seemed he might be about to kiss me. Such a mix of emotion swept through me in that moment – joy, panic, desire, the fulfilment of so many dreams – but the overriding thought was a hope that there was no onion in the omelette I'd had for lunch. But as I geared myself up like a woman in a movie, he leaned across me to retrieve the remote that had disappeared down the side of the cushion.

'Don't suppose you've got any cans in?' he asked, straightening up. He fiddled with the buttons, adjusting the screen brightness. 'I would've bought us some if I'd known.'

'I could pop to the village shop.' I regretted it as soon as I'd spoken. What possible reason could I have to be buying beers in the middle of the afternoon? And that thought led to a whole other train of worries – what was my story for having him here in the house over the next few weeks? How could I keep him hidden from Becky?

Oblivious to my mental dilemmas, Ned's eyes were locked on the TV again. He grimaced at a bad pass. 'You gave that away! Get it up front!'

While my spontaneous offer for Ned to move in with me came from a good place, it had been reckless. Up to that point, I'd done well keeping my secret life separate – my little family with Ned and Dmytro, and our memories of Sunny, was something I cherished. It belonged to me and I didn't want anyone else getting involved and ruining things.

After the match, I dropped Ned back at the pub, using the drive back to contemplate my cover stories. I'd need at least two versions – one for Becky, to keep her at bay until Ned moved out; and one for Mother, in case anyone in the village reported back.

For Becky, maybe Ned could be a remote cousin, a cousin recovering from serious mental health issues, staying with me for peace and quiet, recuperating after leaving hospital. Ah yes! That would work. It was *him* I'd been trying to find a flat for . . . but when I took him to see them, he realised he wasn't ready to be on his own yet. That's it! He needed my support. He couldn't face seeing anyone but me, couldn't be disturbed. Becky and I could still see each other, but it would be best that she didn't come round to the house for a while.

My story for Mother . . . Hopefully I wouldn't need it, but Ned could be a friend of a friend staying for a few weeks. When he needed a room, I'd had no choice but to volunteer to have him stay at The Old Vicarage – everyone knew the place was half empty.

But why did he need somewhere to live? And who had asked me? With my imagination, I was sure I could work up those details before our next Sunday call.

And Ned himself. I could tell him I didn't want the (imaginary) house owner to know I had someone staying. Suggest that he doesn't wander around the village too much as word would soon spread. I could tell him I didn't want to encourage gossip, me being a single woman.

Happy with my stories, I started work on sorting out the house, ready for my new guest. The first thing was to remove anything that might cause questions to be asked. While my office was upstairs and Ned's room would be on the ground floor, he may have cause to come up. Removing my timeline of Sunny's movements from my study walls, it struck me: I'd been so immersed in my search for *her* lately that I'd abandoned my weekly online trawl to find any news of Sam! A good sign that I was moving on. I stashed the papers in a box file for easy reference, before locking them safely away in my desk.

Next came the fun part, setting up a room for Ned. I unlocked one of the unused rooms downstairs, and gave it an airing. Belting out show songs, I immersed myself in creating a cosy space for him. I made up the sofa bed with my favourite duvet cover – the one with the orange and red squares, fresh from the wash and still smelling of the branded fabric conditioner I'd splashed out on. After arranging a side table and lamp, I checked they were within easy reach by reclining against the piled cushions and pillows, which I then had to plump up again. As a final thought, I brought down a picture of Sunny from my room upstairs.

Helping Ned move out of the pub, I got my first view of where he'd been living. I'd imagined something grand after JayCee referred to sharing 'the apartment' with Sunny, but this was basic by anyone's standards. She must've been referring to somewhere else.

'Are they charging you for this?' I asked. A single bed was pushed against the wall to make more floor space, but aside from a pub chair, a dark wood wardrobe and a sink, that was it. 'Where's the bathroom?'

He gestured down the corridor. 'That a way. Shared with the chef.'

As we wrestled his rucksack and suitcase down the lethally steep staircase, I was convinced this couldn't be the apartment that JayCee had referred to.

Back at my house, I showed Ned his room and was suddenly embarrassed, conscious of where he'd been living for the last few months. Had I made too much effort?

'Is it okay?'

'Okay? It's great. Better than most hotels I've stayed in.' He bounced on the bed and took in the room; his gaze resting on the water jug, next to the novelty plastic nose designed to hold his glasses (half price in the sales), and the stack of carefully selected novels on the bedside table; my precious copy of *I Want* on the top. 'You've thought of everything. I bet there's even a Gideon Bible!'

'Sorry, force of habit,' I said. 'My father pretty much lived in one room so he needed everything to hand. I looked after him for years until he died.'

He looked up at me, frowning. 'You never mentioned that before.'

I shrugged. I'd been careful not to volunteer personal information, but this titbit wouldn't hurt. 'It wasn't relevant.'

'All we do is talk about Sunny. There's a lot we don't know about each other,' he said.

★

Once he'd gone to his room later that evening, I embarked on some further property research – if Sunny and JayCee hadn't lived at the pub together, where had they lived?

Trawling through Sunny's photos again, I studied the backgrounds, trying to identify locations. Most were clearly taken in or around the Pheasant. But there was one selfie of Sunny and JayCee where I could just make out part of a sign behind them, their heads blocking out the middle of the building name: Fair ------ ents. Both girls had broad grins, Sunny doing a thumbs-up and Jaycee making a heart symbol with her hands.

I tried various combinations – Fairways Apartments, Fairlane, Fairplain – finally hitting the jackpot with Fairfields Apartments. The place looked pretty grand and the apartments themselves were priced way out of the league of a couple of barmaids.

So how had they financed it? And why had they had to move out and Sunny end up living in the squalid environment of the room above the pub?

Chapter 29

The next day, I popped out to get some extras in case Ned fancied eggs rather than cereal for breakfast. When I got back from the shops, he was talking to someone on his phone, pacing around in the hallway, trying to get the best signal. I started to unpack the bags in the kitchen to give him his privacy, but I could still catch the matey rhythm, suggesting he was speaking to a male friend. It's funny the tone men take when they get together – all back-slapping bonhomie and banter. I used to hear Dad do it when he bumped into a neighbour: 'You see the score?'; 'Don't start. Your lot can't even see the goal'; 'You just wait – we'll show you on Saturday.' A bonding ritual based on sport or politics or health or holidays, depending on age and class.

Ned walked into the room as he was finishing the call, 'Yeah. Thursday. That's great, mate.'

Not wanting to appear interfering, I refrained from asking any questions and busied myself with decanting the Hobnobs into the biscuit barrel. Ned reached across me to grab one and I had to restrain myself from tapping him on the back of the hand as Mother would have done. Instead I passed him a plate to ensure he didn't drop crumbs on my clean floor.

'Dmytro,' he said, through a mouthful of cookie.

Keeping my tone light, I said, 'Oh, what did he want?'

'We've arranged to go for that drink we planned at Christmas.'

My ready-made smile hid my momentary panic. I hadn't anticipated the two of them getting together without me. What if they started comparing notes and worked something out? 'That will be nice for him. I think he's quite lonely.'

'I thought I'd take him to Sunny's pub. Introduce him to a few people. He says she never took him there.'

I had no discreet way of finding out whether it was Dmytro who'd initiated this get-together or Ned. Either way, it wasn't good news, the two of them getting together without me. *And* visiting the Pheasant.

On Thursday the doorbell rang while I was upstairs. By the time I joined the two of them, Ned was bemoaning the skills of some player in the football game he'd watched the other day and a match he'd missed.

'The wi-fi's so bad here, Sonya can't get catch-up on her TV and don't get me started on the phone signal. I have to make calls hanging out the window!'

'That's easy to fix,' Dmytro said. 'Sonya, where is the router?'

'Upstairs, in my office. But you're just on your way out. You can always look at it another day.' But Dmytro was already on his feet. He liked to be useful.

224

'If I take a quick look, I can check what the problem is. It might be easy to fix or I can get you the parts.' He cracked his knuckles, a habit I abhorred. 'Then the problem is fixed and Ned is happy, then you are happy.'

Why did he say that? Was he implying something?

I reluctantly led the way upstairs. Although I was fairly confident there was nothing incriminating lying around to be seen, this was unexpected and I'd not had time for a once-over.

Dmytro squeezed himself behind the desk and examined the router, mumbling to himself under his breath, 'Has this house ever been rewired?' He sneezed a couple of times as he untangled cables that were out of reach of my vacuum. 'You have too many extension leads plugged into each other. It's dangerous. It could start a fire.'

I vowed to pull the desk out and give it all a good clean at the weekend. I like things spic and span. He brushed himself down as he stood up.

'The router looks fine. You need . . .' He mimed plugging something into a socket. 'I don't know what it's called but I can get it for you. It will give you a signal in all of your rooms.'

Even as I thanked him, I was worrying that there might be software to install and he may need access to my laptop. But as I wrestled with that idea, his eyes flicked to something on my desk. A copy of the local paper, news of villages in the surrounding five miles. It was folded open at an article on page 7, part of a regular series on local retailers and trades people, trying to boost traffic in the high street shop. That particular week it had featured the confectioner's shop where Becky had ordered her New Year's canapés, the place where Alice worked. The heading read *Truly Scrumptious*. Beneath it, there was a photo of the staff, the owner and Alice holding a towering iced cake creation between them, which couldn't have been easy for them to balance. I'd circled the image of Alice; her chin raised, head tipped to one side, she looked so much like a smaller, younger version of Sunny.

Dmytro picked it up and studied it, looking from Alice to the Photoshopped composite of Sunny and me on the shelf above, his eyes dancing between the three of us.

Eventually Dmytro asked, 'Who is this girl?'

There was an unnatural pause, as if it was a secret and I was recalling the cover story and didn't know how to answer. My mouth went dry and my top lip felt damp with sweat.

'A relative . . . Alice . . . my niece.'

He placed the newspaper back on my desk, before turning to me with an expression I couldn't fathom. His eyes met mine and I felt exposed as he held my gaze for a beat too long.

I glanced at my watch to break his stare. 'We should get back to Ned. He'll be wondering where we are.'

Dmytro nodded, unsmiling. Following him back downstairs, it was clear I couldn't let the two of them go out for the evening without me.

I made a show of taking my mobile from my cardigan pocket. 'Excuse me. I just need to check this message.' I pressed a few buttons and pretended to read a WhatsApp. 'Oh! Becky's cancelled on me . . . I was looking forward to a night out.'

Ned took the hint. 'Why don't you join us? Can't leave you at home like Cinderella.'

I fashioned a surprised look, ignoring the waves of disgruntlement flooding from Dmytro. 'Oh, thanks. That would be great!' I fumbled in my bag producing my car keys. 'To show my gratitude for an evening out with my two favourite men, why don't me and Ned follow you in my car, so you don't have to run Ned back later, Dmytro?'

In the pub we found a quiet corner and Ned shuffled along the bench seat to make space for me, not noticing the cool atmosphere from Dmytro.

'I'll get a round in. What'll it be? G&T and a beer?' Ned asked.

'Just a lemonade for me, please.' I needed to keep my wits about me tonight.

Once Ned had left for the bar, I turned my charm on Dmytro. 'It's a nice place, isn't it?'

He lent forward, staring at me. 'Why did you want to come here with us tonight?'

I kept the smile on my face. 'Like I said, I was going to see my friend Becky, but she let me down.'

'Becky,' he repeated as if he had echolalia. His lack of intonation, accompanied by the merest twitch of his eyebrow, flagged an element of disbelief.

I felt the need to expand on the story. 'She's having trouble with her son. He is a difficult young man, a teenager.'

He looked me up and down, taking in my outfit, the shoes. 'Where were you planning to go with "*Becky*"?'

'We were going for dinner, near where she lives. They have a band and dancing.'

'Where does she live? Did you go there with Sunny too?' Was I mistaken or was there sarcasm in his tone?

I was about to provide more information on my fabricated night out to waylay his questions about the location of Becky's home, when I was saved by Ned's return.

'A perk of knowing all the staff – speedy service! A lemonade as requested. And a pint for my mate.' Having set down the drinks, he bobbed down next to me then handed me my scarf. 'Here. This was on the floor behind you.'

It must've fallen off when I removed my coat. 'Thanks. I wouldn't want to lose that.' Still ill at ease, I started burbling. 'Sunny chose it for me because of the colour. I bought her a mohair jumper this same shade of orange. It went so well with her hair.'

'I never saw this jumper,' Dmytro said.

Ned frowned. 'Mohair? Not with her allergies. It's like the animal fur – makes her itch.'

I didn't dare catch Dmytro's eye. 'Oh my god, of course. That explains why I never saw her wearing it. Bless her. She never said.'

'That's out of character. She must've been on her best behaviour with you!' He took a sip of his beer then

228

turned to Dmytro. 'That reminds me. I don't think I ever properly thanked you for giving Sonya the rucksack to give to me. I know there wasn't anything valuable but it meant a lot, having her things back like that.'

'She probably left a trail of her stuff everywhere she stayed,' I said, before Dmytro could speak. 'You know what she was like.'

'I'm surprised she didn't ask to move in with you, Sonya, while she got herself sorted?'

'I was away in September. My first proper break in years,' I stopped myself from adding more unrequested details about my fictional holiday, although just in case my whereabouts ever came up, I had a detailed story of a trip to Cornwall, planned and paid for before I met Sunny. 'I suppose she could've stayed at my place while I was away but Sunny was no cat-sitter with her allergies!'

Ned swirled his beer around the glass thoughtfully. 'I've often wondered what happened to her mobile. Not that she used it to actually speak to anyone . . .' He lapsed into an anecdote about the scarcity of her electronic communication. 'I guess she probably lost it for the hundredth time.' He swallowed down the last of his beer. 'Another?' he asked.

'I'll go,' said Dmytro rising to his feet. 'Beer. Lemonade.'

We both watched him push his way through towards the bar.

'I was telling Dmytro about the inquest,' Ned said.

'Oh?' I stopped fiddling with my scarf and gave him my full attention. Maybe that was what had caused

Dmytro's foul mood. It was a huge worry that I kept batting away.

'He didn't know anything about it. I had to explain what it was for. Do you think he'd like to go along to the coroner's court with me?'

'I doubt it. I—' Shouting came from somewhere behind me and Ned stood up to see. Before I had time to register what was going on, he had pushed his way through the drinkers towards the bar. In seconds, he was back with Dmytro, who was white with rage.

'Dmytro, are you okay? What happened?' I said, scanning his face for clues.

He shook his head, his mouth a tight line, unwilling to talk.

'A bit of a ruckus. I'm taking him outside. I think it's best if we leave,' Ned said. 'I'll get him in his car.'

Over Ned's shoulder I could see Rob, the juvenile manager, in animated conversation with John, the married man that Sunny had been seeing. John was fiercely gesticulating, Rob placating. Rob led him off to the far side of the bar, signalling to one of the staff to bring two drinks.

'Can you wait a moment in the car?' I said to Ned, handing him my keys. 'I just need to visit the ladies.'

JayCee was sweeping up a broken wine glass that had been knocked over in the fracas. 'Sweetheart,' I said, 'what happened?'

'It all just kicked off.' She pointed to the mess on the floor as evidence. 'That guy who was with you. He heard me use John's name and then he just lost it.'

'Tell me exactly what happened.'

'Your guy asked John if he knew Sunny. And John just laughed and said "Doesn't every bloke here?" That was when he tried to hit John, but Rob stepped in and stopped it, else there would have been a fight.' JayCee looked around to check if anyone could overhear us, then whispered, 'Tell him he doesn't want to mess with John. I don't think he's right in the head.'

I didn't care to clarify whether her last comment referred to John or Dmytro, but both fitted the bill.

'It was just a bit of a kerfuffle,' I said to Ned back at home. 'I think it was the other chap spoiling for a fight. Probably showing off in front of his girlfriend. Her drink got knocked over and it just escalated.'

'They need to play more sport – get all that aggression out of their systems.'

'I'll give Dmytro a call and check he's okay.'

'He's a good lad but a bit hot-headed,' Ned said, picking up the sports pages as I left the room.

Out of earshot of Ned, I passed on JayCee's warning to Dmytro, but he was full of righteous anger, defending Sunny's honour and his own macho pride. He had it in for John and it was clear no amount of reasoning on my part would dissuade him. I decided it would be best to leave him be for a day or two and let him calm down. It gave him something else to brew on. The way he'd interrogated me earlier in the evening convinced me that he was harbouring suspicions about me.

On the pretext of clearing up, I stayed up after Ned had gone to bed, but really I wanted to examine the composite photo of me and Sunny on the shelf in my office. I was sure Dmytro had noticed something was wrong with it. Searching for signs, no matter how small, I eventually found it: her bracelet. She always wore it on her left wrist. In the photo it was on her right, a giveaway that I'd flipped the image when I'd Photoshopped me, Sunny and the house together. My photo-editing skills weren't brilliant either; I'd done it in a rush and, under close study, it was easy to see how the originals had been collaged into one. We looked unnatural, posed, and now I could see the shadows were odd.

What could be my excuse for creating an image like this? Surely when we found each other after so long we would have taken lots of photos of us together. Where were they? Why would I have gone to such lengths to create one?

What explanation could I give Dmytro?

I gazed at Sunny's face – help me here, sweetheart, help me think.

I thought back to our first meeting. I could see it in my mind's eye. Being part of the selfie generation, she'd snapped us both all the time – me laughing, telling her I'd not brushed my hair, not done my make-up, Sunny pulling me close, 'Smile, Mum!' click, click, click. Our heads together, hair entangled, broad smiles, giddy with our happiness at finding each other. But all the photos she took were on her phone. It was only after her accident I realised I didn't have any copies myself. None of us together. Distraught, I resorted to Photoshop . . .

But then the next question arose: who was this niece, Alice, when I didn't have any siblings? A family resemblance between her and Sunny was, of course, entirely feasible, but why had I never commented how much they looked alike?

And then there was the whole issue of Dmytro's fight with John! I kicked myself for not looking into him before. A quick search threw up John's Wiki page. I skim-read the information: full name, date of birth (old enough to be Sunny's father), early life, career, discography, personal life. He'd joined the band in his teens when he was already engaged to his childhood sweetheart LeeAnn. There was a link to her page, where I learned of her charitable work raising funds for a women's refuge, her trustee role for another charity helping teenagers leaving care. An admirable woman, it seemed.

Nothing there of help. What was that fight in the pub really about?

Chapter 30

After a sleepless night worrying about Dmytro's suspicions, I knew I had to see him on his own to straighten things out. I couldn't risk Ned deciding to tag along on my visit to Dmytro, so I told him I'd received an email asking me to go to see a client – a last-minute project – my (imaginary) property photographer job again.

'Hopefully I won't be too long. I need to snap some photos for the websites. They want to post it as soon as I've done the text.' I was all of a tizzy; my keys were not in their proper place on the hook. 'I don't normally work for this agency but their usual guy let them down.' I tried to stop myself burbling on; providing too much information was a sure sign of a liar.

'Do you think I could use your laptop while you're out? I want to google a few things and do some work on my business website.'

I hadn't planned for that but couldn't think of a reason why not. Was there anything that could incriminate me on the laptop?

'Of course. I'll fetch it for you before I go out.'

My screensaver was a photo of Sunny and Dmytro, no problem with that – it was one Dmytro had given me.

I'd taken the precaution of encrypting all my electronic files on Sunny and any personal files, giving them unappealing names like *Tax Return 2015–16* and *Household Bills*. I'd cleared my search history before Ned moved in, so it seemed quite safe to lend him the laptop while I was out.

On my way back downstairs with it under my arm, I remembered that my password was Janice1968. Too late to change it.

'I'll log you in,' I said, turning the keyboard away from him. 'There. You're good to go.' I picked up my handbag. The car keys were underneath. 'I'll be off now. I'll be as quick as I can.'

'Aren't you forgetting something?' Ned said.

I held my breath, teeth clenched. In my anxious state, what had I forgotten to say or do?

'How you going to take professional photos without your camera?'

Camera.

'Oh yes.' I held my palm to my forehead, shaking my head theatrically. 'Duh! It's upstairs. I got everything ready then left it all on the desk. I'll just nip up and get it and I'll see you later.'

Upstairs I grabbed the empty holdall, wallet file and blank note pad I'd assembled as my 'kit', cursing myself for not thinking this through properly. Of all the props for this pretence, how did I remember the tape measure but overlook the need for a camera?

When I stuck my head through the lounge door to say a final goodbye, Ned was intent on something on the computer.

'You keep your laptop as tidy as you keep your house,' he said, pointing to the neat row of file and application icons.

'Cleanliness is next to godliness, my Gran used to say,' I joked. I waved the camera and holdall as evidence of my project. 'I'll be a few hours, I expect. Be good!'

'I'll do my best.'

When I arrived at Dmytro's he was wearing a track in the threadbare carpet with his pacing. I'd never seen him so angry.

'You know this man John?' he asked, his words staccato, accusing. He was unable to keep still, which was quite intimidating in his small bedsit.

'No, I've never spoken to him. But I know who he is.' There was no point denying it.

'Who is he? How did Sunny know him?'

'She met him in the pub when she was working there.'

'What did Sunny tell you about him?' he demanded.

'Nothing much. I think he offered to help her with her music. He works in the music business.'

'She thought he would get her on TV?'

'Yes, he was famous once. He used to be in a band.' John's rock group was one of those that sounded like Status Quo. No subtlety, just repetitive lyrics over thudding rhythms. Comparing the old video recordings to how he looked now, he'd not aged well.

'I think she hoped he'd get her a recording deal,' I continued. 'You know she wanted to enter a competition, *Britain's Got Talent*.'

236

He slumped into the battered old sofa, staring at his feet, his breathing ragged, his balled fist grinding into the palm of his left hand. Maybe I should have been scared of Dmytro, he was in such a temper, but I trusted him. He knew I thought of him as a son; he would never hurt me. I waited to see what would happen next.

'He is responsible.'

'Responsible for what?'

'He caused the accident.'

'How? Was he there?' I sat forward on my seat. Could John have been there on the bridge with her after all?

'He went to meet her at the station. She was going to London with *him*.'

'How do you know this?'

'I saw him. After I left her at the station, I had to go back – she left her charger in the car. She wasn't there. But he was!'

'Did you see them together?'

'No. But why else would he be there? It's a bit of a coincidence!'

If this was true, it shone a new light on events.

'He is a bad man. I didn't know his name or how to find him. I went to the bridge every day in case he came to say goodbye to Sunny.'

'He paid his respects at the funeral.'

'He was at the funeral?' Dmytro's face reddened. 'He was with her family?'

'No, no. He was there with his wife and people from the bar.'

'With his wife?'

'Yes, LeeAnn. He didn't meet Ned or the family. Ned was too upset to talk to people.'

He looked up at me sideways, through his dark fringe. 'Of course. Ned was upset.' There was a tone of something in his voice – sarcasm? World-weariness?

He was silent for a long time, eyes fixed on the floor. Suddenly he stood and turned away from me. 'You must go now. I want to be on my own.'

I was shaken when I left. Dmytro's fury, his claims that Sunny was with John on her birthday, that John was to blame for her death. While John seemed an arrogant has-been with no redeeming qualities, I felt that Dmytro had it wrong in blaming him. Apart from anything else, John didn't strike me as the type to loiter around on bridges over dual carriageways, even if it was to meet Sunny.

And what did he mean when he said 'of course, Ned was upset' in that tone? It sounded like there was more left unsaid.

In the car, I checked my mobile and found a missed call from Ned. 'Hey, Sonya,' the message said. 'I accidentally logged myself out on the laptop! Are you okay to let me have your password so I can get back in? Cheers.'

Not having come up with a reason for my Janice1968 password, I decided to use the 'no phone signal' excuse for not calling back. I still needed to see Becky and take some photos of her house and garden that I could pass off as the property I'd claimed I had to visit.

I parked near Becky's and was reaching for my handbag in the footwell when I heard a vehicle pull up alongside mine. Expecting someone asking for directions or ready to challenge me for rights over the parking space, I set a helpful expression on my face and pressed the button to lower my window. But suddenly the engine revved and the car sped off.

Blue. It was a mid-blue BMW. Repeating the registration like a mantra in order to remember it, I'd just found a chocolate wrapper to scribble it on, when Becky flung open the front door shouting, 'Sonya! I've not seen you for aaaages.' And the number was forgotten. It seemed a strange incident but I set it to one side to ponder later.

It had been less than two weeks since I'd seen Becky but, with Ned having moved in, I'd not been able to phone her as often as usual. She led the way into the kitchen, flicked the button on the kettle, chatting non-stop. It was nice that she'd missed me.

'Sorry I've not been in touch,' I said. 'I've been working a lot lately, a new project. And my relative has moved in. I'd forgotten how demanding it can be to look after someone else.'

'I guessed as much. How's he doing?'

'It's step by step. Taking it slowly at the moment.'

She nodded sympathetically. 'And you've got work to worry about too? What's the project? Not another ninety-year-old's birthday surprise?'

The project . . . 'Tracking down the genealogy of an adoptee's birth family,' I said. It was the first thing that came to mind.

'Oh, interesting. Is it giving you any ideas that might help you with your search for Samantha?' She'd gone to the fridge to get the milk, held up an empty plastic carton. 'Sorry. Andre's polished off the milk again! Let's go to the café near the hardware shop – they do great doughnuts.'

Pleading deadlines, I managed to keep the visit to the café as short as possible. While it was great to see her, I had a lot on my mind after meeting with Dmytro. As soon as we'd finished the last mouthful, I opened my wallet to get my credit card.

'My treat,' I said, 'since I've not seen you for ages.'

Becky reached across and spun my wallet round to face her. 'What a lovely smile!'

She was talking about the small photo of Sunny, tucked in front of my bus pass. 'Is she family?'

'No, my goddaughter. She lives in Australia now so I don't get to see her.' Too late I remembered that's where I'd claimed my adopted daughter lived.

Becky seemed not to remember. 'That's the godsend of Skype. It might be the other side of the world, but it's only a call away. And it's free, not like the old days.'

My head in a spin, I scurried to the counter to pay. Entering my PIN on the cashcard device, I heard my mobile ring – behind me on our table where I'd left it in my hurry to avoid any further inquisition. I spun round in time to see Becky pick it up.

'Jan's phone!' she said brightly. My heart was pounding as I rushed back – it was the ringtone I'd set for Ned.

'Hallo . . .? Hi . . .? Anyone there?' She shrugged and passed me the phone.

'Hallo?' I pressed the red icon to end the call and carried on talking as if there was someone there. 'Oh yes, thanks for calling . . . Yes, I left you a message earlier—'

Becky gestured towards the hardware shop opposite – the special offer on mixed bedding plants had caught her eye. I nodded my understanding as she mouthed *'See you over the road.'*

Once she was safely out of earshot, I sent a 'bad signal' text to Ned, promising to ring him later.

I joined Becky as she was paying for her seed packets. Feeling the need for a cover story, Ned became an electrician phoning me to arrange a date to inspect the house.

'My Tyrone did an apprenticeship,' Becky said. 'He knows loads of people in the trade. I could get him to pop over and take a look if you like.'

Oh, good grief.

'Let me see how it goes with this chap first and I'll get back to you. He was recommended by a neighbour so I'm more or less committed.'

When we arrived back at her place, she insisted I take half the seed packets: 'Gardening will help you relax. You look really tense; your shoulders are up round your ears.'

'I'd prefer a massage,' I said, trying to draw my shoulders down and back.

'Now that's a skill I look for in a man. When you find a good masseur, give me his number!' she joked, slamming the car door with more force than you'd expect from a small woman.

My cheery wave as I drove off sapped the small amount of emotional energy I had left.

Passing the end of the high street on my way home, I strained for a glimpse of Alice in the confectioner's shop. But there was no sign of her. It was late afternoon and I imagined her at home playing with the baby; then, later, reading her favourite story from a battered picture book. Such a lovely time in a child's life. So sad that I'd had to miss all that.

In the end, the whole saga had taken me the best part of the day. It was getting dark when I rang Ned from the next town.

'Did you get my text earlier? Sorry, the signal's been terrible. I'm by the takeaways. Do you fancy curry, Chinese or pizza?'

Ned was in a grumpy mood by the time I got back. 'I was logged out for most of the day. Didn't get much done. If you could jot down the password, I could just log in when you're not using it.'

I was in no mood for this and fended off his questions about my password with prawn crackers, but after we'd finished our Cantonese Feast for Two, Ned was back on theme. 'So, is your laptop free again tomorrow?'

'No, sorry. I've got to write a load of copy for the estate agent.'

In my office later I checked the day's search history. Among other less worrying things, Ned had looked up DNA sites and searched LinkedIn for Sonya Wicks.

Chapter 31

A few days later, the call from Dmytro was unexpected. He wanted to see me; it was urgent, he said.

I was shocked by the sight of him. His forehead was cut, his eye swollen almost shut and he nursed his arm carefully as he moved. There was blood on his sweatshirt and a strong smell of sweat and fear filled the room.

'What on earth happened? Are you okay?' I asked. The wound looked more than superficial. I reached my hand out to part his fringe to examine it and he jerked away from me. 'Have you seen a doctor?'

'I went to see John's wife.'

'Oh, Dmytro, why?' I sat down.

'I wanted to find out what she knew, about her husband and Sunny.'

Knowing that John was a regular at the Pheasant and Grape, Dmytro had set out on his mission. Several nights he'd driven to the pub car park, sat hunched in his car, watching and waiting as he made his plan. Finally he'd tailed John home, parking a few houses up to observe their routines, waiting to see the times John went out and his wife, LeeAnn, was at home.

That afternoon he'd taken his opportunity – after John left with his golf bag, Dmytro had rung the doorbell.

Apparently, as soon as LeeAnn saw him, she'd tried to slam the door, but he pushed his weight against it. 'I told her I only wanted to ask her some questions, but she started screaming and shouting.'

Before he could get her to calm down, John's car had pulled onto the driveway; he could only have gone a few miles and must have realised he'd forgotten something.

'What happened when John came back?'

It seemed that LeeAnn started hammering on the BMW bonnet, yelling at John.

'Was she angry with him?' I asked.

'More upset, I think. She was crying a lot and kept shouting. Something like, "It's all your fault! Everything is your fault!"'

When John leapt out of the car to stop LeeAnn damaging his paintwork, Dmytro seized the opportunity to make a break for it. He ran to his own car, but the wreck of a vehicle wouldn't start. Meanwhile, seeing his quarry trying to escape, John took a golf club from his boot and proceeded to smash the windows of Dmytro's old Ford to get at Dmytro in the driver's seat.

It would've been far worse had LeeAnn not joined in the brawl, launching her own attack on John, thumping him on the back and screaming her lungs out, according to Dmytro: 'You are to blame. For all of it! It's your fucking fault!'

'I left the car where it was and ran,' Dmytro said. 'He chased me for a while, but he's an old man. Not very fast. I hid behind some garages. He was shouting, "Don't you dare come near me or my family! I know people. I'll fucking find you. I'll kill you."'

'What happened then?'

'I waited until I heard him leave, then I ran back here. It took me two hours.' He shrugged as if this event was nothing, but his anxiety was evident in the grey pallor of his face, his body tight as if still ready for battle.

This was so far removed from my experience of life, I didn't know what to say. In my world, people didn't get into fights in the street; a tut of annoyance might escalate to cursing if someone barged into a queue in front of you, but people didn't openly threaten each other.

'Do you think he means it? Do you think he'll come after you?'

'He is a bad man,' Dmytro said.

Seeing him like this, so vulnerable and wounded, my heart broke. 'What are you going to do? Is there anything I can do to help?' I wondered if I could intervene on his behalf, try to make John see reason. Maybe John would listen to me, as Sunny's mother.

'Can I get you some painkillers? Something for your eye to bring the swelling down?'

Dmytro was staring at a spot on the carpet. He merely shook his head. 'I'm tired.'

The next morning I woke early, worrying about Dmytro and his fight with John. I'd waited until half

246

past six so I wouldn't wake Ned and then gone down-stairs to make a cup of tea. I crept past his bedroom door, not wanting to wake him, but I was surprised to hear him say something and laugh. I wondered if he might be dreaming, but it sounded like one end of a conversation so I stepped nearer.

'Yes, I miss you too, hon. But things have changed. You know that.'

I cupped my ear to the closed door. At this hour he must be Skyping someone in Australia, probably assuming I was still asleep.

'Soon, yes. I'd hoped to see Matt while I'm here but he's not in a good place right now, so I'll be heading back ASAP.'

'What's wrong with him?' A woman's voice.

'Family trouble, he didn't say more. Maybe some-thing to do with his wife? I told him about Sunny's mum being on the scene and he went off on one. Jeez, is that boy sceptical! He wanted to know what proof I've got that she's who she says she is. He thinks she's a gold digger.'

'What do you think?'

'There's something I can't make out. She seems really good-hearted and kind but . . . I dunno. I guess Matt has a point. It doesn't seem to add up, her just appearing like that. She says Sunny was looking for her but, to be honest, it sounds like it was the other way round. Like she was looking for Sunny. Anyway, I'll be back before you know it.'

'Good, cos I'm lonely here.'

'Yeah, but we need to be cautious. Not too public.'

'I'm getting jealous . . .'

'Oh, yeah. And why's that?'

'Well, you're living with another woman!'

'If you'd met Sonya, you wouldn't be jealous. Trust me.'

'What's she like? From all you've said about her, she sounds like a bit of a nutter.'

My pulse was racing.

He snorted a laugh. 'She's pretty obsessive. A bit crazy maybe, but not the whole nine yards.'

'Don't worry, you'll be home with us soon. Me and Taz have really missed having you around.'

'Buy a sack of Bonza for him.'

'When's the flight?'

'Hopefully next week. I'll book it today.'

They started exchanging closing off comments and I was forced to abandon my eavesdropping and rush to the lounge. Fred was sleeping on my discarded *Family History* periodical. I snatched the magazine from under him and he bolted from the room. My footsteps might have been as quiet as I could make them, but I swear anyone could have heard the thudding of my heart. I was furious. Who was this woman? How dare he think he could make a fool of me after all I'd done for him? And how dare he just discard us like this, scampering back to Australia with not even a fare thee well?

When Ned surfaced from his room an hour later, I was in the kitchen, deliberately banging cupboard doors so he'd know I was there.

He came into the room and I kept my expression impassive. 'I'm making coffee. Do you want one?'

He fidgeted about behind me as I was pouring the water in the mugs. I'd used his favourite mug with the footballer on it, the one I'd bought him from the market.

'I had some news yesterday,' he said, 'about the inquest. They're postponing it.'

'Pressures on the court timetable,' they'd told him. There'd been a major fire in a warehouse a few weeks back, bodies found in the burnt-out shell of the building. I'd seen the articles in the press at the time, possible links to people smuggling and/or insurance fraud, depending on which paper you read. Poor Sunny, deemed less important and bumped down the queue.

'They can't give me a date. They'll let me know,' Ned said, 'but from what I've read it could be up to a year.'

'Oh, poor Sunny.' I wasn't going to help him out by directly asking about his plans; he needed to be man enough to tell me.

He was staring out the window, his back to me. Normally, at this time of the morning, he would have been at the kitchen table in his baggy old tracksuit, the papers open at the sport pages; his bare feet jigging, toes flexing as he read, unable to sit still for long. He was wearing the jeans I'd ironed and already had his trainers on, as if ready to go somewhere.

'It changes things. I need to get home, back to my business. There's no reason to stay now.'

'I suppose not,' I said, the calmness of my voice belying the fury in my heart. No reason to stay.

Abandoning me and Sunny and Dmytro just like that to go back to Australia and that woman, whoever she was. How dare he?

'I think I should get a ticket home for some time next week. Get out of your hair,' he said, addressing the window pane, unable to face me.

'Yes,' I said, bending to pick up Fred to give me a distraction, something to cuddle. There was no point in prolonging the agony.

'I'll sort out a ticket then.'

'Yes.' I had to leave the room before I said something cruel, or he said something kind. Fred must have sensed it, or else I clutched him too tightly, because he struggled in my arms, rejecting my need for him, just like Ned had. I opened the back door and dropped him outside without giving him breakfast, shutting it harder than necessary before he could edge back in.

I went up to my office and phoned Dmytro. At least he had never rejected my friendship and support.

'How are you today?'

'Okay. The car's not so good.' He had snuck back to John's early that morning in the hope of reclaiming his car. But all the windows were smashed and he decided to abandon it. On the driver's seat he'd found an envelope with his name on it.

'What did the note say?'

'Meet him at the pub this afternoon, or his wife will go to the police and say I threatened her. They have CCTV of me at the front door.'

'You can't go. He might beat you up again.'

'I have to. I need to find out what he wants. They must not go to police. It is dangerous for me. I will be sent home to Ukraine or put in prison.'

It was in neither of our interests for them to involve the police. I had to do something to sort this out, to help him. 'Let me go and meet him for you.' Ned might give up on his family responsibilities but I didn't.

Chapter 32

By two o'clock, Dmytro and I were sitting in my car in a far corner of the pub car park. While not wanting to be theatrical, I had reversed into the space ready to make a quick getaway if necessary. Dmytro had insisted on coming, but I made him promise to wait for me in the car while I went in to try to reason with John. He was agitated, his knee jittered up and down, reminding me of Ned's nervous energy, and I felt my blood boiling again at the thought of Ned's betrayal. I pushed it down; I had time to think about that later.

In one of the smaller rooms off the main bar, John sat on a bench in a posture of casual machismo that he couldn't quite carry off; his upper arms rested along the back of the seat, his legs spread wide, taking up maximum space. A Stetson, cigar and pair of chaps wouldn't have gone amiss. Despite the fact he looked like a comedy villain, my stomach was jumping; a lot was riding on this encounter. I drew myself up to my full height. I wanted to be assertive without being confrontational, conciliatory and understanding without being a pushover; a mother wanting what's best for her child.

'Hallo,' I said, holding out my hand. 'My name's Sonya.' Since he made no effort to shake hands, I sat down opposite him.

He snorted a laugh. 'The boy's as much of a coward as I took him for.' He stretched languorously and put his hands behind his head in that pose men adopt when they're being cocksure. 'And what are you – his landlady? Or has he fallen on hard times and you're his latest shag?'

I kept my voice even and deep. Shrill female voices lack both gravitas and dignity as many a female politician has learned. 'I'm Sunny's mother.'

'Yeah, right,' he said, his smirk making me switch from anxiety to crossness.

'I am her birth mother. Not that it's any concern of yours but she came from Australia to find me.' Wanting to assert my authority I added, 'She told me a lot about you.'

'If she came to find you, it would only have been for money. Family meant nothing to her. She hated you all.' He leaned towards me. 'How much did she want? Did she tell you all about her exciting musical career? How she needed cash for the photo shoot?'

'Don't speak ill of my daughter.' He had touched a nerve and a degree of shrillness had crept in despite my best efforts. How dare he talk of Sunny this way?

'She hated her dad for what he'd done and felt you were beneath contempt,' he said. 'She told me you handed her over for adoption as soon as she was born. How you rejected her because of her face.'

253

'What about her face? She was beautiful.'

He leaned closer, the smell of beer on his breath battling with his strongly scented cologne. 'Too many drugs in the nineties, made you forget? Or have you chosen to wipe her from your memory as well as your life – just got rid of her when she wasn't the perfect baby you'd imagined for your cosy middle-class existence?'

'You are talking nonsense,' I said, trying to mask my confusion with indignation. I was losing control of this conversation.

He looked at his watch, a Rolex or something similarly brash. 'Tell the boy to get out from under whatever stone he's hiding and get his arse down here. He owes me an apology and then we'll work out what I need him to do to make amends. I'll be at The Grange garages, six tomorrow. It's his last chance. Oh, and you better tell him I've got the mobile. Tell him I "found it" on the bridge. Could be evidence on there that the police would be interested in.'

I was shaking as I got back in the car next to Dmytro.

'Give me a moment,'

I said as I pulled out of the car park. I drove a few miles to park off road at the edge of a copse; it was safer there should John change his mind and come looking for us.

I rubbed my forehead, trying to clear my thoughts. I had no idea what had just happened.

'What does he want?' Dmytro asked.

'He wants you to meet him tomorrow. He said something about a mobile. I think he meant Sunny's mobile.'

'He has it?'

'I don't know. He said so. He said it's evidence. That he found it on the bridge. What does he mean?'

'I told you. He must have been there with her on the bridge. My photo will be on the phone. They will want to identify me, to find me and ask me questions. He wants the police to blame me for what happened.' He drummed his fingers on the dashboard. 'What else did he say?'

'He said Sunny hated her family . . . hated Ned.'

'And you are surprised,' Dmytro said, 'after what happened?' He must've read my confused expression as he went on, 'Sunny didn't tell you? About why she left Australia?'

'No . . . I thought she came here to find me.' He was staring at me, his eyes cold and expressionless. 'At least, that's what she told me. That she came here to meet me.'

'If you say so.' Uninterested in Ned and Sunny, he changed the subject back to John. 'What else did that man tell you?'

My brain was whirring, trying to recreate the conversation with John. 'He kept going on about Sunny's face. Saying I rejected her as a baby because of her face. She was beautiful. There was nothing wrong with her face.'

Dmytro turned towards me in the passenger seat, his eyes scanning me, his expression unreadable.

Eventually he said, 'You are not Sunny's mother.' His voice was calm, like this was a logical deduction, not open to debate.

I shook my head in disbelief. 'What are you talking about?'

He reached a hand slowly towards me and I tried not to flinch, wondering what he was about to do. His forefinger lightly touched the left side of my top lip.

'She had scar. Here.' He tapped his finger on my lip several times. 'She had an operation when she was a baby to make her face right.'

There must have been something wrong with her mouth when she was born. Some sort of birth mark? A naevus? A cleft lip? Something obvious in a newborn but almost invisible in a grown woman, the surgery scar faded with time to a thin pale line. Only ever noticed by those who saw her close up, without make-up.

'You are not Sunny's mother,' he repeated.

I'm not sure why, but I started crying.

Dmytro got out of the car and for a moment I thought he was storming off, but he merely stepped up to a tree and urinated on the ferns beneath and I hurriedly looked away. I dried my eyes on my sleeve and braced myself for the inevitable questions – Who are you? Why did you lie to me? – but my brain wasn't providing any viable responses. All I could think was that Ned mustn't find out that I'd deceived him.

When he got back in the car, he merely said, 'I want to go home.'

It was like I was a bit player in the drama of his life, my back story irrelevant, my role now all but complete. He just didn't care enough to want to know and I felt numb at the thought.

'Home?' I asked, my hand already on the ignition key. 'Yes, I'll take you there now.'

He shook his head. 'Not the flat.'

It took me a moment to register what he meant. 'Home to Kiev?'

He nodded, his gaze locked with mine. 'I need money,' he said, without intonation.

'How much money? How much is your fare?'

'Four thousand. I need four thousand.' The figure hung in the air between us as he stared at me, unblinking. I was the first to look away.

'I don't have that kind of money to give you.' How much was I prepared to pay to get him out of my life, to stop him exploring the truth about me? How much would be enough?

'I understand that you need cash to get back on your feet, to rent a flat at home, see you over until you can find work. I can get two thousand.'

'Three,' he said, drawing the figure 3,000 on the steamed-up window. He pulled his seatbelt around him and the click of the clasp in the housing was unnervingly loud and final.

It appeared the negotiations were done.

Chapter 33

I was so angry. How could Dmytro try to scam me for money after all I had done for him? He would not get away with this, but first I had to find out the truth about why Sunny left Australia.

That evening, as I prepared our dinner, I poured myself a glass of wine and opened a beer for Ned. Things had been a little cool between us recently but I was banking on my kindness giving him a sense of security, so he'd relax and open up. After we'd eaten, I approached my target subject at a tangent.

'So, you're off home soon. Back to Australia.'

'Yeah. Flight's booked for next week.'

'I bet there's a lot you've missed while you've been away. The weather for one thing!'

He laughed. 'That's for sure! That and the beaches and the barbies and the Swans.'

'Swans?'

'Sydney Swans, mate. My team.'

'You must miss your friends too.'

'Yeah. It'll be great to meet up for a few beers.'

'You know, I've been thinking about what Sunny told me about her leaving Australia.'

Ned took a gulp of his third beer. 'Yeah?'

'Something about it doesn't add up. She seemed . . . reticent . . . didn't want to talk about it. As if something had really upset her.'

Ned started worrying at the corner of the label on the beer bottle, tearing off small bits of paper that I'd have to retrieve later. He shrugged. 'She came to find *you*, didn't she? And to enter that singing competition on telly.'

'Yes, but why the rush? Why didn't she make contact with me before she left? Why hadn't she started her application for the TV programme? It's a long way to come on the off chance.'

He fidgeted in his chair, not making eye contact. 'She flitted about. Always doing things on a whim.'

'Yes, but why didn't she tell you what she was up to? And the way she avoided contact – no email or social media. Doing her music under another name. It's like she was running from something. Trying not to be found.'

He looked uncomfortable. Feeling I was onto something, I carried on pushing. 'I know she didn't explain her reasons for leaving, but did she say *anything* to you about it after she left?'

'No,' Ned said. Unable to look at me, he'd now worked the label free and was folding what was left of it into squares. 'We weren't really in touch.'

So they had fallen out. 'Yes, she implied that, but didn't say why. What upset her, Ned? Did you two argue?'

'She thought I was pushing her away, I guess.' He sighed heavily, stared into the middle distance. 'You

259

know what she was like . . . Look, okay – I told you I'd found a new partner . . . It upset her.'

Jealousy, that made sense. I opened another beer bottle and passed it across the table, took a sip from my own glass . . . softly softly . . .

'But you lost your wife years ago. You must've had other partners since then? Surely she understood.'

'It was different . . . I handled it badly . . . I should have told her before she found out for herself.' He cleared his throat. 'She saw us together . . . like, you know . . . Anyway, it was obvious what was going on.' He coughed, embarrassed to say what he meant. 'You know what I mean.'

He can't bring himself to say that she saw them making love. Hiding my own revulsion at the thought of walking in on such a scene, I kept my understanding tone. 'Sunny was a grown woman. It's embarrassing for everyone but, well, I'm sure you didn't mean to hurt her.'

'No. But, I have to admit, I've been . . . selfish . . . but I never thought it would end like this. I thought we'd have time to win her round to the idea.'

'What idea, Ned?' I was trying to convey that I am neither shocked nor shockable.

'Me and Chloe.'

'I'm sure – eventually – she would've accepted a new stepmother.'

'Not this one,' he said. He bowed his head, screwing up his eyes, hiding from the truth. 'Not one five years younger than her. Not her best friend. Her *only* friend.'

I pushed my chair back from the table and left the room. He disgusted me.

So, Sunny ran away because she caught her father with her best friend. No wonder she was ripe for the sordid attentions of an older man like John. Probably looking for a father figure. And Dmytro, did he really care for her as much as he seemed to? Surely if he knew she was with John on the bridge, he should have challenged John straight away. He should have called the police anonymously and told them who she was as soon as he knew about the accident, so my poor Sunny wouldn't have been a Jane Doe for so many weeks. But no. He was too concerned for himself; that he might be accused, sent to prison or packed off home for over-staying his visa.

The three men who should have loved her were all equally pathetic.

Yes, the coroner suggested it was an accident – no defensive marks, 'misadventure'. But all three of them had had a hand in the events that led to her death. If they hadn't played their parts, she wouldn't have been there, on *that* bridge on *that* day.

All three of them had let her down. Not one of them was good enough for her.

And I will get revenge on Sunny's behalf. Make them pay for not loving her enough. I will take away what each of them hold dear.

★

I felt strangely energised when I rang Mother the next day.

'I only have five minutes today,' I said, looking at the timer on my desk. I imagined her eyebrow raising, the lips pursing in disapproval.

'Oh. And why am I downgraded, may I ask?'

'I'm working on something which is time-dependent. It has to be done in the next few days.'

'Well, if you have a few days, you can spare me more than five minutes.'

'Four minutes now,' I said. 'Anyway, how are you?'

I heard the heavy intake of breath. 'In pain. Not that you care.'

She was sulking and wanted me to draw her out.

'What's wrong?'

'It's my hip as always. It's grinding and crunching and hurts to stand, to sit, to walk. I've decided enough is enough and I've booked myself in for the operation.'

'Good. When is it?'

'Three weeks' time. At my usual hospital.'

'St Matthews?' I'm shocked. She cannot mean the hospital that used to treat her, the one twenty miles from me?

'Yes. Where else would I go? They know me there. And I am coming to you for convalescence, so you had better freshen up my room. And I'll tell Georgio to send you some of the recipes he cooks for me and a list of the day-to-day products I need you to get. Bath oil, my special face cream, that kind of thing. If I were to use that stuff you get from the Co-op, my skin would come up in a rash. I've told you that's why you've aged prematurely. I did my bit, keeping you out of the sun when you were young but you've never taken care of yourself.'

I look at the timer. Two minutes to go. 'I'm not around then. I've booked a holiday. I'm going away for a few weeks, with Becky.'

'Well, you'll have to cancel it. I can't move the operation.'

'And I can't move my work commitments and holiday. I will find you a convalescent home you can stay in. I'll give you the details next week or would you prefer that I email them to Georgio to book for you?' That useful *assumptive close*: two options, chose one.

There was silence at the other end of the line.

'Mother?'

'Well, I can't believe—'

'Sorry, I have to go now. I have a Skype call booked with my client. I'll send Georgio some details of places he can book for you and we can speak next week. Bye.' I hung up the phone and literally danced round the room. Assertiveness or rudeness; in that moment I didn't care, but it was the first time I had ever stood up to Mother.

Chapter 34

Oh, I had fun coming up with my plans for revenge. Making the punishment fit their individual crimes. Sunny would be proud of me.

Firstly, Ned 'the loving father and family man', a reputation he no longer deserved and that I was about to shatter. I needed to go shopping first – a quick run to the WH Smith's in the next town. When I got back, I told him I had a work deadline and needed privacy, an excuse to lock myself away in my office all afternoon.

From my desk, I took out Sunny's notebook and my file of screenshots of her online messages. I unwrapped the lockable journal I'd bought at the stationers and cracked the spine.

Four hours later the journal was three-quarters full – song lyrics, magazine cuttings from her notebook, poems, photos downloaded from the net; all glued in around my faked handwritten scribbles and doodles.

Ned's unguarded stories had proved spectacularly useful. I played back his words, the awful things he'd said to me about Sunny in drunken uncensored moments: 'She could be so selfish. Expecting me to be at her beck and call when she wanted something – never bothering to communicate otherwise.' 'I'd only see her when she needed money or wanted to borrow the car.' From his sarcastic comments about her singing and dancing, to her short-temperedness, I remembered them all.

I dated some of the entries around the time I'd said Sunny had first contacted me.

'*I sent a card to Sonya today. It seems too soon to call her my mum but I really hope she gets in touch soon!!!! I hope she likes the photo. It took me aaaaaages to decide which one to send!!*' This one surrounded by doodles of four-leaf clovers and a printout of crossed fingers.

'*I keep checking my phone in case she's called. She must've got my card by now??*'

'*I met her today – my* <u>MUM</u>*!!!! It's really weird but suddenly I felt whole again like I'd found a missing part of me. It was like we'd always known each other. She is* <u>so</u> *like me.*'

'*It's so lovely being around Mum. We have so much fun. I wish she'd been there all my life.*'

Later I included dates of outings we'd been on, reference to gifts we'd bought each other – the torn heart charm on her bracelet, the Dusty CD, her mic nights, a cinema trip. Then other bitter comments began to creep in, her fury at Ned building to hatred as her relationship with me became stronger.

'*I never want to see him again. He is a lying, two-faced bastard. Mum is the only person I can love and trust.*'

I shut the journal and in thick black marker pen I wrote '*PRIVATE*' and underlined it twice. I locked the book and threw the key into my waste bin.

Thrilled with my efforts, I constructed two letters in Sunny's writing – one to Sunny's Aunt Jemima, the other to her godmother, who had also spoken at the funeral. The letters were dated soon after Sunny had arrived in the UK. They both said more or less the same thing.

> Hi
>
> We've not been in touch as much as I would like over the years but as you can see, I'm here in London now and I want to reconnect with my English family. I plan to come and see you as soon as I can but there's something I need you to know before we meet. I'm writing rather than phoning cos I don't think I can say what I want you to know without crying. Basically I'm never speaking to Ned again and I'm never going back to Australia. If you want to know why, you can ask him but I will never forgive him. Please don't talk to me about him when I come to see you.
>
> 'Til soon.
>
> All my love, Sunny xx

I was in a good mood when I finished so decided I'd give Dmytro one last chance. That evening, I locked everything away before telling Ned I had to go and collect some photographs for someone's family tree. I drove to Dmytro's flat and waited in my car for him to come home from work.

The street lamp had been smashed but I didn't want to draw attention to myself by turning on the interior light, so I was forced to sit there in darkness like an undercover agent. In most TV shows they spend their time eating burgers and slurping Cokes but I hadn't thought to bring anything with me; my only entertainment was to stare through the breath-fogged windows at the street.

There was nothing much to see; the parade of shops on its last legs, waiting to be put out of its misery, attracted few people. A lad of about fourteen cycled past my car, his bike far too small for him, forcing him to push his knees out awkwardly, his shoulders hunched. Couldn't be good for his back; he'd need Pilates when he was older, but at least he was getting some exercise. He skidded to a halt by an alley between the shops and made a two-tone whistle. Seconds later an older youth appeared from the shadows. They exchanged good-humoured banter, which I doubted was about the youngster's maths homework. A package was exchanged and the young boy sped off. The older lad looked up and down the street and started walking in my direction. To my surprise, he stopped beside my car and tapped on the window. I lowered it a fraction and the smell of fried food and greasy hair wafted in.

He bent to speak, his voice not unkind. 'You want something?'

'No, no. I'm waiting for a friend.'

'Yeah? Who? Anyone I know?' The lack of overt threat in his tone was somehow more menacing.

Not knowing the local 'politics', I didn't want to say anything I shouldn't. 'He lives above the shops. He's my daughter's boyfriend actually.' The 'actually' sounded painfully middle class. The youth nodded but stayed where he was, breathing Juicy Fruit breath through the gap and I itched to press the button and close the window. The sound of footsteps behind him caused him to straighten, but he kept one hand on the car, a sign that I shouldn't drive off. He wasn't finished.

'Yo!' he said to the approaching person, followed by some other unintelligible street talk. Heart pounding, I turned my head away, determined not to see anything I shouldn't. The passenger door opened and I nearly screamed, before a familiar voice said, 'It is not good to sit here. Come.' And Dmytro beckoned me towards his flat.

Inside, he took a beer from the fridge, opening it against the countertop with one hand, before holding it out towards me. 'I have no milk.' Opening a second beer he tapped his bottle against mine. '*Bud'mo*,' he said, before taking a swig then wiping his mouth with the back of his hand. 'You should not mix with bad men.'

'I wasn't. I was waiting for you.'

'Lucky I arrived then.' He sat down, still wearing his coat and gloves. The gloves I'd bought him for Christmas.

'Thank you for dealing with that man.' Maybe Dmytro still cares about me, still has some respect for me, for my kindness to him.

'That's okay. My mother taught me to protect old ladies.' Another mouthful of beer. 'You have the cash?'

'No. It's not easy for me to get the amount of money

268

you want.'

He took a swig of beer. 'Life is not easy.'

'Why do you need so much money?'

'Maybe I'll go back to college. Maybe I'll travel.' His tone was cold, his eyes locked with mine. 'Maybe I'll find a new girl and have a big wedding day. You do not need to know.'

'If I give you the money, I need to be sure you will never contact me again.'

'Why would I contact you?'

'You must promise me. Please.'

'*Obitsyayu,*' he sneered. 'We are not children. Promises are just words. You must trust me.'

He was right. What choice did I have? He stood up and it was clear he expected me to leave. At the door I told him – without guilt about lying – that I would try to get the money.

'Thank you.' He paused, smiling his Mona Lisa smile. 'What do I call you now?'

It took me a moment to figure out what he meant. 'Sonya. Just Sonya.'

I heard his door shut behind me as I descended the stairs. He had blown his opportunity to turn this around. He was now in my sights.

Chapter 35

The next morning, I told Ned I'd been to Dmytro's.

'He got in a terrible fight with that John from the pub.' I explained how Dmytro had been to John's house, described the wrecking of the car, the physical threats.

'He should go to the police,' Ned said. 'Is there anything we can do to help?'

I refrained from saying 'there is no *we*' – he had snatched away all my hopes for a little family group united around Sunny. Instead I commented blandly, 'I told him he must report it, but he won't consider it. I think there are things he's kept from us.'

'Like what?'

'For one, it turns out he's working here illegally. I think he might also be involved in something dodgy. He certainly knows some unsavoury characters.'

I had Ned's attention. 'What, something like drugs?'

I shrugged. 'I don't know. But he's in some kind of trouble and he told me he needs money. He says he plans to go back to Ukraine and I think he's running away from something.' I waited a beat or two for that to sink in. 'I don't feel comfortable around him anymore.

I don't think you should answer if he calls you. He'll only try to scam you for money too.'

Ned shook his head. 'God, what a mess.'

'Oh, and he gave me a few things of Sunny's that he still had.' I handed Ned a carrier bag. In it were the meagre possessions I had retained months ago, my faked letters and the journal I had edited.

He tipped the contents out onto the table and sifted through. I reached for one of the letters. 'She must've written these letters and never got round to posting them. This is for her Aunty, Jemima,' I said. 'If you have the address, I could post them this afternoon.'

'Hmm, yes . . .' He was distracted – he'd spotted the journal. He held it in both hands, tried to open it, inspecting it from all sides as if there were a hidden switch. 'It's locked. Can you see a key anywhere?' he asked.

'I didn't look but, if there is one, it's in the bag.' I stared at him coldly and pointed to the cover of the book. 'It says private. She didn't want anyone to read it.'

I turned on my heel and left. I had no way of knowing whether he would post the letters or read the diary. But whatever he did, he'd be punished for hurting Sunny. If he was a moral person, which I hoped he was, he'd act appropriately. He'd post the letters, set the diary on one side. But he would be constantly wondering, wanting to know the contents, to find out more about his daughter's last months after his ill-chosen affair. If he lacked all decency, he would open the letters, force the diary and suffer the consequences. It was in his hands now.

That night, when Ned's snores reverberated through the walls of the house, I seized the opportunity to creep downstairs to the lounge. He believed he had lost his charging cable a few days ago, after I'd acquired and hidden it when he left it in the kitchen. Thoughtfully, I had brought my own down from my office, plugging it into a socket in the lounge so we could take it in turns to use it. He'd left his mobile there to charge overnight, ready for the long journey ahead.

I would never have imagined myself stooping so low but, driven by anger, bitterness and necessity, I unlocked the phone with the code I'd seen him use many times, Sunny's birth date. After scrolling through Ned's contacts to find the entry for Dmytro, I blocked the number then typed a made-up entry under Dmytro's name. Job done, I knew I should turn the phone off again but, my curiosity aroused, I had to look further. This was no time to take the moral high ground.

I looked for Sunny's despicable friend in his Whats App. There were reams of messages, full of exclamation marks, icons and trivia. I focused on the most recent.

Last week: 'Looking forward to your return! I'll bake you a cake. Xx'

Ned hadn't responded.

Her next message read: 'Not been to the park since you left. Not the same without you', followed by a sad face and a muscle man icon and a dog.

Ned had replied: 'I'm getting too old for all that exertion' plus a winking-smiley. In response she'd sent a row of cakes and the mysterious text 'Never too old for my lamington!!! Xx'. It was like they were communicating in code; I would need to google these references.

Ned had not deigned that message worthy of acknowledgement. I noticed a pattern – two or three messages from her for each reply from Ned. Maybe he was carrying some guilt, after all. Her most recent message read: 'Don't get a cab. Me and Taz will pick you up from the airport. Text me when you know ETA. Xx.'

I made a note of her details from the contacts file. Force of habit.

Before I turned the phone off, I had a quick look at his photos. First up was a selfie of Ned with his arm slung round the shoulders of a young woman; they were both wearing tracksuits and looked dishevelled – he smiled at the camera, she smiled at him. I assumed this was Chloe – her WhatsApp profile picture was a selfie of her lips so I couldn't know for sure. She was reasonably attractive if you liked that type of look: short and rounded, still carrying some puppy fat.

There wasn't much else of interest so I plugged the phone back into the charger and turned it off.

I was up early the next morning, the day Ned was due to leave, his taxi prebooked for the first flight. Over breakfast I casually asked if he'd like me to post the letters Sunny had written. He acted as if he'd forgotten about them but when I pulled out my sheet of stamps, he had little choice but to look up the addresses on his phone.

Ned went to do some final packing while waiting for his cab to arrive, as if he was avoiding me. I don't know what I'd expected, but some acknowledgement of all the emotion we'd shared. When it came to it, our goodbye was fairly formal. A brief hug and kiss on the cheek; a thank you for being there for him; mumblings about keeping in touch, meeting up again when the inquest eventually took place. Empty words from a man with no heart.

Watching his taxi drive away, I had a pang of sadness for what might have been. But there was no time to brood. Next in the crosshairs was John.

Chapter 36

It was lunchtime. My next stop was designed to put the metaphorical cat among the pigeons. A visit to see John at the Pheasant; according to information I'd picked up, he and LeeAnn often went there at midday during the week.

In the car park I parked near a blue BMW. I seemed to be seeing them everywhere since that strange incident near Becky's house. I was edgy, not used to moving in this strange world inhabited by men like John and Dmytro.

John was sprawled on his usual seat – legs akimbo, arms spread wide, taking up more space than he warranted in his feigned bravado. LeeAnn was perched beside him, upright in her seat, as if ready to jump at his bidding should he want a drink or ask her to leave. Beneath her eyes were the dark shadows of too many sleepless nights.

I stood beside their table and launched into my planned speech. 'I thought you might like to know. Dmytro has reported you to the police. He's told them you were there with Sunny on the bridge when she fell and died.'

LeeAnn gasped. 'But he wasn't!' Putting a restraining hand on his forearm, she looked from me to John. A flash of fear in her eyes made me wonder if he took his temper out on her when no one was around.

He flicked her hand away without even looking at her and leant towards me. 'The stupid fucker!'

LeeAnn was shaking her head, as if she couldn't believe what she was hearing. She looked straight at me, her eyes bright with unshed tears. 'He can't do that. It's not true. I know it's not true.'

'When did that little bastard contact the cops?'

'I'm not sure. I only just found out.'

'He's more of a fool than I took him for. If anyone would be in the frame, it would be him.' John rubbed his chin as he thought. I waited, silent, my eyes on LeeAnn, who had lowered her head, trying to cover her upset. Eventually John sighed deeply and snorted out a breath. 'Tell him if the cops come after me, we'll give them the mobile. We'll say my wife found it on the bridge in the undergrowth when she went for a walk there.'

I felt my temper rise as he tried to draw poor LeeAnn into this.

He warmed to his story. 'She didn't know whose it was, couldn't unlock it, so couldn't return it. If the police come looking for me, I'll just hand the mobile over and they will be onto him. Prime suspect – his photo on the camera, his dabs all over her phone. Oh, and tell him they can get the CCTV from the station which will show I was there at the time she fell. I heard the sirens as they drove over there.'

276

'You told me you phoned her from the train station! That will prove you weren't there on the bridge. They can look at the phone records.' LeeAnn looked up at John, a hopeful expression as if expecting praise, but John glared at her.

'That's enough,' he snapped at her and she bit her lip like an anxious teenage girl being admonished by a parent. 'Your makeup's smeared. You might want to go and sort out your face.'

I watched as LeeAnn dutifully headed for the ladies. 'Why were you meeting Sunny that day? Were you taking her to London like she said?' I thought I may as well ask him, even though I doubted I'd get the truth.

'Why do you think? You really think I'd go away to London with that mad box of tricks? I was going to tell her to stop hassling me for money. Now go and tell your lapdog that LeeAnn's got the phone and we'll use it if the police come knocking.'

As I was leaving the bar, JayCee stopped me. 'Is everything okay? I saw LeeAnn crying and wondered what was wrong.'

'Everything's okay. I wanted to know if John had been with Sunny on the day of the accident. I just want to know what happened.'

'It must be horrible not knowing.' She gave me a spontaneous hug. 'I feel so sorry for you and Ned.'

It was only later when sorting out my handbag I wondered if the hug was not so spontaneous, after all. I found a note, scribbled on the bottom half of a page from an order pad. 'Back off,' it said. 'There are things you don't understand.' My guess was that JayCee had dropped it in my bag, but it raised two questions: was this a gentle word of advice with my best interests at heart, or a threat of some kind? Either way, there was clearly more to find out.

Meanwhile I continued with my plan to pay Dmytro back for rejecting my kindness. I phoned his mobile, knowing full well he would be at work and unable to answer. I left a short message, which I hoped sounded serious without being overly dramatic. 'John thinks you've reported him to the police and he's sending someone to find you. You'd better get out as soon as you can. He's serious.' I wasn't 100 per cent sure what I was trying to do, but I hoped Dmytro would rise to the bait and go after John again and all hell would break lose. However, knowing that Dmytro was an intelligent young man, I also had a back-up plan.

One more quick call: 'Becky, are you in? . . . Can I come round to see you about something that's worrying me?'

Over coffee in Becky's kitchen, I shared my concerns.

'You know I've had my cousin staying with me, after he had that breakdown?'

'Yes. How is he doing?'

'Much better. The peace and quiet did him a lot of good. He moved out last week, so I'm on my own again.' I paused, a look of concern on my face. 'That's the issue . . . I'm not sure whether it's my imagination, but since he left I think I've seen someone hanging around outside the house.'

'No! Have you any idea who it is?'

'No idea. I've seen something several times now. It looks like a young man, watching the house. Once I saw him at the end of the driveway. But I'm sure I've seen movement near the house a couple of times.'

'Have you told the police?'

'There's nothing really to report. It's not like I have any evidence to show them.'

'You ought to get some security cameras put up.'

'That's a good idea. I'd feel a lot safer. Do you know anyone who can do that sort of thing? I wouldn't know where to start.'

'Our Tyrone can easily sort that out – I'll talk to him and he can get a camera from work. I'll give you his mobile number and you can arrange it with him.'

Step one of the plan complete.

As I was leaving, Becky gave me a hug and said, 'If you think you see anyone again ring me straight away. And if you ever want to come and stay here, you know you're welcome any time.'

'I really don't know what I'd do without you, Becky.'

I was right. Everything went to plan.

Dmytro turned up at my house just as I expected, his own expectations of ready cash and a quiet exit disrupted by my failure to pay up and the potential threats from John. He'd tried to phone me several times during the day, but I'd let the voicemail pick up and he'd not left a message.

It was late afternoon when he arrived. I was well prepared: the doors and windows, all locked tight; my car hidden in the garage; upstairs curtains shut and lights turned off, as if I wasn't at home. And, thanks to Tyrone, the security cameras installed, ready to catch people approaching from all angles. Belt and braces. I sat poised at my bedroom window with my camera, ready to focus on anything else that might be useful.

He must've parked his car out on the country lane that runs past the end of my driveway, not wanting me to hear the engine as he pulled up. Annoying but not a huge drawback to my plan. He strode confidently towards the house, stopping several yards away to look up at the building, scanning the windows for signs of life. Training the lens of my camera on him, I held my breath, gently pressing the button to catch his upturned face. He was a striking young man with handsome, distinctive features, his dark hair tufting from his red beanie hat. I could see why Sunny was attracted to him.

Dmytro was distracted by Ginger who had emerged from the cats' Wendy house and was seeking attention by winding her way around his legs. He took off his gloves and bent down to stroke her, picking her up and holding her to him, his lips moving soundlessly as he spoke to her. She struggled and he put her down. He walked round the side of the house and I followed his path on the security footage beamed to my laptop, imagining I could hear the sounds of his tread on the gravel, the rattling as I watched him test each window in turn. Returning to the front of the house, he strode to the front door. I waited to hear the doorbell, but the rattle of the letterbox told me he had lifted the metal flap to peer in. It clanged shut and I watched as he walked back up the driveway, putting on his gloves again without looking back.

I allowed myself a moment to feel sad about my lost dreams and then got on with the next task. I cleared down the hard drive of my laptop, removing all my electronic records of Sunny. As if reading my mind, the machine prompted, 'Are you sure you want to delete this file?' and initially I paused, finger raised above the key. No, I am not sure, I thought, but there was one thing I did know: this mass of data was no longer necessary; her story would be etched on my heart for ever.

I retrieved the hardcopy documents that had made up the timeline of her movements on my wall, handling each sheet with the care afforded the mementos of a loved one. I piled each item with the contents of my paper files – the cuttings, the maps – aligning the edges of the sheets, forming a neat stack. A tidy environment equals a calm and tidy mind.

Perched on a low stool, with a Dusty Springfield CD playing to keep me company, I fed the sheets one at a time into my crosscut shredder, quietly chatting to Sunny about our journey together over the past months. I was about to shred a pile of photos when something caught my eye about the image on the top: Sunny and JayCee, both wearing sunglasses and baseball hats, broad smiles on their faces. *What is it that's wrong with this picture? What's nagging me?* And then I spotted it, hiding in plain sight. Sunny's auburn curls cascading over her shoulders, the blue baseball cap perched on her head; next to her JayCee wearing a dark red cap, *her hair cropped short*. No extensions! I flicked through the pile. In early shots she had a long blonde weave, then this. Between having her extensions replaced she sometimes left her hair short. While not as tall as Sunny, she was probably about five foot seven and, from a distance with short hair hidden in a cap, it's possible she could have been mistaken for a man. Was it her who was spotted on the bridge after Sunny fell?

Chapter 37

The next afternoon I phoned Becky.

'That man was here again last night. I just checked the footage.'

'Oh no. Did he do anything?'

'No, he just looked in the windows and then left.'

'Do you think he's a burglar? Will you report him?'

'There's really nothing at The Old Vicarage worth stealing,' I laughed. 'Maybe he was casing the place but I doubt he'll be back.'

'You must come and stay with us tonight. I don't like the thought of you being there alone.'

I allowed myself to be easily persuaded and agreed to come over later when I'd finished my work and packed up the few valuables to bring with me.

I slept that night in Becky's room while she made do on the couch. When I'd thanked her for everything, she said, 'That's what friends are for. You'd do the same for me.'

And she was right, I would.

A gentle tap on the door woke me. Momentarily I couldn't think where I was; unable to place the lacy pink duvet – half on/half off the bed – and the large fluffy duck watching me with beady eyes from the lace-trimmed pillow next to mine. It had teetered forward at some point in the night and its orange-felt beak rested inches from my nose.

'Morning, campers! Rise and shine!' Becky sounded unnecessarily bright and breezy as she made her way across the room with a laden tray.

'What time is it?' I mumbled, unable to focus on my watch in the semi-darkness of the room. I needed to get back to my house to find out if my plan had worked.

'Half eight.' She tossed the *Daily Mail* on the bed and placed a mug of tea and a plate of buttered toast within reach on the bedside table. 'I need to leave for a photography job soon, but there's no need for you to get up.'

She straightened the duck on the pillow next to me and I sat up, pulling the covers around me so I didn't expose my bra and pants.

'I just need five minutes and I'll get myself sorted and head home,' I said. 'I don't want to get in the way of your boys.'

'Believe it or not, they're all out at work. Even Andre!' I raised my eyebrows and Becky shrugged. 'I know. I have to pinch myself each time I think about it.' She paused for dramatic effect, eyes and mouth wide, miming awe. 'He's got himself a job working in that cash and carry on the industrial estate. Says he's saving up! So the place is yours,' she mumbled through a mouthful of bread, covering her mouth with her hand as she chewed. 'Take as long as you like.'

'Thanks, but I'd better be off home. Feed the cats before they try to eat the ducks!'

At the door she paused, waving the rest of the slice of toast. 'See you at the weekend? Girls' night in Friday? Pizza and a DVD?'

I gave her a thumbs-up, grinning.

Before heading home, I stopped off in the high street to sort out a few things I needed to embark on my plans. First, I nipped into the hairdresser's to book an appointment with Cathy for later in the week – it was time for something completely new – then the stationer's. I also wanted to get something to thank Becky for being there for me; a card didn't seem enough, but I had an idea.

At the confectioner's, my arrival announced by the ting-a-ling of the bell, I was met by a warm smile from Alice. Her hair was pulled back in a chignon and for the first time I really took in her face: her features were much softer than Sunny's, her looks natural rather than achieved through layers of make-up. One of those people who was beautiful both inside and out.

'Hi. You're the lady from New Year's Eve. I haven't seen you for a while. How are you?' she asked.

'I'm well, thanks. And you? Your daughter?'

'Suki's fine, thanks. Into everything at the moment. Her personality is really coming through.'

I pointed to a cake in the window display. 'Is it possible to get something like that iced with a message and delivered today?'

'Yes, of course. I'll do it myself. Is it for a special birthday? Suki has seen them in the window and she's already told me what she wants on her birthday cake, and it's not 'til September!'

'September? What a coincidence! That's when my goddaughter was born.'

I studied Alice as I dictated the message to be iced on the cake. She was an admirable young woman, bringing up a young child on her own and working all hours to support them both. I wondered how she managed. Whether she had supportive family around her . . .

'For a wonderful friend with the hugest heart x', she read back to me. 'We could all do with friends like that.'

Did I imagine a trace of wistfulness in her eyes?

I drove back to my home humming a slightly off-key rendition of 'I've got the Whole World in my Hands'.

When I approached my house it was like a scene from a TV crime show. Blue and white tape across the drive and a police constable standing by the pillars at the entrance. Getting out of my car in the lane, I was waylaid by one of the workers from Woodley's Farm, the property where the cats were meant to live. But it was clear he wasn't there to berate me about enticing their rat catchers away.

'You can't go in there.' He was eager to play his role as the bearer of bad tidings. 'You've had a fire.'

I frowned at him. 'What do you mean?'

'There's been a fire. Round the back of the house. Quite a bit of damage, I gather.'

'A fire?' I mumbled, concerned and confused. 'Have they said what caused it? Was it the wiring? The house hasn't been rewired for years.'

'I don't know, but that's the woman in charge.' He pointed to a detective in an unflattering forensic jumpsuit who was making her way towards us.

'Good morning. Are you the home owner?'

I nodded.

It's so pleasing when a plan comes together.

Chapter 38

My framing of Dmytro for a fire that I'd started worked perfectly.

Before I'd left to go to Becky's, I pushed the cats out and shut the door that connected the kitchen to the rest of the house. I'd then left the house via the front door, as could clearly be seen on the time-stamped security footage. But what the recordings couldn't show was the activity off camera: me donning a pair of men's wellies and doubling back through the woodland to get to the back door and start the fire five minutes later, the trampled undergrowth marking the route that Dmytro was deemed to have taken. Aside from the surveillance recordings that placed him outside my home the night before, the forensic team found his fingerprints on the windows and letterbox, as I knew they would. There was also the pair of men's gloves I'd discarded near the bins round the back of the house, gloves that smelt of petrol and were duplicates of the ones I'd bought Dmytro for Christmas.

The fire had been started with a small amount of petrol poured through the cat flap in the backdoor, allowing it to catch on a nylon doormat and travel to the blankets in the wicker cat basket and a cotton dressing gown I'd left over a nearby armchair.

While they didn't find Dmyto's prints in the AFIS database, they reproduced a photograph of him from the surveillance footage and posted it on the internet. He was deemed 'a person of interest'. I was naturally cross-examined by the curious staff in the local shop, all eager for gossip, and after I described seeing a car that was the colour, make and model of Dmytro's, several other people agreed they had seen such a car in the area, driven by a young dark-haired man. So easy to lead the witnesses with a few well-chosen statements.

Needless to say, Dmytro disappeared fairly quickly after that.

Now *Sonya* had one final task before I could wrap her up for good and go back to being Janice full time.

After finding the note that I took to be from JayCee, I had sent a message to her c/o the Pheasant. On the back of the torn scrap of order pad I wrote *'Meet me at the place where all this started. If you don't turn up I will go to the police with all I know. I want the <u>whole</u> truth.'* I added a date and time, but not my name. She would know who it was from.

As that evening approached, I became more nervous; scared of the unknown, what might transpire.

I parked at the Gressingdon side of the bridge, leaving my car under a street light, hiding my keys on top of the front tyre. The only things I carried with me were my mobile and an attack alarm in case I needed to attract attention, both safe in my zipped pocket. I was wearing my walking boots in case I needed to run away. If you'd asked me what I was frightened of, I couldn't have said – I was only meeting JayCee for a conversation. But it seemed bigger than that. Walking towards the bridge, it felt as if I was outside my body, watching myself, unable to believe that this was real.

As I passed round the scrubby bushes, a small animal rustled in the bracken and I jumped. It was with relief I spotted JayCee, already on the bridge, standing on the far side, looking over the barrier. She must've heard me approach as, without turning round, she said quietly, 'I wondered when this would happen. I've been waiting for this day.'

I stood next to her, looking down at the evening traffic flashing past below. People heading for their homes after a long working day. I felt numb just thinking about it.

'She didn't stand a chance,' I said.

'No.'

Neither of us said anything for a while, the noise of the traffic swishing in and out like waves, the headlights coming and going as the cars passed under the bridge below our feet.

'Why did she come here that day?' I asked.

'Because I asked her to.'

Not what I'd expected. 'Why? Tell me what happened.'

'It was a surprise. I thought she'd be pleased . . . I swear I didn't know.'

'Didn't know what?' I took hold of her shoulders and turned her to face me so I could read her expression. 'Start at the beginning. What was this surprise?'

'Her brother.'

That didn't make any sense. 'What do you mean?'

'He told me he wanted to surprise her on her birthday. Apparently they'd not seen each other for years. He—'

'Stop a moment. How did you meet her brother?'

'It was about a week before the accident. He came to the Pheasant one day asking after her, but he didn't say who he was at first. She'd been out with lots of different men so I had to be careful. I told him she wasn't working that week. He came back another time and said he wanted to get in touch with her. That was when he showed me the photo of him and Sunny when they were kids and told me who he was. He wanted to know where she lived.'

'Did you tell him?'

'I didn't know where she was staying – I told him I thought she'd moved in with a man she was seeing.'

Dmytro. Chucked out of the pub, Sunny had immediately fallen back on loyal Dmytro as someone to stay with.

'He said he wanted to surprise her on her birthday, that she'd be thrilled to see him . . . He said they hadn't been able to see each other for years because she lived so far away. I swear, I didn't know they'd fallen out. I told him she was going to London with John on her birthday – she'd been showing off about it for weeks. That was when I suggested that he could meet her on the bridge near the station, before they left for London. He asked me to help him make it a lovely surprise for her. I really thought she'd be pleased. That's why I got her the balloons too, to make it fun for her . . .'

'So, what did you tell Sunny to get her to come here?'

'I said there was someone who wanted to meet her, pretended it was an admirer from the pub who had a birthday present for her. I said that he'd sworn me to secrecy, but she'd be pleased when she found out who it was. That hooked her. I arranged to meet her here on the bridge, just before she was due to get the train with John.'

'So, what happened?'

'When I got here, she was all geed up and giggly, guessing who her admirer was and what they might have bought her. She said she hoped he had lots of money and then she could swap him for John. We had to wait longer than I'd hoped and she started messing about, climbing on the barrier with those stupid balloons . . . She'd already been drinking.'

She paused, looking past me, screwing her eyes up as if trying to focus on something in the dark and I half turned to see what it was.

'No!' she shouted, pulling me sideways as a tall figure in a black hoodie rushed towards us from the far side of the bridge, the light glinting on something in an outstretched hand. Before I could work out what was happening, JayCee ran forward, swinging her holdall at the man. The bag hit him hard in the arm and the knife he'd been holding skittered across the bridge, falling between the railings to the road below. With the man off balance, I took my chance and knocked him sideways. He let out a groan, fell to his knees, losing his glasses. Another swipe from JayCee's bag and he was down on the ground.

'Run!' she shouted.

Crouched down beside my car, I fumbled for the keys on top of the tyre.

'Hurry! Hurry!' JayCee implored beside me.

The man appeared from the behind the bracken, limping slightly, and I grabbed JayCee's arm, pulling her down to hide behind the car. Crouched on the pavement, I rued parking under a street light, scanning around for bushes we might hide in. It was then I remembered the attack alarm. I inched it from my pocket and signalled to JayCee to cover her ears before pressing the button.

The screeching blare rang out and a man and woman appeared from the off-licence, summoned by the noise. 'What's going on?'

'There was a man following us,' I said, standing. There was no sign of him.

JayCee pointed back towards the bridge. 'He went that way.'

'How frightening. Do you want me to call the police?' the man asked.

'No,' I said firmly. 'Thanks, but we're okay.'

Chapter 39

Once we were in the car I drove off quickly, my ears still ringing, my heart pounding.

'Matt,' I said. 'That was him, wasn't it? Sunny's brother.' I'd recognised him; the solitary man who had sat at the end of the pew at Sunny's cremation. The man who had left before the end of the service.

'Yes. They hated each other, but I wasn't to know. He lied to me.'

'Do you know what car he drives?'

'A blue BMW. Why?'

'I think he's been tailing me over the last week or so.'

I drove us to a hotel an hour away, taking a circuitous route and constantly checking in my rear-view mirror to ensure we weren't being followed. We found a quiet table in the corner of the bar where we could talk without being overheard. JayCee told me the full story of what happened that day on the bridge. Far from being pleased to see her brother, Sunny was furious with JayCee and swore at Matt.

'They started arguing. I wanted to leave – I assumed it was family stuff, nothing to do with me - but Matt grabbed my arm and held me there. He said he wanted me to know what my friend was *really* like.'

JayCee told me everything that Matt had said to Sunny that day; if all he accused her of was true, her behaviour was appalling. Apparently when she'd first arrived in London, Sunny had turned up at his office in the City unannounced, 'looking like a prostitute' as he'd described it. At first he hadn't recognised her; they'd not been in touch for over ten years. She'd got his address from Ned's computer before she left Australia.

As soon as they met, Sunny had told him she needed money so he gave her double what she wanted and made her promise not to contact him again. But then it started. She'd seen he was successful and realised he had cash and wanted more. When he refused to see her, she started phoning his secretary, pretending to be a client so she could get an appointment with him, hanging around the coffee shops he frequented, calling his mobile in the middle of the night. Then, one day she took it too far. She went to his home and spoke to his wife. His wife who didn't know he had an estranged sister. His wife, who believed Sunny's lie that she was actually Matt's lover. His wife, who took up Sunny's suggestion that she check the bank account for missing money, ask his secretary about the appointments, look at his phone to see all Sunny's calls and texts.

It was all too much for Matt. Not only had she destroyed his happy childhood home, she was intent on robbing him of what he had now.

'The more he described everything Sunny had done, the angrier he got. He was all red in the face and almost spitting. It was really frightening. He said his wife wouldn't believe him.' She rubbed her upper arm at the memory of where he had gripped her. 'My arm was bruised for weeks.'

'What did Sunny say to all this?'

'She didn't say anything. She just perched there on the barrier fiddling with the string of those bloody balloons, watching him.'

'So how did she end up falling?'

'When he stopped shouting about all the things she'd done, he was really revved up. He was jabbing his finger at her, saying, "I want you gone. Out of my life for ever. You destroy everything that's good!" It was awful. And you know what she did? She just yawned. Like she was bored. She said something about having a train to catch and started to climb down from the railings. That was when he charged at her . . . It all happened so quickly, I don't know if she fell or he pushed her. I ran to look and saw she'd landed on that car.'

'Why didn't you go to the police?'

'I wanted to but I was scared. He threatened me. He knew I worked at the pub. It would be easy for him to find me. Oh God! He knows where I work.' Her hands shook as she clutched at my sleeve. 'What should I do?'

It would take me a while to come up with a plan but firstly, I advised JayCee that we couldn't just wander into a police station that night and report her story – it would open up too many questions and, at the end of the day, what actual evidence did we have to support our case against Matt for Sunny's death? It would be JayCee's word against his.

'Oh no. He could say that I pushed her. Everyone knew that me and Sunny had a lot of arguments about her seeing John. They might think I was angry with her for going to London with him and we had a fight.'

'People might think you were jealous.'

She grimaced. 'Even if he looked like Roshon, I couldn't do that to LeeAnn. She was always so good to me.'

'Don't worry. There's clearly no forensic evidence to say that *either* of you were there, otherwise they'd have used it by now. What happened to Sunny's travel bag and mobile?'

'Matt grabbed it before he ran from the bridge.'

So John had been bluffing when he claimed to have Sunny's mobile. What a liar!

'From what you've told me, the evidence on her phone would potentially incriminate Matt – all the calls and texts they must have exchanged. Not to mention the money he paid her. It provides evidence of a motive. He's probably destroyed it. Did you tell anyone you were going to the bridge that day?'

'No.'

'And the only person seen by witnesses was a man in a red hat peering over the barrier after Sunny fell.'

'That must've been me! I was wearing the hat to hide the state my hair was in.'

'You'd had your extensions out, hadn't you?'

'Yes. I had the pink dreadlocks put in by my mate later that day. I chose bright ones deliberately as no one would say they'd seen a woman with long pink hair.'

'Clever thinking! And there's your alibi. It's highly unlikely your friend would remember the exact time she did your hair.'

With JayCee calmer, I popped out to a nearby pub to make a phone call to Steve, the young policeman. Changing my voice and giving a fake name, I reported the 'attempted assault' that day. I suggested they search under the bridge for a knife and speak to the people from the off-licence as witnesses. My description of Matt was pretty perfect, including the likelihood of broken glasses and the blue BMW. And I threw in the fake 'fact' that under his hoodie he was wearing a red hat 'just like the man on that bridge when that young girl fell last year.'

That night, I got us two rooms in the hotel so JayCee didn't have to go home and I was nearby if she got scared. Once she was secure in her room, I stayed up all night thinking about how to keep us both safe. I hummed and hawed but eventually came up with an idea which, while not without risk, had the beauty of being best for us both. At two in the morning, there was a smile on my face as I rang room service: 'Could I trouble you for a large Merlot and a prawn sandwich, please?'

While I waited for my order to be delivered, I settled down to rehearse how I would broach my idea with

298

JayCee when she woke up. I toyed with several versions of my opening sentence, finally settling on:

'Sweetheart, there's one thing I need you to know. My real name is Janice Thomason.'

Chapter 40

The next day I told JayCee a version of the truth and apologised for lying to her about being a family friend of the Ryans. I truthly explained that I was actually Janice Thomason, a researcher, often employed by people to investigate their families and track down the details of their history. I told her how I became intrigued by Sunny's accident and wanted to use my research skills to help Ned and her family discover the truth. Which was also true.

My guess was that when Ned had told Matt about me, Matt had been suspicious and assumed I was investigating his role in all this. He only had to ask Ned where he was living. And then he'd started tailing me, finally following me and JayCee to the bridge that night.

'You probably saved my life,' I told her.

I told JayCee about the fire at my house, implying it might have been Matt. 'I'm renting a house for a while before I buy somewhere. It's your choice entirely, but if you want to lie low for a while you are welcome to come and stay with me for a few days. There's a spare room with ensuite!'

Before we'd even left the hotel, she'd phoned the Pheasant, calling in sick with a stomach bug.

I went back to Gressingdon briefly the following week. Incident signs had been placed near the bridge, asking for witnesses to the 'assault on two women'. I popped into the off-licence, confident that my new sassy blonde hairdo would be enough for the manager not to recognise me in my guise as a tourist. In response to my casual enquiries – 'There was an assault? Here? In a quiet place like Gressingdon!' – he spent a few minutes basking in his embellished role as the saviour of the two women and furnished me with a useful update. The police had followed up on information given in an anonymous call and they had found a knife.

After explaining my story to JayCee, wrapping up my old identity as Sonya was comparatively easy, as the only two people who really knew her were hundreds of miles away. All it took was a new mobile phone number, a PO Box forwarding address and a deleted email account, and I was back to being Jan full time.

Thanks to Gran's foresight and dislike of Mother, the house had been left to me along with my trust fund. But Mother was surprised when I told her I was selling The Old Vicarage instead of having the damaged part rebuilt. I claimed I was unable to face living there anymore after the shock of the fire. Becky had found me a property developer who was keen to knock the old house down and build several starter homes, which had many benefits, including a higher sale price for me and affordable housing to bring some much-needed youth to the village.

The second that I heard the money from the house sale had transferred and the deal was completed, I knew I could start the next phase of my life.

I felt so much better for it.

Then the icing on the cake was when I read in the Daily Mail gossip pages that *'the seventies rock star John Blue Jackson was being divorced by his long suffering wife LeeAnn'*. I raised a glass of prosecco in her honour.

I still thought of Dmytro and Ned now and then; wondering what they were up to, how they were getting on. It was only natural.

In the first couple of months, I had complicated dreams that Ned had come back to declare his love for me, decided he couldn't live without me. In the dream we'd be all set up in our country idyll when we'd discover Becky and Dmytro lived next door. I'd have to hide behind curtains/only go out at night/disguise myself as an old woman, so they didn't see me. Funny what the subconscious can do.

One day – after a particularly fraught variation of the dream, which had involved digging a tunnel so I wouldn't be seen – I thought I spotted Dmytro in the town shopping mall. It was only a glimpse through market-day crowds but it was the man's walk that caught my eye – Dmytro had had a distinctive bow-legged stride, a way of throwing his knees out as if he was on a ship. Pulse racing, I pushed my way through to trail the chap, but he turned out to be the mustachioed owner of a stall selling Turkish snacks. I celebrated my small moment of relief by buying half a kilo of baklava, most of which I devoured on the walk home.

★

As Matt Ryan wasn't in any police databases, the police hadn't been able to identify the man with the red hat who assaulted two unknown women, let alone link him to Sunny's fall. Consequently there were no criminal proceedings. It was a major moment of release for me and JayCee when the inquest was finally held. I wasn't required to attend or provide any further statements, so that was the *official* end of any connection between me and Sunny. I'd toyed with the idea of going along to wait outside the court, see if I could spot Ned, just for one final look. But sanity ruled. I'd come this far.

It was soon after that the dreams stopped.

As anticipated, the verdict was misadventure. Which in fairness, it probably was. Sunny: a hard-hearted young woman, out to manipulate money from any gullible source. Matt: a hard-working man, whose career and family life were threatened by her scheming and lies. The fuse was already lit before her baiting him on the bridge. As JayCee said, in the heat of the moment, no one really knows whether she slipped or he pushed her.

I could accept misadventure.

But I couldn't forgive his unprovoked attack on me and JayCee. I was watching him.

Chapter 41

It was September already, nearly a year since the accident.

The time had gone so quickly and so much had changed in my life. It was getting near the anniversary of the accident and I wanted to mark the occasion. It felt fitting to say a formal goodbye to Sunny. Although it was clear that she wasn't always the charming, happy-go-lucky young woman I'd imagined, I couldn't help but wonder if she'd have turned out differently with proper parenting. If that dark side could have been tamed.

I was ready. I planned to take her flowers one last time.

I drove to the cemetery where Paula was buried, where Ned had scattered Sunny's ashes. There was something important I needed to do.

It was the wrong season for planting a rosebush but I'd bought a potted miniature rose instead – a token gesture. Brushing away the first fall of leaves, I dug a small hole near the headstone with the trowel; the damp heavy earth smelt of compost and mould. From my pocket, I removed the engraved wooden box I'd had made, just large enough to hold the treasured charm bracelet. I was ready to acknowledge that I wasn't meant to keep it for ever – it wasn't a gift. It had been a catalyst, which sparked the search for her story.

Our story.

I tucked the box in the bottom of the hole, the dappled light dancing on the silver plaque: 'They broke the mould' it read – Ned had been right about that. A golden-brown leaf fluttered down to land on the little casket and I left it there, gently scattering some soil before planting the miniature rose on top. Originally it had been passed from mother to daughter and it belonged here, with them.

'Goodbye, sweetheart,' I said.

The purchase of my house was a brand-new start and I was thrilled when JayCee took up my offer of a permanent room. I immediately deleted all my files on Alice, the young woman from the confectioners, and her child. Obviously, I'd done my due diligence and researched JayCee thoroughly online. I knew all about her time in the care system and assumed LeeAnn must've taken her under her wing when she left, probably finding her the job at the Pheasant. I had evidence of *those* teenage parties, her brief modelling career, her aspiration to become an influencer. She seemed quite naïve; such a charming, lovable girl. Bright and willing to have a go at things, to help me out she was earning extra cash photographing and selling the antiques and collectables from my old house. She was also working in a local restaurant, where they'd already seen her potential; she'd be assistant manager soon enough. I wondered if she might like to go to college one day and sent off for some brochures.

As I got to know her better, I came to think of her as more like a daughter than a lodger. And Becky welcomed her with open arms. She'd 'got in quickly' and already invited us both over for Christmas lunch that year 'in case we got booked up'.

Seeing the youngsters together at Becky's, I often imagined how it would be if JayCee dated Becky's Tyrone. I let my imagination run freely, playing it out over time like a film in fast-forward, JayCee marrying Tyrone. Maybe me walking her down the aisle, her surrogate mum. Helping set them up in their first home. Becky and I becoming part of one big blended family . . . sharing the grandparenting of the babies when they came.

It was a warming thought and I started scheming, thinking of ways to get the two youngsters together . . .

Meanwhile, I stewed on Matt. I doubted that he really intended to harm us that night on the bridge. His plan was probably to scare us into silence. Well, that's a game I could play too.

It had taken me a while to work out, but when JayCee had told me about all the sums of money Sunny had prized from Matt, I knew! I'd forgotten all about those scrawled columns of numbers and dates in Sunny's notebook; the ones I'd scanned into my laptop so long ago. Suddenly they made sense – it was a record of the cash Matt had

306

given her in the vain hope of getting her out of his life.

My plan took shape.

Having previously mastered Sunny's scrawled writing, it was easy. One last time, a diary entry, dated after the last payment that she'd recorded in the notebook.

I think Matt's really furious with me. I thought the cash he gave me was a gift but now I'm frightened that if I don't pay it all back, he'll come after me. I'm really scared he'll try to kill me, he's so angry.

I scanned the faked diary entry, printing a copy with the list of dates and figures, which could no doubt be tied back to his bank account. He'd given her a lot of cash in those five months, before she upped the stakes by involving his family and he realised, no matter how much he paid her, he couldn't make her go away.

I typed a note to accompany the copies: '*I have the original diary pages. I'm watching you. Keep looking over your shoulder because if you put a foot wrong, I'll know.*'

I put it in an envelope addressed to him at his office, marking it <u>Private and Confidential, Addressee Only</u>. I wouldn't want his wife or secretary to see it; I'm not spiteful.

I was just sealing the envelope when JayCee shouted upstairs to me. 'Do you fancy a cup of coffee? I got us some cakes from the shop.'

'Thanks, sweetheart. I'll be down in a minute.'

I looked out the window. Not a cloud on the horizon. Life was bright again.

Acknowledgements

My thanks to:

- Shivanthi Sathanandan, Diane Wilson, Anna Davidson, Tamara Henriques, Stella Barnes and Elizabeth Price, for feedback on various drafts and unwavering moral support. And Lucy W, David G and David H for still being part of the herd, albeit remotely. Wouldn't have got this far without you, Pals.
- Emma Haynes and Fiona Mitchell, for starting me on this journey by voting an early draft of this story the winner of Blue Pencil's First Novel Award.
- Rhea Kurien, my editor at Orion, for her insightful editorial advice.
- Liv Maidment for her support, ideas and guidance. If you're looking for a great agent, look no further.
- My friends Ken Hummerstone and Carolyn Simon for their backing and encouragement in all my creative endeavours. My friend Rosy Forward, for her feedback on an early draft and for many shared arty activities.
- My partner, Martin, for his support through the ups and downs of a writer's life.
- And, to everyone who read and reviewed my debut novel, *Her Little Secret*. It means a lot.

**If you loved *The Accident*,
don't miss Julia Stone's thrilling,
unputdownable and chilling debut . . .**

*It started as her harmless little secret . . .
but now she's trapped.*

As a therapist, Cristina always keeps her clients at a
professional distance. Until she meets new client Leon.
Charming. Seductive. Dangerous.

Leon comes to her grieving after the death of his
married lover, Michelle. A woman Cristina realises used
to be her client. As they work through his feelings
in regular therapy sessions, ignoring her attraction to
Leon is at first difficult . . . and soon impossible.
Their relationship becomes her little secret.

But as she unravels the truth about his obsessive
affair with Michelle she questions what he *really*
wants from her?